# SILENCING SARAH

# Silencing Sarah

M.L. Cordle

Resplendence Publishing, LLC
http://www.resplendencepublishing.com

Resplendence Publishing, LLC
P.O. Box 992
Edgewater, Florida, 32132
Copyright © 2007, M.L. Cordle

Original trade paperback printing November, 2007

# ACKNOWLEDGEMENTS

*At one time I thought that this would be my favorite part of being published. It isn't. I know on an intrinsic level that I will overlook someone.*

*I must give it a shot, however, because without the help and guidance of a number of individuals, this book would not have become available to so many.*

*I would like to thank Brett Cordle and Leah Cordle for sharing their lives with me. You make my heart beat and let my imagination take flight. Also, my unflagging gratitude to Resplendence Publishing for seeing the hope in this otherwise diamond in the rough. Many stars now rest in your crown and I'm so proud to be one of them.*

*A running thank you to Leigh Collett for her patience with me while I'm still learning the ropes, and to Jessica Berry for being available no matter what and for her keen editor's eye.*

*Also to Tiffany Mason whose editorial input has been so critical and appreciated, and to the other Resplendence authors for their kind words of support and who, in my opinion, are the best group of writers ever.*

*To my MySpace following, I so appreciate the endless flow of support and validation. How did you know I needed it so much? And on the home front, hardly the least of my champions, I need to thank so many. Deb Harmon, you were the first to read this book and have gone out on a limb more than once to keep me on track, writing or otherwise. Thank you for continuing to be a keeper of the flame.*

*Anita Perry, you've done so much to promote Silencing Sarah, but one of the high notes would have to be Christopher Newport University. Thanks for leading this horse to water.*

*Steve Meade, I never thought I'd have a lawyer go to bat for me. Thanks for putting in a good word for me at CNU.*
*Much gratitude to my retired editor friend, Steve Lorton, from Time Warner, who took time in his travels to read my work and who reminded me that writers generally receive enough rejection slips to wallpaper their house but I had what it took to move beyond the mountain.*
*To Debbie Kilgore, a kindred spirit and one of my biggest fans in Big Stone Gap – thanks for all you do (and there's a lot)!*
*Dorothy Perkins, you've been sewing me into the wonderful fabric of life since you gave birth to me – thanks to you and Dad for what you've both done for me along the way to mold me into who I am.*
*And a big thank you to: the rest of my family and friends for their collective support. Also, Mary Barnette, Alice Cordle, my friends on the* other *side (you know who you are), Carol Nelson, Angela MackIntosh with Women on Writing, Adriana Trigiani for stoking the embers of my Appalachian heritage and finding time in her busy schedule for me, and Sandra Brown for years of inspiration.*

*Requiem aeternam dona eis, Domine.*
*(Grant them eternal rest, O Lord.)*

*Seeking warmth*
*They inhabit my being; curious souls*
*And whisper softness beneath my skin*
*Beseeching me to search their ways*
*I endeavor to know their plight*
*I open my soul wide*
*And behold the gifts*
*I am the voice*
*Carefully I listen*
*With my heart, my mind, my bones*
*As they petition for rest*
*And gain memory from mine haunted eye*

never
underestimate
the power
of dreams.

*For Edward and Brett.*
*Te decet hymnus*
*(To thee is due a song of praise)*

# CHAPTER ONE

Will had no clue why a woman would be on his property, much less caught in his trap, but he never questioned the voice in his head. Sarah Chambers' whisper was both pervasive and accurate.

*Steel trap. At the spring.*

He cut across the short swath of sun baked ground between his wood-working shop and his house, hearing nothing beyond the screaming in the woods, and the ghostly Sarah whose feathery words continued to float over his fevered conscience like a caress from the grave.

*Time has come.*

He ate up the distance between the yard and the woods, his long strides carrying him toward the stream and whatever he was about to find there.

How long had this woman been crying for help?

His fear pushed him to run faster, to ignore the burning in his lungs. With his own racket of wood saws filling the better part of the last hour, she could have been out there in the brush for at least as long as it took a person to bleed to death. Her voice was raw, hoarse from screaming.

He ran headlong into a flock of chickens, impervious to the distress he caused them. Plowing through the flurry of feathers and frantic squawking, he fled the lawn, jumping the split rail fence that bordered the woods. He was soon swallowed by the shade of looming poplars and enveloped by the smell of pulpy undergrowth.

Beneath the canopy of the young but towering timber it was noticeably cooler, but the change in temperature had no effect upon his body. A vicious chokehold of dread, and its accompanying adrenaline rush, had his sweat glands laboring like the pistons on an old steam engine.

He spotted her as soon as he stepped into the small clearing that comprised the spring box. She was on the ground. She was in the trap.

*Sacrifice.*

He skidded to a halt, his legs refusing to carry him any further. He took a step back, willed Sarah to be quiet.

The woman writhing on the ground was small. Clad in camouflage pants and a tank top, a spray of freckles across her nose, she might have been a child. Wet ropes of auburn hair plastered her cheeks and forehead. Her eyes, dark and glittering with fear, were like deep pools of misgiving.

The trap had caught her just above her boot, and the brutal steel mouth of it had sawed through her pants and skin. Blood saturated the earth tone fabric, the crimson stain spreading through it and into the white of her sock. Dread tightened his throat.

"Help me." It was a raw gasp that escaped the narrow white column of her throat. "Please!"

*Sacrifice.*

He took another step backward.

He couldn't help the woman. He shouldn't get near her. Why was Sarah doing this to him? Placing him in an impossible situation? He had to get away from here, away from the strident pleas for help. He would find someone else to get her out of his trap. Anyone else.

She bellowed for him to come back, fear and rage building in her voice with each subsequent expulsion of words, but he didn't slow down as he ran toward his cabin. He didn't stop until he saw his wife standing on the porch, her arms crossed over her breasts like tightly folded wings.

Her brows drew together in a fierce glare. *"I can't find my name in the book, Will. I can't."*

Though he didn't want to hear this, wanted to turn around and run back into the sheltering woods, he didn't.

He wanted to face the woman in the trap even less.

****

Will McGomery opened his eyes, blinking away the dream's sticky tendrils.

He groped in the dark for his blanket, found it on the floor and yanked it over his chilled body. His bedroom had the semi-dark quality of pond water. Staring through it, he thought of Sarah Chambers. Wondered if the cold, murky light was all she had seen when dying.

Huddled beneath the blanket, he fought the tremors racking his body and ordered himself back to sleep. But when he closed his eyes, he could see only one thing: Marshy Owens' daughter in the woods, bleeding a small river into the dirt.

# CHAPTER TWO

Marshall Owens entered the morning-bright kitchen like an overbearing salesman at a car dealership—the kind that never took no for an answer.

"Ah, the prodigal daughter," he said, his usual good 'ol boy demeanor intact. "Sleep well?"

Madison forced a smile. "Yeah, Daddy, wonderfully."

A huge overstatement since she'd spent half the night staring at, via the nightlight, the spackling patterns in the ceiling of her old bedroom. That and rehearsing what she would say to her parents when the sun came up.

She watched her father cross the room, tried to gauge his mood. His shoulders were broad as ever, and from this angle, his slight paunch not visible. He looked to be much younger than what he was. His posture was rigid, which might mean her presence made him uneasy. Or not; it was difficult to tell.

Did he still think she was a headstrong brat, some whirling dervish destined to cause emotional catastrophe wherever she went?

Despite the early hour, he already had his customary pipe clenched between his lips. With each puff, he spread the scent of cherry flavored tobacco throughout the kitchen, reminding her of when she'd been a child and thought him to be an old man simply because he smoked it. Now, he was retired, but seemingly unchanged from her childhood memory.

Her mother brought a cup of coffee to the table and smiled when Madison eagerly reached for it.

"I've got fresh eggs from Will McGomery in here," she announced, maneuvering to the heavily stocked refrigerator across the room.

Madison shot her father a look when he laughed. His voice was a ruddy sound, reminding her of sandpaper on sheet rock.

"And bacon, and a ham, and some deer meat in the freezer," he said. "He's always bringing you something."

Madison frowned, wondering why the name sounded so familiar. Will McGomery. She was certain she had heard it before. "Who is he?"

"A clockmaker," her father said.

He stood in front of the window, pushing his woodcutter knuckles into the small of his back as he stretched. Morning sunlight caught strands of silver hair from the top of his head, causing them to shimmer like Christmas tinsel.

Her mother's plump arm jiggled as she whipped eggs in a bowl and picked up the thread of conversation.

"His name most likely sounds familiar because of that scandal he was involved in years back. His wife committed suicide when she discovered he was having an affair with that Chambers girl."

Madison felt the kind of rush she experienced when hit with an idea for a book. "Didn't the Chambers girl drown? It was speculated her boyfriend was behind it."

"Aubrey McGomery," she vouched, lifting a hand to scratch her scalp, which was shrouded beneath cropped hair the color of corn silk. She sighed and caused the weight of her generous bosom to shift up and then downward. "Will's own cousin. Only Aubrey's trial resulted in a hung jury and he walked."

"Will McGomery is a generous enough neighbor," her father said, aiming a scowl toward his wife. "I would think you could show him a little respect and not gossip about him."

"Is he the one responsible for the clock you have in there on the mantle?" Madison asked, ignoring his gripe.

Her mother smiled faintly, her round face devoid of lines that would indicate her age. "He just up and brought it to me one day. I was tickled to death to receive it. It's quite lovely, isn't it?"

Madison pursed her lips. "Impressive workmanship."

Her heart was like a worm that had been suddenly skewered on something sharp. Once upon a time, she had considered herself to be quite impressive. Confident in her ability, she had stood at the pinnacle, basking in her accomplishments as a writer. And then Jim had walked out on her. Just like that, her life had been turned inside out.

The memory was indeed a barbed and rusty old hook.

Now she just wanted to fill her life with simplicity, forget the hard won battles that had nonetheless resulted in tremendous personal failure. And she knew just how she would get that simple life she so desired. She would leave behind the carnage of her broken marriage and reclaim what had once been her private haven. Yes, it would be a place where she could rethink her life, find renewed hope, and maybe even dream about loving again.

Drawing a deep breath for courage, she set her plan in motion.

"How would you guys feel about me moving up on the ridge now that I'm back?"

Heavy silence descended over the kitchen. Her father's scowl deepened into something downright ferocious, his chin jutting at a mulish angle.

She had anticipated him putting up a fight as well as putting her on the spot, but that foreboding look; it made her anxious. Her nerves jangled like keys on a fob in a fidgety hand, she hadn't expected such animosity.

She didn't want to have to defend her decision to move up on the ridge. She wasn't asking her father for money. She wasn't asking for anything that hadn't already been promised her. There was nothing illogical about what she planned to do. And yet, here he was, on the verge of saying something she would likely resent. Something that might, in fact, hurt her terribly.

Her mother stood motionless by the stove, looking like a woman who had been plucked out of the fifties in her long housecoat and plush slippers. In her hand was the fork she'd been using to whisk the eggs, but she'd moved it to the side of the bowl. Raw egg dripped onto the countertop.

Madison put her coffee on the table, but clenched the mug with both hands, trying to resist the urge to spring up from the chair like a hostile teenager.

"Why the twin looks of surprise?" she asked, her voice a smooth mockery of blasé. "This has always been in the works. Years ago—"

"Years ago?" Her father laughed. The sound of it rumbled through the kitchen like a rockslide. "You mean when you were ten years-old?"

Her stomach knotted and she scolded her body for its traitorous reaction. She hadn't come all the way back to Virginia to play little girl with him, but here she sat feeling exactly as though she were one. Lord, she was the antithesis of the prodigal child. She was the proverbial thorn in her father's side, and she would never get lucky enough to slip by without him making her answer to it.

She forced herself to meet his gaze. "If the cabin is too far gone to refurbish, I'll have it dismantled, piece by piece. I want it to be an exact replica of the original."

He shook his head back and forth like a Terrier with a rat. "It's absolutely nuts and besides that, impossible."

"Madison, honey, what planet have you been living on?" her mother asked. She placed the bowl on the counter and turned the stove down so she could give Madison her full attention.

"William McGomery bought that land from us a goodly number of years ago. Don't you remember your father talking about it? I'm sure he must have mentioned it when you were down on one of your visits."

Madison blinked, dumbfounded. Mentioned it to her? That was one thing he had never done. "I'm sure I would remember something like that and clearly I don't."

She glared at Marshy as he joined her at the table, her fingers now splayed over her chinos and curling into the cotton covering her thighs. "A widower who makes clocks and brings Mama animal meat...so essentially, you found his money and a piece of fatback a temptation you couldn't resist?"

Her mother stared at her in amazement, as if she couldn't believe her daughter had a right to be angry. To Madison, her guileless reaction was too incredible to be genuine.

The woman knew how much she had always wanted that land. Both of her parents were fully aware of what that place had meant to her, and yet they'd sold it right out from under her, and to the scourge of their community.

"We didn't have no use for that brush pile up there," her father said, amazingly subdued now. "Not at our age and you weren't coming back as far as we could see. We decided to sell it and do something useful with the money. We put it into trust funds for Lorna's kids where it will do some good. McGomery paid more than our asking price. When we received a better offer, he matched it, was just crazy to have the place."

Lorna's kids?

Madison struggled to maintain control of her temper. If her parents had wanted to do some good in regard to her sister's children they could have sold the land to her. She would have made an offer for it that would have made that clock making farmer's generosity seem like a pittance in comparison. They had to at least suspect that she had made a bundle on her last book. Their failure to consider her as a potential bidder was an egregious oversight.

"I told you years ago that the land and cabin was all that I expected in regard to an inheritance. Although you promised to deed it to me, I came prepared to make an offer. You could have at least given me an opportunity to place a bid."

Her father might have been the biblical Methuselah for his stark, white hair and sober expression. Head slightly bent, huge hands folded over the table, he sat there while her mother twittered like a small, rotund bird.

"You should have called before coming, Maddie. I could

have saved you the trip if that was all you—"

"Now listen here, little gal," Marshy cut in, suddenly drawing himself up and raising steely, battleship gray eyes to Madison's. "You can't just march in here and run roughshod over everybody. You made your choices. We didn't make them for you. In fact, I recall trying to talk you out of marrying that pretentious sum bitch. If you'd stayed around here like your sisters and found yourself a decent local boy, I might've honored that whimsy of yours."

He jabbed a finger in her direction as if to drive home a point. "You didn't. You married a buckeye who couldn't keep his diddler in his fancy trousers, and far as I'm concerned, you reneged on our deal, not me."

Madison flinched as his words hit their mark. He'd never tried to hide the fact he considered her love for Jim a betrayal, and now here was the unmitigated proof that he had thought her marriage to be an act of treason. As if to punctuate his hurtful statement with a physical response, he curled his blunt tipped fingers into a fist and thumped the surface of the table.

"You and your big ideas about becoming a writer. I don't see that it did much for you, except maybe fatten your bank account." He raked her with a derisive sweep of his eyes, made a rude noise in the back of his throat.

"You have no marriage to speak of and you want to move up on the ridge to do what? Write another book? You don't belong up there. You left us, and this place, behind you in the dust a long time ago."

Madison's heart shuddered as the vortex of angry words spun through it.

Nothing had changed. He spoke to her no differently now than he had when she had been younger and they'd been as opposing as the north and south in the Civil War. No different than when she'd left Virginia to live with her aunt in Ohio so she could experience life outside the shadow of these mountains and away from his scrutiny.

She sat motionless, as if fused to her chair. She had tried to brace herself for the balking, even the insults, but not this all-out assault on her character.

Ever the diplomat, her mother offered up an encouraging smile. "You'll find your bearings, Maddie. Just give it some time." She turned back to the stove, pouring the eggs in the cooling skillet, leaving Madison to wonder if she was capable of defending anyone other than her husband.

The man had just said that his daughter was a total failure. Did that not warrant at least a measure of disdain from Hannah Owens? Apparently not.

"You're welcome to stay here for as long as you need," her mother said, ignoring the tension, which continued to thicken the air like a dense, toxic cloud. "After breakfast, we'll go see Lorna and the boys. She's off today and it will be so nice for all of us to get together."

Undaunted by Madison's lack of response, she went about cooking breakfast, her birdsong like sharp fingernails scraping along Madison's nerve endings.

"I'll call Rachel a little later and tell her you're in," she chirped. "She can drive over from Bristol for a visit. Maybe we can go shopping. Oh, that would be nice."

"The cabin, did he tear it down? Is it gone?"

Her father's ominous expression showed sudden and definite signs of lightening.

"To the contrary," he said. "He used the logs to raise himself a barn, then he built with his own hands a right smart looking cabin out of the poplars that grow up there."

He gave his head a shake, clearly in admiration of the man most people in the area had considered for years to be a pariah. "It's almost to the square inch of being like the original cabin, except for the new logs. It suits a man like him, nothing fancy, just a place for him to hang his hat and rest his bones…in his case, you might say skeletons."

He chuckled. "You should see it. I tell you what. I'll drive you up there sometime and show you. I'm sure he won't mind."

Madison bit down on her lower lip so that it wouldn't tremble. Some farmer had stolen her dream and she didn't even have a right to be mad at him. He hadn't known any better; had just paid for the land and obliterated her dream—happenstance, a quirk of fate, her parents being total shits.

Their blatant disregard of her feelings was inexcusable, and damaged profoundly any lingering respect she might have felt toward them, especially her father.

She caught her mother's pitying glance and immediately stood from the table, fighting to keep her voice level. "I've got a headache, Mama. You go see Lorna without me."

Not waiting for a response, she turned and made her way toward the stairs, forcing her body to hold itself erect—shoulders squared, head held high. She made it to the second level of the house and shut herself inside her old bedroom.

Pressing her back against the door, she drew a breath and locked it. Then she crossed to the antique dresser and pulled open the top drawer to remove the battered scrapbook she'd put in there the night before. It felt heavy in her hands, heavier than she knew it really was. Memories of her childhood seemed to weigh down the pages and, even more so, her heart.

She wandered over to the bed and sat down, opening the book over her lap. Her favorite photo rested in its usual place. She ran her finger around the curling edges, the image blurring as she gazed at it through a veil of unwanted tears.

At the time, she had been eleven, maybe twelve. She stood on the sagging porch of her great-grandparents' log house, smiling audaciously for the camera as her sister Rachel snapped the picture. The cabin had been a favorite haunt of theirs, but it had been Madison's special place, her sanctuary.

Now the land, the single grain of hope that hadn't slipped away in the aftermath of her disastrous marriage, belonged to some philandering clockmaker.

She traced her fingertip over her child likeness, searching

for some connection to that smiling young girl. The unruly auburn hair and splash of freckles across her nose remained the same. But on the inside, she and that girl might as well be galaxies apart.

Her eyes burned with tears of mortification. She was not the rambunctious dreamer she'd been once upon a time. She didn't know what had happened to that eager young creature, she only knew that the woman sitting in her place shared none of her boundless enthusiasm.

What had she done? Come crawling home in search of sanctuary where none existed?

Yes, that would sum it up quite efficiently. And for a bonus, she was unable to write, had been suffering from a crippling case of writer's block for months.

Disconsolate, she closed the book and set it aside. She buried her face in her hands and took a deep breath. Then, disgusted with herself, she succumbed to the tears she had managed to contain while in her parents' presence.

# CHAPTER THREE

Madison ventured from her parents' house and into the thick midmorning air, grimacing at the heat. Despite the early hour, humidity hung over the land like a wet dishtowel. Clouds stacked one atop another, cumulous monsters dwarfing the majestic sprawl of mountains below them.

Later that evening, Russell County or one of the surrounding counties stood a good chance of being awarded a show of lights or a downpour from one of these thunderheads, but then again, maybe not. It was a toss up.

Like her future.

Sweat beaded on her brow and her thin cotton tank top stuck to her skin. By the time she slid in behind the wheel of her Jeep, the article of clothing felt as cloistering as a too-tight bandage. She tugged at the strap that had slipped over her shoulder, and with her other hand, turned the key in the ignition.

She had to meet this Will McGomery. She had to at least make the man an offer for the land.

Her land.

She tightened her fingers over the steering wheel as she bounced along the first bend in the wagon trail, determined not to let her father's low opinion of her dampen her enthusiasm. So he was of the opinion that she had spitefully left her family in the dust. She knew the truth, knew she had done nothing in spite, had only done what she had needed to do to find herself. And she had several bestsellers to show for that decision. He could not fault her. Well, he could, but his accusations would be unfounded. Jim had been a mistake, true, but only a minor setback, as she was about to get herself back on track, or was very close to getting herself back on track.

It was easy to conclude that this McGomery character was someone who enjoyed his solitude. On that count they should be able to relate, for there was little that she cherished more than the serenity of being along. She'd had her share of chaos and scrutiny with her and Jim's divorce and the hoopla of the book tours. Now she wanted some down time, some time to catch her breath and heal her heart.

She had convinced herself that this Will McGomery was a kindred spirit. He was someone who had made his share of mistakes and wanted nothing more than to live them down silently. Perhaps his past had left him with scars, but he was not completely embittered and mistrustful, she decided, because a man like that would not be bringing her mother eggs on a regular basis. He would not have given her one of his clocks.

At the moment, her kindred spirit was in the barn behind his cabin. She could see him as she drove across the clearing that topped the ridge. He wasn't wearing a shirt, just faded overalls. She could see the muscles in his chest and arms as he tossed rectangular bales of hay from the bed of his truck onto the low loft.

He paused to watch her as she eased to a stop in his drive, but resumed with the hay when she disembarked from the vehicle. After that one, cursory glance, he had seemingly formed an opinion of her, and had decided she was not someone he needed to take a break for.

It wasn't easy to steady her breath. This was not the man she had conjured in her mind's eye, after all. He was not the beer-gutted, hairy-necked hermit she had expected to find. He was something worse, something far worse—he was a man who, from this distance, looked like one of the cover models she had encountered at the romance writer's conference she'd attended that spring. He was bronzed and fit, with shoulder length, brown hair streaked with blonde.

It was perhaps one of the hardest things she had had to do in a while, but she forced herself to cross the lawn at a leisurely pace. Will McGomery's dog barked at her but she was not intimidated by the animal. No, it was the dog's virile master giving her pause.

"Settle down, Clovis."

His voice was low and deep, far more sensual than she had had any right to expect. Her heart skipped and she silently scolded herself for it.

What was the matter with her? She had come across attractive men in her line of work many times. Why did this farmer trip her up? Maybe it was because he was so out of context, so unexpected, so different than what her mind had drawn up.

She stepped inside the barn, simultaneously tucking her hair behind one ear. "Going to be a scorcher today, huh?"

He grabbed another bale of hay and pitched it into the loft. His sultry voice lacked emotional inflection as he spoke into the chorus of morning birdsong. "No going to be about it."

This lazy, almost remote tone was not surprising. If he'd had tattoos emblazoned all over his torso and a wad of chewing tobacco in his jaw, it would not have been surprising. What was very surprising was his remarkably gorgeous face.

A face to go with the amazing long, lean and muscular body.

Good Lord.

His incredible countenance set her immediately on edge; enough so that she began to grit her teeth like a child heading for the doctor's office. Men as good-looking as Will McGomery could be real pricks. Jim had taught her that. It was something inherent to them and she did not savor the idea of having to deal with yet another inflated ego.

She forced a smile when he paused to look at her, then she crouched in front of his dog. She distracted herself from the heart-stopping blue gaze he fixed on her by focusing on his mongrel's peculiar, mottled eyes.

"Hey, funny face. You're a true Heinz 57, now aren't you?" In the subdued atmosphere of the barn, her words sounded like they were being pulled out of her against her will, and she hated it.

This was not the time to freeze up, make a bad impression. Her future hinged on her ability to appeal to this man's better nature. To get her land back, she had to appear to be a competent, rational thinking woman, not some infatuated dolt. And there could be no stalling simply because his hawkish appraisal intimidated the hell out of her.

Her fingers slid over the canine's head. She stood and tried to widen her smile without it appearing stiff. McGomery stood at the end of his truck, still watching her in brooding silence, and her eyes were inexplicably drawn back to his.

She wondered how anyone's stare could be that blue.

The color reminded her of a Blue Tang fish she'd seen once while dining at an exquisite little eatery in New York. The restaurant had featured a large aquarium running the length of one wall and on one occasion while waiting for a table, she had spent several minutes entranced by the colorful inhabitants.

Swallowing and entranced yet again, she struggled for something—anything—to say.

*Are you wearing contacts?* No, that was lame. She cleared her throat. "That certainly is a lot of hay you've put up this summer."

"It'll be enough for my animals this winter with some leftover to sell." He reached for another bale, then paused, his eyes locking with hers once more.

"Something in particular I can do for you, Miss?"

She chewed the inside of her cheek for a moment. When he continued to stand there, his impassive expression giving away none of his thoughts, she shrugged. It was best to appear casual. It wouldn't do to have him discern how off balance she was.

"I could use some breakfast," she said, smiling. "But I'd settle for a conversation."

He glanced meaningfully at the bales of hay still stacked in the bed of his truck. "Look, I don't mean to be rude, but I've got to get this—"

"I'm sorry," she said, suddenly desperate to make a good impression. She stepped over and extended her hand, and was tremendously relieved when he finally clasped it in his own larger, callused hand around hers and shook it. "I should have been more straightforward. I've come to talk to you about the land. I would like to make you an offer for it."

"The land? What land are you talking about?" He scratched the stubble on his cheek. "You're mistaken. I don't have any land for sale."

"I'm Marshall Owens' daughter," she said after a lengthy pause, swallowing dryly because her salivary glands had suddenly stopped functioning. "I was hoping that perhaps, since the land was in fact supposed to be deeded to me, you might be willing to sell it. I would make it worth your while. More than worth your while."

He leaned forward and pulled a bale of hay toward him, then took a moment to mop the sweat off his forehead with the back of his forearm. Turning his eyes onto her again, he smiled faintly.

"By chance, were you up here poking around earlier this morning?"

She studied his face for traces of insincerity and found none. Her heart hammering because she had, in fact, taken a walk up the ridge, she moved her eyes away from him. "I wanted to see the spring but I didn't want to disturb you so I went through the woods. I didn't stay long."

He shook his head. "I'm not sure I believe you, Marshall Owens' daughter. If you didn't want to disturb me, you would've left a minute ago when you saw that I was working."

"My name is Madison," she said, "and I apologize for disrupting your work." She tilted her head to one side slightly. "You look miserably hot."

When he said nothing, she pulled her lower lip through her teeth. "With exception to the early morning walk, this is my first trip up here since returning to Virginia. I assure you."

"I'm glad I put away my traps." He reached up and fingered the brim of his hat. It was a floppy concoction with no particular shape to it, like something her grandfather would have worn to work in the fields. "It pays to play it safe, obviously."

She pondered his words for some time before speaking. "What were the traps for?"

"Coyote, and coon," he said. "One rides my corn down, both make off with my chickens."

"Funny you would think to play it safe all of a sudden." She glanced away from his open stare. "I saw the No Trespassing signs on my way up here. Has someone been ignoring them?"

"Not recently, unless I count you."

"I just wanted to see the cabin you built, enjoy the spring for a few minutes," she said, becoming flustered.

He lifted one shoulder in a shrug. "So you've said. I'm not interested in selling, Miss Owens."

Her hand flew up, first to tuck hair behind one ear and then the other. "I can make you a really generous offer."

"Not interested."

"You destroyed the house," she said with a measure of disdain. "I would've never done that."

"I believe you're looking at the house," he said, extending his arms out from his sides to indicate the barn around them.

Her eyes flitted over him, took in everything. And there were a lot of really amazing things to take in—the muscles in his arms, the soft-looking hair matted to his solid chest, his eyes, his mouth, his sun-kissed, wavy hair. "You're being sarcastic with me?"

"God forbid," he said. A smile flirted at the corners of his mouth. "I used the logs from the cabin to build the barn." He gestured toward the house. "But I really liked the layout of the original place, so I copied it as best I could. Would you care to see the inside so that you can come to grips with how badly I botched things? I could fix you that breakfast you were talking about."

Was that his idea of a pick-up line? In the end, she realized she didn't much care. She wasn't going to pass up an opportunity to see the inside of his cabin. He was more than an interesting diversion from her family woes. He was more than just the man standing between her and the land she had come back to claim.

Will McGomery was fascinating, had done more to intrigue her than anyone or anything had in two years.

"Breakfast sounds really good."

# CHAPTER FOUR

Will led his beguiling guest down a short hallway and into the kitchen. She had dropped a bomb on him when she said she wanted to buy his place. He hadn't seen that coming. Perhaps he knew she would show up, but he'd had no idea she would make him an offer for the land.

He could feel her eyes on him as he walked over to the cabinet, took down a glass, and filled it with water. He brought it to her, and when their fingers brushed, a small river of excitement flowed through his gut.

She was very attractive, this Madison Owens. Lush hair, the tank top and camouflage pants hugging her amazing figure, made him want to stare long and brazenly. At a glance, her face was only that of a girl—huge, expressive eyes, cheeks strewn with freckles. But there was no mistaking she was a woman. Too many curves... soft, inviting curves.

Life could be awfully cruel.

He did not need the temptation of her, of this beautiful, girlish vision in her ridiculous camouflage knickers. Why the hell had he let her finagle her way inside his house in the first place? Why had he invited her? Could he be any more of an idiot? Or was he just allowing his brain to be overruled by a different part of his body?

She trailed her fingertips over the granite countertop that separated the kitchen from the living room and he watched, feeling as though he had been cast into a trance.

"Very quaint," she said, her eyes roving his living room and clearly missing nothing. "I like the Norman Rockwell prints over by the bookcase. Very Americana."

Her lips parting over the rim of the glass in her hand, she sipped her water and continued to survey the two rooms. Appearing pressed for something else to say to him, she flashed him a look. "Oh, sorry. Thanks for the drink."

He nodded and pulled out a chair for her at the kitchen table. After she wandered over and lowered herself into it, he took one across from her.

So she had come to see what he had done with her family's land, to make him an offer for it? He could be a condescending jackass, piss her off. Maybe then she'd suck it up and go on home. Associating with him would bring her nothing but suffering and he'd seen enough suffering in his time. He could only hope that she would tire of him, forget all about this encounter.

*Sacrifice.*

He closed his mind to Sarah's voice, prayed that this one short visit from Madison Owens would be her last.

"Are you surprised?" he said, trying not to think of the dream he'd had about her.

"About?"

"About the fact that I have appliances and running water? The outhouse is a prop, you know. I just liked the idea of keeping to the original layout of the place."

"I figured that one out already." He raised a brow and she continued. "I saw your water box down by the spring."

She gingerly smoothed her hand over the surface of the rustic dining table and his eyes caught the subtle movement. Did she suspect that the table was one of his creations? Would she even give a damn?

It didn't really matter.

She didn't matter.

Only, he couldn't quite make himself believe that. He was acutely aware of his appearance for one thing, and he never was. He hadn't shaved that morning and knew he had a shadow of beard covering his jaw. She probably thought he was some illiterate hillbilly, some crazy old hermit living up here away from the world. For whatever reason, that bothered him. That meant her opinion of him mattered. That meant she mattered even if he didn't want her to.

"As for the appliances," she said, "I'm surprised the utility company ran the electric lines over from the Tignor place instead of from my parents' house."

He didn't say anything, just watched her as she lifted her glass and drank some more.

His eyes followed the movement of her throat as she swallowed. When she lowered the glass and licked her glossed, shell pink lips, his gaze settled longingly over her mouth. It was a mouth a man didn't soon forget, full and succulent looking, ripe for the taking.

She smiled. "God, there's no water in the world like this."

There was no mouth on earth like hers. The way she skirted his gaze, he was certain that she was at least partially aware of his attraction to her. She offered a quick shrug and dropped her eyes to the table.

"I used to love drinking from that spring out there. The water in Columbus is atrocious. You know how city water is."

Actually, he didn't know Jack Shit about city water. But he wasn't going to tell her that.

What he really wanted to do was bury his nose in her wealth of rich auburn hair, absorb her sweet, womanly scent, and lose himself. Instead, she met his eyes and he tried to simulate some kind of rational thinking. Her voice was soft, but riveting, and nowhere close to being something that could jerk his thoughts back to where they needed to be.

"Do you live up here like this because of what happened years ago?"

At that, his mind was jarred back to a rational place. He rose from the table, crossed over to the refrigerator, and opened the freezer compartment. He removed a package of frozen strawberries and tossed it into the microwave mounted over the cook range. He turned to face her.

"It was closer to come over from the Tignor place with the electric lines. That's why they ran them from there instead of from your folks'."

After several moments in which they just stared at one another like two people beholding something remarkable and unexpected, he turned to grab a saucepan from a lower cabinet and placed it on the stove. He took the fruit packet from the microwave and dumped the semi-thawed contents into the saucepan.

A plate of biscuits, leftover from his breakfast, remained on the back of the stove. He grabbed the plate and put it in the microwave, glad that he'd forgotten to add the biscuits to his slop bucket that morning.

He stirred the melting contents of the saucepan, grateful for the task. Heavy silence permeated the room once more. He told himself that she would be gone soon even though he didn't relish the thought of her leaving at all.

Whether it was a good idea for her to be there or not, he wanted to spend time in her company. Her curiosity beckoned to be answered, and his curiosity about her was already nearing an insatiable level.

"You know, most people assume I bite," he said. "You don't seem at all wary of me."

"I don't scare easily," she replied, and he caught a shimmer of mischief in her eyes. As they moved cautiously over his face, she ventured a smile. "You bring my mother gifts. How could you be scary?"

She wound a strand of her hair around her pinkie, and his heart did something funny in his chest. The last time he'd felt that kind of kick, he'd been another man, a young man with dreams and—

"Pardon me for saying so, but you look like you just stepped off the set of some Civil War epic," she said, a playful note in her voice. "All you need is a beard, maybe a musket. Actually, you put me in mind of Legends of the Fall. What was his name? You know Brad Pitt's character?"

"Seems you've decided that, by today's standards, I'm a

social reject." He said, ignoring her question, and added sugar to the saucepan and stirred the liquid until it began to fill the kitchen with the rich smell of warm strawberries.

He turned his head, his attention shifting from her startled expression to her camouflage pants. "I may look like a Confederate roughneck, but you look like you're thinking about pulling duty for the National Guard. Funny… you don't strike me as the type."

"Your hat," she said, clearly of a mind to ignore his sarcasm. Her eyes moved away from his and fixed on the top of his head. "Do you never take it off?"

He removed the item of question and hung it over the straight back chair he'd been sitting in moments before. "I'm not used to visitors and having to use proper etiquette." He shrugged. "I forget I'm wearing it, actually."

She didn't let anything slip by. Something about the way she looked at him now, those huge curious eyes probing at him like beacons, perturbed him.

"You can't possibly remember with clarity what happened years ago, and yet you seemed completely comfortable enough bringing it up." He stared hard at her. "You asked me if I live up here because of what happened."

She actually blushed. "I didn't mean to offend you. My mother knows everybody's business—past and present—and last night, she elaborated on yours. Unlike the norm, I paid attention. I admit, I found it all very intriguing."

"Thus your visit today." He rolled his eyes. To her, he probably seemed like the worst kind of trespasser, the kind guilty of infidelity. Yeah. Likely she believed what her mother had told her, believed the worst about him. Just like everyone else in this blasted place.

"You've been in the public eye," he said after a moment, "you know how it feels to have people intrigued with your dirty laundry. Why would you want to come up here and try to inspect mine?"

Her mouth fell open, and her gaze narrowed over his face. "I came to make you an offer on this land and to have a conversation. That's all." She continued to stare at him, and then blinked rapidly as though totally disconcerted by his question. "You don't even know me, Mr. McGomery. How do you know I've been in the public eye?"

"Your Pap may have mentioned that you're a best selling novelist." He jabbed out thirty seconds on the touch pad of the microwave with his thumb. He brought a cloth potholder to the table, set the saucepan on it and then produced a tub of butter from his small refrigerator. "I would say he seems mighty proud of you."

She made a rude noise in her throat and he wondered why that particular statement offended her. He didn't inquire however. The less they knew about one another's dispositions, the better.

He went about placing two ceramic plates, the biscuits, and the saucepan on the table, and then filled two glasses with milk.

"I can't believe you fixed me breakfast," she said.

"I can't believe you actually showed up."

Once again, he joined her at the table and, fooling with her ear, she surveyed him curiously.

"You say that as though someone told you I would."

He shrugged and silence drew out long and heavy between them, until he could sense her unease.

"I noticed your milk isn't in a carton or jug," she remarked finally, taking the knife he extended toward her, along with the plastic container of butter. "Is it from that cow you've got out there?"

Was she serious? He gauged her expression and laughed, sensing that she was incredibly serious.

She paused in her action of spreading butter on the biscuit she had pulled apart. After a long moment, she resumed with a flourish, her cheeks suffusing with color.

"What do you find so amusing? It seemed like a legitimate

question to me."

He leveled his smile. "It's just that old Dib's been around longer than a coon's eye. I don't imagine she has any milk to give these days. I buy milk at the supermarket and put it in glass containers because the glass somehow makes the milk taste better. A trick I learned from my Grandmother."

He watched her spoon a dollop of steaming strawberries onto her biscuit, and was amazed by how quickly she recovered from her embarrassment. She flashed him a look. "So the cow serves what purpose?"

He took the knife from her and dipping it into the butter, he shook his head, feigning indifference. "No purpose really. Except I'm partial to her."

"You're partial to a cow? Sorry, but I fail to see the appeal of bovine." A hint of a smile played at the corners of her lips. "I don't know that I've ever met a man who had a cow for a pet."

"Hey, she's a gem." He grinned, couldn't help it. He found that he liked being around Madison Owens; figured he might as well make the most of the time he had with her. "Dib's retired. I'm just making sure she enjoys her golden years."

"I get the picture," she said, laughing softly. "So, do you believe Dib really cares one way or the other how you feel?"

"Let me tell you a story and then you can decide for yourself if she is capable of feeling."

She waved her hand in a way that was amusing, like she was the superior gesturing for her minion to indulge her. Only, she wasn't aware of how she looked to him. Suddenly and irrevocably, he wanted to lean across the table and press his lips over hers, taste her, know her.

"By all means," she said. "I love stories."

He leaned back in his chair, allowing his eyes to roam over her face. It wasn't easy to squelch the impulse to kiss her, but he somehow managed to do so. "I used to breed her so I could have milk… long time ago. Each time I would sell her calf, she would wander around for days, looking for it. I would glance out the window and she'd be standing where the truck and trailer had been, great ribbons of slobber streaming from her mouth where she had been bawling for hours.

"Does she care about how I feel?" he asked. "I doubt it, but do I think she is capable of suffering? You're damn straight, I do, and I'm seeing to it that she doesn't anymore."

He could see the emotion as it flickered in her eyes, compassion and sadness for poor, old Dib.

Just as he'd expected, she was a complete softie. Camouflage or not, Madison Owens was no army brat. She was a bleeding heart, and God he wanted to touch her. He wanted to make sure no one else got to. He wanted to touch her, be with her.

Protect her.

She bit into her biscuit, chewed slowly and deliberately. Then she made a sound of pleasure and licked strawberry from the corner of her mouth.

At that moment, his throat actually seized up. Could she have any idea that she'd just rendered him completely speechless, almost incapable of breathing?

Her eyes darted across the table just in time to catch him shifting in his chair.

This was definitely not what he needed, her catching him with this shot through the balls grimace on his face. She continued to chew slowly while he watched her, and he tried to ignore the sweet, tugging pain in his groin.

They finished the meal in silence—or rather, she finished. He'd barely eaten a thing.

She rose from the table, gathered up the plates and the saucepan, and took them to the sink. She filled the single basin with water and added dish detergent, glancing at him as he set their glasses down on the counter near her.

He put immediate space between them, feeling as though he'd somehow been sucker-punched. "You don't have to clean up," he said. "You're my guest."

"Inviting oneself does not constitute being a guest." She smiled benevolently—so benevolently, he thought she just might actually want him to kiss her.

What the devil was he about to get himself into?

"Those strawberries were out of this world, by the way," she said. "Did they come from your garden?"

He nodded and grabbed the towel hanging from the oven door. He took three steps, which brought him to her side. He reached for the dish she had just rinsed.

His breath went thin. She looked so soft, smelled so sweet. Like a meadow run through with wild roses. One smile from her and he was simply stunned, as if he'd been zapped with a jolt of electricity. She handed him the plate and he felt his heartbeat pulsing in his eardrums. He wondered what it would be like to pull her against him.

He was pretty sure it was her hair that was going to completely undo him. The smell of it was the kind of distinctly female scent a man wanted to get totally lost in. To get lost in for an indeterminable length of time. Until...

"Are you okay?" she asked, her brow furrowing as she looked at him.

God, it had been a long time since he'd been this moved by the sight and the scent of a woman. His hands were like the uncoordinated appendages of a drunk. It was any wonder he hadn't dropped the plate in his hands.

He swallowed with difficulty. He needed to put that space back between them but he couldn't. He couldn't do anything, it seemed, not even catch his breath.

"McGomery," she whispered, her voice was so tentative he wondered if she had read his mind, had sensed his inner struggle.

His eyes were on her mouth, pleading for the words to escape her lips... Yes, I want you to. Kiss me. Explore every inch of me.

Instead, she set the dishrag aside, moved to tuck her hair

behind her ear, which was pointless since she had already secured it there numerous times already.

"What is it?" she asked.

"You came here to inquire about the land," he replied, clearing his throat. "But it's not why you had breakfast with me. Why did you have breakfast with me? I need to know."

She submerged another dish in the soapy water, but made no move for the dishrag. "I don't know. I... don't know."

She nibbled her lower lip, looked into his eyes, and he was brought instantly back to the time he'd fallen from a tree as a kid and had the wind knocked out of him. He felt the same way now, like he couldn't suck in enough air.

Her hands came out of the water and one of them reached for the towel he held. She worked the towel over her fingers, then laid it on the counter, shaking her head back and forth slightly. "I should go now."

He caught her wrist lightly as she moved away from the sink, and she immediately turned to face him. His voice sounded strange and thick to his ears. "Wait a second. Wait."

"I'm sorry, I can't do—"

Her words were lost when he kissed her, soft, tender. With so much reined in, he trembled. Her hands camp up, her fingers curling into the denim bib covering his chest. She made a sound of pleasure when her lips parted and his tongue gained access to the interior of her mouth.

Then whimpering with need, she responded readily, meeting the thrust of his tongue with the sweet, moist pressure of her own.

And then it was over. She pushed against his chest and he lifted his head. He did not step back, however. He placed his hands on her slim shoulders and pressed his forehead to her own. "Jesus, I'm sorry... I am and I'm not."

"I've had bad luck with this sort of thing in the past," she croaked and sighed raggedly when he angled his head and kissed her again, more slowly than before and without doing anything more than grazing her lips with his own.

"And I haven't?" he whispered. "Between the rumors and whatever your mother told you, you have to know that I come with some baggage of my own."

As his lips lingered lightly over hers, she lowered her hands, allowed him to scoop her against the hard length of him. She turned her head to the side, barring him from kissing her. Then she clutched his biceps, simply clung to him, her breath coming in a fast, uneven rhythm.

He held her and thought his heart would pound right out of his chest. "I've been waiting for you to come, Madison."

Possibly the wrong choice of words because she wrangled back and looked up at him with alarm. "I shouldn't be here with you."

He took a step back, leaned against the sink in an attempt to seem less threatening. "It's up to you, of course."

She immediately moved across the kitchen and had almost made it to the front door when it occurred to him that he might never see her again. It was for the best, but he couldn't stand it, could not leave well enough alone.

"I think we got started off on the wrong foot," he said abruptly. "Tomorrow morning, early, I'm canning my tomatoes. I'd love it if you would come…you know, hang out with me for a while. I'd enjoy the company. No strings attached."

"I don't know," she said, looking back at him over the half wall that separated them. When he said nothing, just stared at her, hoping that she'd see that he was just as rattled as she was, she sighed. "I have to think about it."

After she left, that was all he could manage to do—think about it.

# CHAPTER FIVE

Madison blew at her long bangs and placed the tomato Will had suddenly tossed at her in the pail on top of the few she'd already picked.

She shot him an irritated glance and wiped the sweat from her brow with the back of her hand. "Well, you've got this tomato picking down to a science. I'll give you that."

They had been in his garden for only a few minutes, but already, her tank top stuck to her skin like wet gauze. The humidity gathered in her hair, making it feel heavy, like a thick curtain pressing against her neck. She wished fervently that she'd put it in a ponytail.

She also wished that the tension in her shoulders would ease up. It had been there since she had visited McGomery's bathroom upon arriving and she discovered the photo he'd left for her on the toilet.

It had taken a lot of nerve to come back up on the ridge in the first place, and now it seemed she had more to be concerned about than just their attraction to each other.

She could only wonder what kind of game Will McGomery was playing.

"I mean it," he said, breaking into her thoughts. "You don't have to help me pick these. Sit over there in the grass and enjoy the morning."

She gave him a look. "I don't believe in watching others work when I'm capable of helping out. Just don't expect me to keep up with you."

One hand poised over the metal pail he'd provided her, she peered into his magnificent blue eyes and remembered how she had felt when she'd discovered her land belonged to someone outside her family.

Someone she clearly couldn't trust, someone who was

playing with her head.

Anger surged through her, and the words escaped before she could debate the wisdom of them.

"Okay, I'm just going to say it. I saw the pills and the photograph when I used your bathroom. You put them where you knew I'd never be able to miss them, didn't you?"

She rose and dusted her hands on the thighs of her pants. "Yesterday, you said that maybe we got started off on the wrong foot. Now I'm thinking that maybe you're just a head case. If you have something to say to me, then just say it, McGomery. Don't play games. Why are you on Ativan and Phenytoin? And why did you want me to see that photo of the two girls?"

He slowly stood. "You misunderstand. It wasn't my intention for you to see anything."

He was lying through his teeth. He had used the prescription bottles to prop up the photo on his toilet lid. She had had to move it all just to pee. He was clearly either a coward or a lunatic.

"What are you being treated for? Anxiety, Schizophrenia, what?"

"I'm an epileptic," he said, making a pass over his forehead with the back of his hand and avoiding her eyes.

She was silent for several beats. "That's why you're here. You bought my land so you could hide from the world. I talked to my mother about what happened. You've been plagued with seizures since the car accident you had following your wife's suicide, haven't you? And you can't stand the thought of people knowing."

"Despite what you think, I'm not interested sparking your curiosity about my past." He frowned and crouched again to pick tomatoes. "I'm not happy to know that your mother told you things that you otherwise wouldn't have remembered."

"Look," she said, her voice tight in her throat like an angry fist. "I'm sorry a coma rendered you an epileptic. Truth is, I was promised this land when I was a little girl and I can give you a great deal of money by which to find yourself another place to convalesce. Yesterday was a mistake. I shouldn't have allowed it to happen, but I did, and I regret it, especially in light of your...issues."

He surged back to his feet. "Then climb in that Jeep over there and get the hell off my ridge. If you think I'm a freak, then just take off, get out of here!"

"Why did you do it? Why did you leave those things for me to see?" She pushed her fingers through her hair. "Who are the women in photo? Is that your wife and Sarah Chambers?"

"I don't have to justify anything to you," he said. "And the photo is none of your business."

Madison thought about the girls in the photo. They had been young and beautiful at the time of the candid shot. She was dying to know who they were, and why he would pull such a stunt.

And dying to know why it only made her more intrigued with him.

She swallowed, searching her mind for a way to salvage the morning. "I think we should just drop the subject for now, get these tomatoes picked."

Anger tightened the features of his face until his expression was as formidable as a tornado-laden storm front. "No, I'm pretty damned sure the subject is dropped for good. And for your information, I'm not selling this place to you no matter how much money you've got, so you'd do good to just leave me the hell alone."

She bent, snatched a tomato from a vine and tossed it at her bucket. It hit the ground with a juicy splat. She placed her hands on her hips and sighed loudly.

"You're playing games with me. I just don't know why."

It took him about two seconds to skirt the row of tomatoes between them. He moved into her space—so close she could see right through the buttonholes on his shirt—and fixed her with a bone-melting stare.

She blinked, clenched her jaw, and said nothing.

His gaze was hotter than liquid metal. It coursed over her, through her, until she felt flushed and dizzy. Canonized.

If she had the nerve, she could walk away from him, escape those blue lasers, but she didn't. What she did have was an attraction to him so pure and so strong, she wanted to come up on her toes, take his face in her hands, and smother his mouth with her kisses.

He began talking again, though, barring her from action in the wake of his molten words.

"You think yesterday was a game?" With his face bent over hers, his lips very close, he softened his voice until it was little more than a whisper. "I didn't lure you up here. You came of your own accord, asked for breakfast, and I fixed you something to eat."

It was difficult for Madison to meet his hostile glare, even more of a challenge for her to formulate the few words bouncing around in her head. Finally, clamping her lower lip between her teeth, she looked at her feet, realizing he had said it all.


Resigned, Will stepped back from Madison.

What should have made him feel triumphant left him feeling cheated instead. What had he been thinking when he'd invited her to come back up here?

That was just it. He hadn't been thinking. He'd been feeling—had been overcome by his attraction to her. This was what he got for it too. Now she thought he was some sort of flake or nutcase when in truth, he'd had nothing to do with what she had come upon in his bathroom.

He squeezed his eyes shut, brought his fingers to his temples.

Why him? Why was his life polluted with dreams and seizures, plagued with the paranormal? And why had his unique situation brought him the one person he had no wish to hurt, but would undoubtedly destroy in due time.

He wished he could shrug it all off—the visions, Sarah's whispers, everything—and convince himself the things he saw weren't really glimpses of the future. But he couldn't. The dream about Madison Owens getting caught up in his trap could have been literal, but stood just as good of a chance of being symbolic. The bottom line was that he knew having her up on the ridge boded bad things to come.

For her.

He wished Sarah Chambers would leave him the fuck alone. The dead shouldn't be able to torture the living like this. It was against everything he'd grown up believing.

*Sacrifice.*

Yeah, he got it. His life was one big sacrifice and Madison Owens was someone he couldn't have, couldn't allow into his world. He got it.

His fingers curled into fists by his sides as Madison spoke to him. Her brave voice only made her seem smaller and more wary of him.

"I think you need to take a deep breath and calm down, Will."

She was right, of course, but what he wanted to do was kiss her again. He could think of so many delicious ways to get his mind, and hers, off of the damn photo. And therein lay his real problem.

In a matter of seconds, this ongoing thing between them had become overtly sexual once more, or maybe it had never stopped. He not only wanted to bed her. He needed to bed her, and she wanted him to. Consent was right there in the depths of her chocolate-caramel eyes.

In them, he beheld her soul, the damaged little girl, and the woman who was in desperate need of validation. He saw her attraction to him, raw and inviting. She might have been a naked flower trembling before him in the brutal morning sun.

He could have her, but he would do better to jump right off the edge of a cliff.

To become intimately involved with her, no matter how much his body demanded it, would be crazy foolish. On many levels she was a threat to him, to his secrets, and to his wellbeing. And he was a threat to her.

A huge one.

A romp in bed, however tempting, was an extremely risky thing for both of them. That was why, in the end, he left her standing there in his garden with the sticky smell of tomatoes clinging to her beautiful, dewy skin.

# CHAPTER SIX

Madison eased her Jeep to a halt in front of the cabin, pulling alongside McGomery's truck. She eyed him cautiously as she got out. Despite the fact she'd been telling herself all afternoon that a little time to calm down was all he needed, she half expected him to detonate the second she opened her mouth to speak.

He sat on the front porch, a fiddle tucked beneath his chin. He sawed the bow in his hand over the strings in a mournful fashion, creating a melody just as forlorn and sad. She paused on the top step of the porch and leaned against one of the wooden beams supporting its roof.

After a few more tenuous strains coaxed from the instrument like a whisper, he put it in its case. His eyes remained far away from hers as he snapped the metal clasps and lifted the case to his lap. "You don't know when to leave a thing alone, do you, Owens?"

She tilted her head to one side, looked at him thoughtfully. "Mama told me you were wearing jeans when she first met you. What's with the overalls?"

He didn't answer, but her eyes snagged his as they finally lifted to her face. She decided to press further.

"And she said you didn't have long hair. You quit wearing it short after Sarah and your wife died, didn't you?"

He pulled his lips to one side as if debating how he should answer. "There about, I'd say."

"You know what I think? I think you not only hide from the world, but you to try to hide from yourself."

"I think you want to buy my land so you can try to do the same." His eyes moved to her tank top, skimmed her breasts, and then slid in another direction. "Please go away, Madison. This morning proved one thing. Like everyone else, you don't trust me."

She thought of Jim and how much it had hurt to discover he'd been unfaithful to her with another woman, one who had been more or less a kid at the time. Perhaps she had overreacted in regard to the photo and pills that morning. Maybe Jim's betrayal had left her predisposed to distrust any man that came into her life.

This man who had assumed ownership of her land, the man her mother said locals often referred to as Slick Willie, wasn't playing games with her. If anything, he had tried to give her a glimpse of who he was by leaving her with a couple of clues. Perhaps she had read too much into what she'd found in his bathroom, and now she felt horrible for the way she had accused him.

She didn't miss it when his intoxicating eyes landed on her mouth. When he said nothing, only continued to penetrate her with a stare, she turned and gazed in the direction of his garden.

"You can stop looking at me like that, McGomery."

"No," he said, "I can't. My eyes are thirsty for you."

Her heart beating fast and hard, she forced herself to keep staring across the yard. "Why did you grow out your hair? I'm curious."

After a moment's hesitation, his voice came out, low, almost pained. "I don't care to look like the man I used to be, a man I'll never be again."

She turned and found that his eyes were no longer on her, but on his dog instead, who had come to stand, panting, by the rocking chair.

"And who was that man?" she asked.

"One with at least half a shot at a future." He stood and moved toward the door, fiddle case in hand.

"Won't you invite me inside?" she said. "I'd like to talk to you."

He pivoted and his gaze was suddenly cold, clashing with hers. "Why? So you can try to convince me to convalesce somewhere else? Accost me about being an epileptic? No, I don't think so."

She winced. "I deserve that, I guess."

"No," he said, "You just need to find some new land to bid on because I'm not selling."

"McGomery," she began, "Perhaps you would sell me a parcel of your land, just enough that I could have my own place up here on the ridge. I had my heart set—"

"No," he said, cutting her off. "I don't want to be rude, but you don't belong up here. You shouldn't be anywhere near me."

"You didn't feel that way yesterday, or this morning," she refuted. "Not until our argument anyway."

"Let's just say I've come to my senses." He opened the door and disappeared inside the house.

Madison stared open-mouthed at the door for several seconds after he closed it in her face. Then she turned and went to her Jeep, her shoulders painfully tight.

She came back to the porch carrying the scrapbook she had been stashing in the chest of drawers at her parents' house and sat down in the rocking chair McGomery had vacated. She gazed at the horizon and tried to believe that he would come back out and join her.

The encroaching sunset promised to be swallowed by the ominous storm clouds rolling in from the West. She drew her knees up so she could wrap her arms around something solid.

Thunder rumbled like distant canons, interrupted only by the sound of a crow's caw. The macabre note was like a song for the dead, reverberating through the wasteland that was her heart.

When all that remained of the sun's exit was a swath of purple tinged in volcanic red, her heart settled heavily in her chest. He wasn't coming back. She had cut him down, and now he would want nothing to do with her.

How could she have thrown his infirmity at him like she had? He was an epileptic. You didn't harangue someone about being an epileptic. What exactly had she said? She tried to remember, feeling despicable.

In truth, Will McGomery the man was far more captivating than Will McGomery the urban legend. He was a paradox, a man she couldn't begin to fathom, and she had freaked out over nothing. She had to do something to make up for her bad behavior, but what?

She had to think. Think.

Lightning zigzagged across the sky and she flinched. When the cabin door opened and McGomery poked his head out, she catapulted to her feet.

"Just as I thought," he said. "You're still here."

Her mouth went suddenly bone dry. What ushered from her parched lips shocked her plenty.

"Of course I'm still here. My eyes are thirsty for you."

****

Rain collided with the slope of the cabin's metal roof in popping corn sounds that made it necessary for Madison to raise her voice.

"Storm moved in fast," she said, hovering on the edge of Will's living room sofa, trying not to squirm as her unwilling host sat in the rocking chair across from her and stared at the scrapbook balanced over her thighs.

Nervous, she glanced down at it. "I thought you might reconsider about selling if you saw how much this place has meant to me."

He reached over to the small table next to his chair and switched on a lamp. Unfolding from the rocker, he came over and extended his hand. She passed off the thick, tattered book.

She watched him take it back to the rocker, her eyes moving over him in blatant exploration. He was at least six-foot-four and though his overalls fit loosely, she could discern that every inch of him was rock solid. The way his white shirt played over the muscles in his back, the way his forearms looked below the rolled up sleeves—she was transfixed. Only when he sat down and opened the book of her youthful memories, did she glance away.

The rain was coming down harder than ever now. She studied his sleeping dog on the cushion by the half wall, and then crossed over to one of the windows in the small room. Her hands sliding, palms out, into the back pockets of her shorts, she peered outside. Lightning forked across the sky, illuminating the darkened landscape. A sudden gust of wind sent house to shivering upon its foundation. Will McGomery's voice came to her, caressing, like a ribbon sliding along her nerve endings.

"It's obvious from the photos that this place was a sanctuary for you."

Her eyes didn't stray from the window. "Yes. Then I grew up and thought I needed to go far away to find sanctuary. I got married and then divorced. Did my mother mention that to you?"

She could feel his eyes on her. "Yes," he said.

She made a scoffing sound. "Of course she did."

"I wouldn't have kissed you if she hadn't told me you were unattached." He closed the book; she could hear, even with the rain, the crackling sound of the pages being pressed together.
"I would've wanted to kiss you." He added, "But I wouldn't have."

She angled a look over her shoulder, peering at him through an auburn curl. A current flowed between them, like electricity channeled from the storm outside. She wanted him to channel all that intensity into kissing her again, into making her forget the disaster that had been her marriage.

Jim had crushed her spirit. She had vowed to be extra careful when love came knocking again, had told herself that she would feign indifference until she knew for sure that what she had was real, but could she engage sexually with Will McGomery and actually remain emotionally detached? Indifferent?

The answer to that, of course, was no. And becoming emotionally involved with him felt like a mistake. A big one.

Damnably, she already had feelings for this man with the gold streaked hair and denim overalls. If she wasn't careful and this thing between them led to a night of passion, these feelings were liable to explode into something she might not be ready for.

She watched as he laid the scrapbook on the table and rose from the rocker. Watched as he moved toward her. Then she quickly turned her face back to the darkened window and closed her eyes, wondered how she would find the willpower to turn away if he touched her.

Spurning him was impossible now. She knew what it was like to be held by him, knew the scent of him, the taste of him.

Heat emanated between their bodies like sun-worshipping grains of sand on a beach. He closed in the space between them, and she anticipated his touch with an excitement that was at once incredible and consuming. She didn't care about the risk to her heart. She just wanted his mouth on her.

When he didn't say anything, just stood there so close, the whisper of his breath a tease to her straining ears, she braced herself for the inevitable physical contact. She felt her body responding to the excruciating pleasure of her anticipation.

Lightning, accompanied by a jarring tumble of thunder, penetrated the moment of delicious promise and, startled, she flinched away from the window. Her bare shoulders brushing against McGomery's shirt, she felt his hands—strong and warm—catch her upper arms.

The nape of her neck tingled. Her eyelids fluttered closed again and she reveled in the sensation of her body shaking.

Or was it his trembling she felt?

Her insides shuddered at the possibility. She couldn't remember the last time she had felt this vital in someone's embrace, delicate and yet potent, like she could render this man powerless to her with a word or a touch.

Did she dare to speak? To touch him?

Her senses endeavored to absorb the moment; they

quivered like the fragile, pregnant strains she'd heard Will coax from his fiddle. Her heart thudded with the imminent weight of need. She found it exquisite, this sublime assault, this sensual orgasm. Within one heartbeat she had become his, completely and unequivocally his for the taking.

Air escaped her lungs in a sudden but soft sigh. Her heart caught, then resumed pounding in her chest with the impetus of the rain pelting the cabin.

When Will didn't release her, pressed closer in fact, she sucked in a tiny breath and held it.

His ragged breath fanned her neck. Then she felt the soft tug of his lips on her hair, the heat of his mouth as he pressed it closer to the delicate folds of her ear. "You might be my sanctuary, Madison."

She remained there, quivering like a leaf exposed to the storm outside. Afraid any movement would break the spell and he'd vanish into thin air.

His chest was right there, whisper close to her tank top, and she sensed the powerful thud of his heart through his straining muscles. She yearned to feel his lips on her skin, released her breath in a tiny thread that was accompanied by a whimper of need.

His callused fingers still encircled her left arm. With his other hand, he pushed her hair out of the way and positioned his mouth more intimately over her ear, slipped his tongue evocatively into the sensitive interior. A prism of desire shot through her, turning her knees to jelly and making her heart quicken like the wings of a startled bird.

He laved the shell-like interior of her ear, once, then again, taking his time with the sweet torture. After plundering that secret part of her a third time, he breathed deeply, like a fisherman that has waited many months to gain the plush smell of earth. She reached blindly for the window casing and held on.

He moved closer.

"Turn around, sweetheart. That's all you have to do."

The words alarmed her. They put way too much power into her hands. She glanced at their reflection in the window, wanting to see his face pressed close to hers, seeing instead someone standing just to the side and back of him.

A girl.

Cavernous eyes, her wet hair plastered to the sides of her pale face.

*Oh, God!*

She jerked away from Will just as his dog started barking wildly, and when she turned to face him, she found that no other person was in the room with them.

"What's wrong?" he asked, his riveting blue eyes registering his surprise.

Her throat tightened as she continued to stare at the place where the frightening image had been. Her eyes landed on the floor where the girl should have been standing, and she noticed with no small amount of foreboding that there was a puddle of water. He turned, following her eyes with his, and stared at it, then at the ceiling.

Directing a finger at his dog, he made a gruff sound in his throat, and the animal lowered to his haunches, ushering a low growl.

He didn't say a word, and that perhaps, was what unnerved her the most, even more than the peculiar sight of his dog's hair standing on end.

"I saw someone in the window," she said, the words coming out in rapid succession. "I mean their reflection...behind you."

One of his brows shot up. "Behind me?"

"A girl. Where the water is on the floor." Her hand came up and, rather savagely, she pushed her hair behind her ear. Eyes moving back and forth between him and the water, she swallowed convulsively. "She was soaking wet but I think she was the girl from the photo...in your bathroom. Sarah Chambers?"

The chill radiating from his eyes could have rivaled that of Antarctica's glacier tipped waters. "What would you like for me to say, Madison? I'd tell you that you're imagining things, but then, I can't explain that water, now can I? Or my dog acting up."

Her gaze cut across to her scrapbook on the table. Maybe she needed to think about this before anything else was said. She wasn't sure what to make of his sudden bristling. And she really didn't know what to make of what she had seen in the window or of the water on the floor.

"I've got to go. My... they're going to wonder where I'm at."

He ran his tongue out, tucked it into the corner of his mouth like he was conflicted by his thoughts. Finally, he spoke, and his voice came out husky. "I'm sorry. I didn't mean to snap at you."

"Don't worry about it," she said, moving toward the rocker. She could feel him watching her as she picked up her book and hurried across the room for the door, and was not surprised when he didn't say anything.

What was there to say, after all? A ghost had cropped up in his living room and nearly scared her to death.

And she suspected that he knew any explanation would be moot.

She needed to think about what she had seen.

And about what would have most certainly happened between her and Will McGomery had Sarah Chambers not decided to make a surprise visit.

# CHAPTER SEVEN

Madison squinted at the numbers on her digital alarm clock and groaned. Two mornings in a row of waking early had left her physically depleted. At least the previous day, the early rising had been her choice. This morning her alarm clock was in the form of her sister slamming the bedroom door.

"Mama told me you you've been going up on the ridge to see Will McGomery," Lorna said, her pale eyes flashing like mirrors being turned to the sun. "Is it true?"

Their mother.

Oh God, she should have seen this coming. Madison's sisters, Lorna and Rachel, would have been the first ones Hannah Owens told about her youngest daughters treks up on the ridge. And she wasn't ready for the ensuing lectures.

She rolled her eyes and attempted to shift onto her other side. Her sister's hands seized the comforter. As it went airborne, she felt a prickle of irritation set in and she sat up in the bed, aiming a glare at her unwanted visitor. Lorna was small, with the figure of an adolescent, but her anger made her seem almost gremlin-like—a blond waif capable of curdling someone's blood with a single moonstone stare.

"What is the matter with you?"

Lorna's lips thinned. "I asked you a question."

"No, you were being unspeakably rude. Furthermore, I don't owe you an explanation."

"So it is true. You've been going up there." Lorna's blond pageboy had swung forward and covered her left eye. Her exposed eye glowed with accusation. "Don't deny it."

Had Lorna bought into the rumors about Will cheating on his young wife? Was that it? Did she believe, like many had, that his betrayal had propelled Molly McGomery to commit suicide? Did she think he was unfit to associate with?

"I'm not denying it, Lorna," she said, slowly. "I'm just not going to try to justify my actions with you."

"Are you sleeping with him?"

She sighed. "I guess I might as well get up since you're not about to let me go back to sleep." Sliding her legs over the side of the bed, she sat there for a moment and then met Lorna's pointed stare. "What gives, Lor? Why do you have such a bee in your bonnet over me going up there?"

"You need to find something other than Will McGomery to occupy your time," Lorna said. With a mocking laugh, she flung up her hands. "I mean, Christ, Mad. He was screwing Sarah Chambers. He got her pregnant. Is it such a stretch to think he was the one who drowned her? It's obvious he wanted to be rid of her. And you're gonna what, camp out up there? Write a book about his exploits? In a sense, glorify what happened to that girl?"

Something was way off here. Lorna's was not a version that complied with anything their mother had said in regard to the Chambers' murder investigation and subsequent trial.

"What are you talking about? Will McGomery's cousin was arrested and went to trial for that murder."

"His cousin took the rap for him," Lorna said vehemently. "McGomery is a lying, cheating, son of a bitch. You're going to stir up a shit storm. Is that what you want?"

"With who?"

"For starters, his cousin Aubrey. You know, the one he hung out to dry?"

Madison frowned at her. "How do you know this? Who have you been talking to?"

Her sister eyed her shrewdly. "Drop him, Maddie. He's not worth the trouble."

"Lorna."

"Fine," she said, flipping her glossy blonde hair. "I talk to Aubrey. I know him. I've known him forever. I went to school with him and Sarah, and Will's wife, Molly. Couldn't stand any of them back then."

Madison couldn't hide her surprise over the fact Lorna had been Sarah Chambers' classmate. That little detail had totally escaped her. "Why? Why didn't you like them?"

Lorna snorted. "You might recall that I was an honor student, Mad. I didn't hang out with skanks."

Oh, she remembered all right. Lorna had been an FBLA representative, cheerleader, homecoming queen, and the list had gone on and on. At eleven years old, Madison had aspired to be just like her. "But you're thick with Aubrey McGomery now? How did that happen?"

"We have memberships at the same gym." Lorna's delicate features screwed up with her defiance. "I feel sorry for him, okay?"

"And he's told you what, that Will had better not ever become involved with anyone? He won't stand for it?" It seemed a ridiculous notion, but Madison pondered it nonetheless.

Lorna's face relaxed in measures. She came over to the bed and sat down on the end of it. Slipping a wedge of her hair behind her ear, she peered out the room's window into the brightening day. "He despises Will. I don't want to see you get involved with someone who has such bad blood in his family."

Madison rubbed her eyes then combed her fingers through her tangled hair, willing to lie for the moment. "All I want from Will McGomery is my land. Dad sold me out and it's unfair. I refuse to accept such a raw deal."

"So you're hoping to screw your way into getting McGomery to sell. That's why you're going up there?"

Madison laughed. "You know what, Big Sissa? Kiss my ass."

"It's a bad idea to make friendly with Will McGomery," Lorna said, her voice grave as she swiveled her head to look at her. "People who get involved with him end up dead."

Madison couldn't deny it. She had considered that fact.

Whether McGomery had been involved with Sarah Chambers or not, his wife had believed they were lovers, and had killed herself because of it. Or so the story went. The man was a jinx at the very least, someone despicable at the worst, maybe someone who had, in truth, earned the moniker Slick Willie with his adulterous behavior.

After last night, she even believed to an extent that he was cursed.

That, of course, didn't mean she was any less interested in him.

Unfortunately, she was extremely attracted to him, couldn't stop thinking about the way it had felt to be touched by him, kissed by him, seduced by him.

"Why didn't you tell me Daddy sold the land to him? He's been up there a long time, and neither you nor Rachel said a word to me. All the times I was in for Christmas. Nothing."

"You didn't ask."

"That's lame. Come on, we're sisters."

"I have to get to work," Lorna muttered. "Mama says that after Darius catches the bus you're gonna take her and Chastin to Rachel's for awhile. Watch Mama and don't let her give Chaz too much sugar. It makes two year olds spastic and he kills me after he's been with her all day."

"Lorna, if anyone would have made it a point to mention the land to me it would have been you or Rachel. Why didn't you?"

Lorna sighed. "We didn't find out until after the deal was finalized. Rachel said what you didn't know couldn't hurt you."

"And what do you say?"

After a moment of deliberation, Lorna spoke. "At one time, I was in the same position as you, Maddie. I met McGomery here...downstairs in Mama's kitchen. He was bringing her a ham. To be honest with you, I found him irresistible, began going up there to see him. A few weeks later, the roughneck cut me off and trampled my heart. He said I wasn't ready for another relationship. In fact, he told me I wasn't going to find what I needed in him, that he was only interested in finding someone to fuck around with."

Madison's blood went icy even as her conscience nagged her not to jump to any conclusions. What she and Will had shared...that kiss and last night, it had meant something to him.

It had.

"You're saying you stayed up there with him for several weeks?" she asked. "You were his lover?"

Lorna shifted her slight figure over the end of the mattress. "I visited him, yes. I have two boys, though. I couldn't just move up there."

"So it was more like what, conjugal visits?"

"I fashioned myself in love with him, and you will too if you don't already." Lorna's salon-tanned face darkened and she directed a French-manicured finger at Madison. "You go up there, you'll see. You'll be hurt."

Madison's chest tightened as she watched her sister rise from the bed and walk stiffly across the room. When Lorna opened the door and disappeared into the hallway, she actually felt a lump forming in her throat.

The last thing she could afford was to have her heart trampled again and yet, already, Will McGomery had the power to do just that.

It had been smart to leave his cabin when she had. Would be foolish to go back.

She slumped back in bed and stared at the ceiling, wondering if the girl she had seen in his window thought the same.

# CHAPTER EIGHT

Cecilia Onate perched on the edge of the apartment's kitchen counter, her fingers splayed over each of her denim-clad knees. She strummed them over the fabric as though to some internal rhythm, a tapping that would grate on even a saint's nerves.

Lorna gritted her teeth. She was no saint.

What was this little tramp's problem? They'd known one another for less than a month, and yet the woman had assumed the role of alpha dog—queen bitch. It was hardly worth the trouble of fooling with her for the sake of Aubrey's voyeuristic sexual appetite.

It wasn't the petulant curve of Onate's mouth that had her so worried. It was her eyes. They were the eyes of a possessive spouse and she had already been down that road, thank you very much.

*Señorita* Cecilia was proving to be more of predicament than she had bargained for, and now she regretted having used the lesbian to satiate her curiosity. The last thing she needed was Cecilia drawing attention to something she had no desire to broadcast around town.

It would not do to have the public at large knowing that little Lorna Owens was not above playing from both sides of the deck. If that got back to her Daddy, she would have a whole lot more to deal with than Madison taking up with Will McGomery.

Her eyes honed in on the pretty Hispanic's face. In a matter of two evenings, under the watchful attention of one Aubrey McGomery, Ceci—as she liked to be called—had gone from being her fitness trainer to a sexual dalliance, and now it had to stop. Her pulse quickened.

How invested was this woman?

"Why did you want me to stop by?" she began, gauging

Cecilia's face. "I have to pick up my boys at Mama's soon."

Cecilia's gaze was calculated. "You nervous about being here alone without your boyfriend, *chica*?"

Lorna glanced around the kitchen, looking for a distraction. "I thought you wanted to put down some roots here, Ceci. You've done nothing to make this place yours, you haven't even hung a picture on the wall."

"Maybe I was holding out for someone to share it with," she said. "I told you, I am looking to settle down, find someone to share my life. That is why I wanted to talk to you. It cannot go on like this. I am not interested in a threesome, Lorna. I told you that already."

Now Cecilia's face twisted into a dark scowl. "Why you want to whore around all the time? You told me the thing with Aubrey was pretty much over, but it is not, is it? You never had any intention of ending things with him. You just used me to get him worked up."

It had to be Cecilia's boss filling her head with crap again. "What has Miranda been telling you, Ceci?"

Cecilia's head tilted to one side. "She tells me nothing. When I am not around, you are there fawning all over that pot smoking hippie because that is the way you operate, Lorna. You think I am stupid? I am not stupid, you are the one who does not see the whole picture here."

"What's that supposed to mean?"

Cecilia made a longsuffering expression. "You are dancing with the devil himself when it comes to that man."

Lorna smiled. All she had to do was make sure Cecilia Onate's opinion didn't change. If little Ceci thought *Señor* Aubrey was going to be a part of their future, she would bow out and quickly—problem solved.

She crossed over to the counter. If this was poker, she had a full house and couldn't go wrong. She slid between Cecilia's plump thighs and cupped her hands around her dark, cupid face.

"I've been involved with him long enough to know I can't

up and change dance partners just like that," she whispered. "He's not so easy to get away from, Ceci. I'm trying to put some distance between us, but it's going to take some time."

She paused to let that sink in. She thought of something else that would be serve as the icing on the cake. "He's every bit as domineering as he was with that girl I told you about. He was a masochist with Sarah Chambers in high school. I saw him with her. You want me to take a chance and piss him off? No, of course you don't."

She saw Cecilia's lips as they parted, and pressed a fingertip to them to keep her from speaking. "Ceci, listen, you see how religious he is about working out. He's vanity with a temper. We can't just exclude him from our relationship. Cutting him out of the triangle now would insult his ego. Until I can figure out how to break it off with him, we're dead in the water."

Cecilia's gaze was cool as it always seemed to be, but in the depths of her dark, metallic colored eyes, hostility shimmered like newly minted coins.

"Then you can just exclude me because I am not interested in feeding his inflated ego." She clutched Lorna's hands as they were dropping from her face, squeezed them hard. "You are going to keep it up until he kills you. You are addicted to him, and addicted to using people just to make him jealous. I am not going to be your puppet on a string, *chica*, you hear me?"

"You're not my wife, you fucking dirty whore, so stop trying to lay a guilt trip on me." She pulled away from Cecelia violently, stalked across the room so that she could contemplate her from a safer distance.

Cecilia slid off the counter with the ease of a serpent. She padded over to a stainless steel refrigerator and her curvaceous figure disappeared behind the door for a moment.

She came out with a Corona, popped the top, and wasted no time partaking of the amber liquid in the bottle. After she wiped her mouth with the back of her hand, she fixed Lorna with a dour look. "If you ever call me that again, you will have to pick yourself up off the floor, *puta*. Got it?"

Lorna chewed the inside of her lip, crossed her arms over her chest. "I'm not addicted to either one of you. You don't scare me, Cecilia, and neither does Aubrey."

"And that is why you are going to end up floating in a pond like that girl...what was her name...Chambers?"

Lorna turned for the door, her shoulders rising in a flippant shrug. "We'll talk later, when you can be less of a drama queen."

Feeling the woman's dark eyes burning into her back as she left, she told herself that there would never be another talk with Cecilia Onate. The nay-saying twit had crossed the line when she'd equated her to Sarah Chambers.

She would never wind up like Sarah. She was too smart.

# CHAPTER NINE

Mental exhaustion had set in.

After her daylong excursion to Bristol to visit Rachel, the last thing Madison felt up to was another paranormal episode with Will McGomery. But she drove up the ridge anyway.

Lorna's words had haunted her throughout the day. She needed to hear his version of things, needed to ask him point blank if he'd slept with her sister.

A random thought struck her as she cleared the woods. If he'd had a dalliance with Lorna, he would have known the potential for her finding out. He wasn't that stupid or brash.

Was he?

Her troubled thoughts dwindled when. As she drove across the meadow, she saw a black truck with an abundance of chrome and purple pin striping parked in his drive next to McGomery's rattletrap Ford.

Great. He had company and it was too late to turn around. They had surely seen her by now.

She drove the rest of the way across the field and eased her Jeep to a stop behind Will's truck, her eyes darting to the porch. He and his grizzled looking guest were seated in wooden rockers, the younger man holding a fiddle, the older a banjo. Both watched her as she got out of the vehicle and their music promptly dwindled to nothing.

Mounting the porch steps, she dared a look into Will's eyes, butt he glanced away from her. The strange incident of the night before had changed him somehow. She felt it intuitively.

His eyes landed on the other guy who was, in the awkward silence, fiddling with the tuning knobs on his banjo, his gunmetal gray hair hanging limply over his bony shoulders like aged cornhusks. Her attention fixing on him as well, it occurred to Madison that he looked like an aged elf. He had large ears that poked out beneath his cap and through his hair like props, and a nose that was not large but elongated to the point his heavily lined face was thrown off balance.

His leathery fingers remained busy at their task as he gazed back at her as though she were some kind of mystic creature, a mermaid perhaps. No treachery gleamed in his murky gaze. He was merely curious—curious enough now that his banjo picking was not likely to resume.

She stood on the top step of the porch and leaned against one of the support posts, feigning an ease she did not feel, her eyes cutting back to Will while her palms sweated because she was incredibly nervous. With a pointed look toward his guest, she prompted him to make an introduction and he didn't disappoint.

"Dow, this is Marshy Owens' daughter," he said, a glint in his eyes. "She's writing a book about her great-grandparents who lived up here."

Okay, so he was proving that he could lie and do it convincingly. Writing a book about her great-grandparents? Why was he telling this old man such a thing?

Dow tipped his head at her, a gnarled finger touching the brim of his cap. She now noticed that it boasted the embroidered words, *Modern Chevrolet*. His tobacco stained lips curved upward at the corners and he transformed from an elf into something Grinch-like, making her want to glance away from him.

"Didn't think my nephew had any lady friends no more. Guess I figured wrong, huh?"

"Madison, this is Dow," Will said, his eyes flat now. "Dow McGomery."

She immediately stuck out her hand and Dow rose to shake it, all the while grinning unabashedly at the other man, his toothless maw impossible to ignore. When he released her hand, he set about putting his banjo in the case.

"I'll get Clarence to burn you a copy of that CD, Willie,"

he said. He glanced at her and winked. "And don't worry about your lady friend here. Secret's safe with me."

She gave him a strange look. "I hope you're not leaving on my account. I would love to hear the two of—"

"I have your word on that?" Will asked the other man, cutting her off. He put away his fiddle and latched the metal fasteners on the case, left it sitting by the rocking chair. Standing, he crossed his arms over his chest and leveled a stare at his uncle.

"Shoot, you know I ain't gonna say nothing, Willie," the older man said. "Never know what that sorry shit Aubrey's capable of. Shamed to even call him my son, truth be told."

Will visibly relaxed, and even stretched as he stood. Clovis came to his four paws and stood at the ready next to his master's denim-clad leg, as if he suspected they were going somewhere.

Will leaned against a porch beam a few feet away and angled Madison a look, a look that made her heart stand still because it was accompanied by a smile so boyish, so at once open and inviting, that he was instantly transformed. Gone was the cynical man that had emerged after the ghostly vision in his living room. Gone were the drilling blue eyes and hard mouth. The man standing before her was a man she would never be able to resist should he turn his affection on her. She rested her head against the beam she leaned on and just stared back at him.

"Dow plays claw hammer style," he said. "Ever seen someone play a banjo that way, Madison?"

She forced a glance in Dow McGomery's direction and puzzled over his tense expression. Was it her imagination or was he suddenly ill at ease, ready to get out of there?

"Not in years," she answered. "I wish I could have seen it today."

"Tell you what," Dow said after clearing his throat. "You come to the fair September Six. Me and the band will be playing that night."

He tipped his scraggly chin at Will. "In fact, you should

come too. Play with us this year. It would do you some good, man."

"Sure it would," Will said, gazing across the yard toward his garden. He said nothing else as the light extinguished from his eyes. He made a swipe at a mosquito and, after a moment, stepped over to the front door, leaning inside the cabin to flip on the porch light.

Dusky shadows dissipated with the warm glow of the small globe situated high beside the jamb. Insects immediately drew in for the attraction, but just as they were compelled to hang around, Dow McGomery was just as anxious to get away.

"Well," he said. "I gotta scoot. Ada will have supper on for me and I've done been late for it once already this week. It was nice to meet you, Miss Owens, and remember, if you fancy Bluegrass, you need to come on over to the fair. We're pretty good for a bunch of old geezers."

She smiled at him, and then watched as he took off in the direction of his truck. Dust billowed from his tires as he started across the field, and she surmised he was relieved to be finished with them. She turned, caught Will staring wistfully at her, and her breath hitched in her chest.

"Why did you do that?" she asked, finally finding her voice. "You told him I was writing a memoir."

"What, it doesn't sound reasonable?" The unnatural looking smile that curved his lips slipped a little. "I couldn't tell him the truth."

"That I want my land back?" The words sounded spiteful coming out of her mouth and she regretted them instantly. "I'm sorry, but I don't understand. Whether you're interested or not in selling, why not tell him? Why the secrecy?"

He stepped over and propped himself against the post on the other side of the steps. His eyes scanned the yard restlessly. "If I'd told him you were here to talk to me about the land, he would have wound up trying to talk me into selling. He pesters the living hell out of me about the way I live, says I'm a hermit, and I don't want to listen to him."

It was a bizarre thought, Dow McGomery lecturing his nephew about being reclusive. He looked closer to fitting the bill than Will did.

"Um, we need to talk," she said, squelching the need to fidget.

He nodded. "About what you saw last night. Look, emotions were running high. I'm not saying you didn't see something, but I don't think it was what or who you think."

The ghostly image in his window was not the subject she had been about to broach with him, but his trivializing the incident was discomfiting. "I know what I saw, Will."

"The water came from the rain," he said dryly. "I inspected the ceiling and found that it was leaking. I had some drywall mud leftover from patching a leak in my woodworking building and fixed it."

She nibbled the soft lining of her lower lip. "I see, and your dog's behavior?"

"Apparently he gets a little freaked over leaky ceilings," he said.

Her heart beat faster with a surge of anger. "Okay, fine, whatever you say. It's not what I want to talk about. I want to talk to you about my sister, Lorna."

He was silent for a beat. "What about her?"

"She used to come up here," she said, gauging his expression and finding it suspiciously blank. He raised his hand and bit at a fingernail.

"And?"

"And you led her to believe she had a future with you."

"I don't know what the hell you're talking about."

"Will, don't do this. Don't lie to me." His eyes shone bright with his anger and she felt her belly tighten in response. "You told her she was expecting too much from you."

"I told her I wasn't interested in her wares and that she should take them elsewhere," he said, pushing off the porch post and stepping toward her.

She folded her arms over her breasts and looked at him, torn. "You're saying you didn't sleep with her then?"

"Hell yeah, I'm saying that."

"So, you're above reproach. That's what I'm supposed to believe? That my own sister lied to me?"

"Would that be out of character for her? To lie?"

She sighed, wondering why the hell she was compelled to believe him instead of Lorna. "I haven't been around my sister much in the last decade. I went to live with our mother's sister in Ohio, attended OSU and married a professor. She stayed here, married an insurance agent and had a couple kids. If not for our subsequent divorces, she and I probably would have never even had our conversation this morning."

"Or dealings with me."

"You are what stands between me and my land," she said, his close proximity making her feel unsteady on her feet. "That's the only reason I started coming up here to have dealings with you."

One side of his mouth quirked up and then he closed in the remaining distance between them, lifted his arm, and cupped her face in his palm. His thumb made passes over her cheek and she stared at him, wishing she could inoculate herself against the hungry look on his face.

When his gaze moved from her lips back to her eyes, simply holding her gaze, she felt a stirring of awareness that frightened her. He intended to have her, one way or another, and she could not let that happen. Not until she knew the exact truth about Lorna. Turning away from him, she sought the far end of the porch, looked across the darkening field.

"My sister clearly put out the welcome sign for you," she said. "She's beautiful and you live up here like some backwoods relic. You must think I'm a simpleton, Will McGomery, if you expect me to believe you weren't attracted to her."

She heard the scuff of his boots as he walked over to stand

beside her, and she looked askance at him. He swatted the air then blew at a lock of blond brown hair that had tumbled over his brow.

He shrugged. "Ever heard the saying, pretty is as pretty does? In any case, I take exception to being called a relic. I'm not a fossil...yet anyway."

The barest of smiles curved his lips as he narrowed his eyes over the deep shadows of the landscape. Lit from behind by the porch light, his features were shrouded in mystery, lending him an almost ghostly appearance. She longed to touch him, make him real, but instead, darted her tongue out to moisten her lips.

"How does the, pretty is as pretty does, adage apply to Lorna?"

He drew one of his hands down over his face. "Let's just say your sister has some issues."

"With you," she acknowledged. "My sister despises you."

"She's got a problem with me all right."

She shifted her weight, looked hard at him. "What do you mean?"

"Put it this way," he said. "If Lorna was a doctor, there would be no way in hell she could hold to the oath of first, do no harm. She's morally corrupt."

At her look of shocked dismay, he sighed. "Your sis is an adulteress, Maddie. She threw out that welcome sign you were talking about, long before she was divorced...at least in regard to me."

Maddie? Was he trying to endear himself to her even as he besmirched Lorna's reputation?

"You, the man everyone knows as an adulterer?" she said, unable to keep the mocking lilt out of her voice. "Talk about the pot calling the kettle black."

"Believe what you will, but I don't uphold infidelity. Guess you could say I've seen how it destroys people. My wife killed herself because of it."

She stood completely still, studied him at length. She knew

exactly why Lorna had been drawn to him. It was the same reason she herself could not look away for very long when in his presence. Despite that almost hard glint in his eyes, he had a haunted look about him, seemed completely vulnerable. At times he exuded vulnerability.

"People stray," she said carefully. "At least you learned from your mistake. Right?"

He seemed to be holding a great debate in his mind, but finally imbued her with a judicious smile. "You're not interested in that scandal. You're here because you're dying to get the low down on your sister. It eats you alive to think I might have fucked her."

For a moment, she was too astonished to speak. Evidently, unpredictable was the word she was going to come to know him by, and somehow, at the moment, she found this sudden foray titillating.

"To the contrary," she said, having to clear her throat. "I do want to know about the past. I wish you would set the record straight about it."

"That a fact?"

"Yes." She scratched the corner of her eyebrow but held his stare.

His blue eyes, almost velvety in the dusk, were steady, very steady. "Sarah was in trouble. Molly and I were the ones she turned to."

"What kind of trouble?" she said, surprised he had said this much.

"She was pregnant. She was afraid of what my cousin Aubrey would do if he discovered it and she wanted us to help her get an abortion. Her parents were deeply religious and she didn't want them to know, plus she needed money for the procedure."

She counseled herself to keep her expression even. She hadn't expected him to actually indulge her and if she exhibited too much intrigue, she suspected he would instantly shut down.

"So she must not have thought the baby was Aubrey's if she feared telling him."

"Aubrey isn't capable of fathering children," he said. "When he was around twelve years old, my old man beat him within an inch of his life. Among other injuries, he suffered gross testicular trauma from one of the kicks he sustained."

At her startled expression, he offered a dry explanation. "My father was a drunk; nine times out of ten a mean one. Aubrey got in his way. I did myself, on occasion, but fared a lot better than he did because I was older, could hold my own. Trust me when I say no one mourned his passing when liver cirrhosis finally did him in, least of all Aubrey and my mother."

"Did you foot the bill for Sarah's abortion?"

"No. She decided to have the baby but miscarried."

She stood up straighter. "But she was pregnant at the time of her death."

"Your mother is a walking history book, isn't she?"

She offered a shrug, unwilling to admit that she had accessed the computer in her father's study the night before to peruse the archives of the Bristol Herald Courier. "So she was pregnant with her second child at the time of her death?"

He nibbled the inside of his upper lip, which might as well have been a verbalized yes.

And her next question would be even tougher.

# CHAPTER TEN

Will's eyes were hooded and his body tense.

Was he standing there next to her wondering if he'd fathered not just one child with Sarah Chambers, but two?

She waited, had almost gotten up the courage to hit him with the question again when he spoke gruffly.

"I don't want to talk about this, Madison."

She pretended not to notice the way his jaw had tightened. "Who was the father of those babies, Will?"

"I said I don't want to talk about it."

"Maybe you need to talk about it," she said, wanting to touch his shirtsleeve and, at the same time, afraid to embrace her presentiment. "Is that why Molly hung herself, because you were the father, because she thought you were the father and she couldn't deal with that along with losing her best friend?"

"I don't know. I asked her when I found her hanging by her neck in the barn, but she seemed all choked up." His mouth twisted with anger. "Look, I don't need to talk about the past. I'm humoring you because you have that kid-in-the-candy-store look in your eyes and I'd hate to send you back to your Mama without any fodder for gossip."

She would have to ignore his bitter sarcasm if she hoped to get deeper into the truth of what had happened to Molly McGomery and Sarah Chambers.

This was not a tenable situation. It called for finesse and tolerance. "You must have an idea about why Molly did what she did."

"Are you familiar with the biblical account of Ruth and Naomi?" he asked, eyes burning with an emotion now that was beyond anger.

"Yes. Of course."

His appraisal of her drew out, each second bringing more

antipathy to his expression. "Ruth had her heart set on going wherever Naomi went, right? Well, I believe Molly was no different when it came to Sarah, and the afterlife became her choice of destination after Sarah drowned."

"Murdered," she said. "You mean after Sarah was murdered."

His expression went blank.

She leaned back, surveyed him with skepticism. "Why would she want to join, in the spiritual realm, someone who had sullied her chance of having a happy marriage, someone who had betrayed her profoundly?"

"Perhaps to hunt her down and make her pay?" he said, his voice suddenly crackling with scorn. "Look, I was just yanking your chain. Sarah and Molly were no Ruth and Naomi. They were screwed up, that's what they were."

He cocked his head to one side, his beryl-blue eyes losing some of their heat. "My wife did feel betrayed by Sarah, and by me. As retribution, she went to Aubrey and told him that Sarah's second pregnancy was my doing. Guess you could say she was trying to kill two birds with one stone. In one fell swoop, she hoped to get Sarah and me both. Only I don't think she counted on Sarah drowning, and I don't think she counted on becoming a suspect in the ensuing investigation."

She considered his words and then spoke into the heavy silence that followed them. "I tend to think Aubrey killed Sarah in a moment of jealous passion. Drowned her in your grandparents' pond and then walked because more than half the jury couldn't absolve themselves of the doubt your wife did it. He showed his propensity for revenge and violence again when he burned your house down."

"I can see you've been doing quite a bit of studying on this," he said. "Thing is, I'm finished humoring you, Owens."

He glanced down to where Clovis was sprawled between them, panting while he dozed, and nudged the dog with his boot. "You hungry boy?"

Without another word, he turned and moved for the front door, the animal right on his heels. Allowing Clovis to precede him into the house, he angled her a look. "You coming in or are you too afraid of Sarah Chambers' ghost?"

She crossed the porch and held his stare as she stepped across the threshold. He followed her in and walked around the end of the counter that divided the living room from the kitchen. He produced a bag of dog food from the cupboard next to the refrigerator and made a kissing sound. After he poured some of the morsels into one of the bowls situated over a pet mat on the other side of the refrigerator, he ran his hand over the eager dog's back.

"Yeah, you're starving half to death, aren't you?" He issued a pat to the animal's head and Madison watched with her mind still locked on Molly McGomery and her friend.

"Aren't you worried that it will set your cousin off, me being up here?" she said. "Lorna seems to think that you're involvement with me will rankle him."

"I can't argue that Aubrey is volatile," he said, replacing the bag of dog food to the cupboard. "Truth? I think my cousin would find you a very intriguing diversion from what he has going on, and I can't say he's ever gotten over the idea of me sleeping with his girlfriend. I don't know that he wouldn't view you as a way to get back at me. I don't know that he wouldn't hurt you in an attempt to ruffle my feathers."

"Are you trying to scare me away?"

"No. I'm telling you my theory about Aubrey."

"Do you think he pushed Sarah into that pond?"

"It wasn't an accident."

"You're evading the question."

He came back into the living room where she stood on the rug a good ten feet away from where the water had been the night before. He took up a position in the rocker, appearing mostly as he had just before he'd approached her during the storm and did that erotic thing to her ear. She shivered and his lips thinned as his eyes ravaged her face.

"Sarah was involved with Jacob Davidson around the time of her drowning. In school they didn't belong to the same clique, but after they graduated, she believed the social boundaries no longer existed and started a thing with him behind Aubrey's back."

His expression bland, he continued. "Jake was the sheriff's son, bound for medical school, and she was wrong to think they could have a relationship. With or without the complication of Aubrey, it couldn't have worked. The second he would have figured out she was pregnant, he would have bolted, been desperate to escape any kind of scandal."

So maybe he hadn't betrayed Molly.

She felt incredibly relieved by this new information.

It was easy to imagine what it would have been like for a young, idealistic Sarah Chambers to be in love with the sheriff's son. The girl had probably thought that Jacob Davidson would be her ticket out of the southern mountains of Appalachia—not unlike the way she herself had supposed in regard to Jim Eckhart. Aubrey was sterile and not without emotional baggage. Jacob would have seemed like a prince in comparison.

God, the girl had drowned in a pond that Will's grandfather had allowed, for decades, to be a place for the community to picnic and swim. What once had been a haven for fishing and swimming had, for a young, pregnant woman, turned into a watery grave.

Jake's father, Tritt Davidson, had been the sheriff of Russell County for years. Was it possible that there had been some kind of cover up? It seemed so convenient that the murder had taken place on McGomery land. How ideal if you were planning to frame a McGomery for that same murder.

Who had had more reason to want Sarah Chambers out of the picture, Aubrey McGomery or Jacob Davidson? Aubrey would have been livid over the pregnancy, but Jacob would have had much to lose by being the father—possibly the future his parents had mapped out for him.

"Nothing I've heard indicates the sheriff ever knew that his son was involved with Sarah," she said. "You didn't come forward with what you knew, didn't reveal your suspicions about who the father was?"

"Implicating Jacob Davidson would have gone over real nice with his Pap, don't you think? I'm sure Tritt would have jumped right on it, brought his son in for questioning, let the local media eat his family alive."

"If Sarah did, in fact, inform Jacob Davidson about the pregnancy," she said, "he had a motive to kill her."

"He didn't kill her. I only told you about him because I want you to realize that there is more to what happened to Sarah than what you've read or heard. It's dangerous to form opinions on hearsay and old newspaper articles."

How had he put it together that she had done some research of her own on the Chambers' case? Was she that terrible of a liar? "You believe your cousin did it, don't you?"

He stifled a laugh. "I don't know why you think I would enjoy a conversation about my cousin."

"You enjoy living up here on my land with your ghosts?" The words, spawned from her anger over his refusal to open up, were out before she could stanch them.

His eyes suddenly flinty, he glared at her. "I enjoy my solitude, what little I'm able to find now that you're back on the scene. And this isn't your land, little lady. Not by a long shot."

"It is," she said, her voice suddenly bubbling with emotion.

"No." He shook his head, straightened from the chair and approached her. "The land is mine. Would you like me to show you the deed of trust?"

She picked at an imaginary speck of lint on her shorts, refused to meet his eyes. "No. I would not."

"I think what you would like is for me to kiss you again."

Her teeth sank into her lower lip, even as her insides fluttered with sudden arousal. God, could he be any more right?

And it was terrible, so awful for her to want him to kiss her again. Lorna's words would not go away with that kiss, with what would surely, sweetly follow it. They would be right there waiting for her when all was said and done.

But.

Will McGomery wanted her. And she needed him.

He touched her hair, tucked it behind her ear. Her eyes lifted to his. "Do you believe in taking chances, Maddie? I want to be with you. Stay with me tonight."

The window in which she had seen the girl was a few feet away, but it could have been a thousand miles from where they stood. Will McGomery was simply too potent for the memory of that to matter. She watched as he tilted and lowered his head, and then her eyes drifted closed as his mouth settled over hers.

"You're in my blood, girl," he mumbled against her lips. "Already, I can't get my mind off you."

She opened her mouth and he filled it with the salty sweet pressure of his tongue. Gripping handfuls of his shirt on either side of the denim bib covering his chest, she was shocked to hear her own strangled cry of passion.

He responded by splaying his fingers wide across her back, and pulling her snuggly to the front of him. They became a tangle of limbs and hungry, desperate fingers. Hers slid through the strands of his long hair, and his roamed over the swell of her hips and down her bare thighs.

His mouth leaving hers to trail kisses down her neck and across her collarbone, he spoke her name, more or less, breathed it against her feverish skin.

"You hurt me without even trying," he whispered against the hollow of her neck. Dipping his tongue into that sensitive place, he made a sound of pleasure like a deep purr in his throat. "You make me ache."

He palmed her breast through her tank top and bra, kneading gently, then squeezed the mound. In turn, she arched into the solid length of him, felt the pressure of his erection against her lower belly and gasped.

It was no longer a question of whether they would follow their passion wherever it may lead. They were going to consummate this thing that had started the moment they had laid eyes on one another. He was tight and hard with arousal. She was more than ready to give him what he needed.

She fumbled with the fasteners on his overalls until they gave way, and then with that accomplished, she attacked the buttons on his blue button down shirt until the worn fabric fell open to reveal a muscular chest matted with soft, dark hair. His fingers were on the metal button of her shorts and then on the zipper. She helped him rid her of the barrier of her clothing, removing her tank top and tossing it aside as he worked her shorts and panties down her legs.

As she stepped out of her sandals and the pool of clothing at her feet, he crouched to remove his boots. When he stood again, he gave his overalls a hard tug, and they unfastened at his side. He let them drop, stepped out of them, and stood before her in nothing but a pair of black boxers.

She backed toward the sofa, sat demurely on one of the cushions and watched him, her chest rising and falling quickly and her head muzzy with desire and anticipation.

He smiled boyishly and she knew that he had figured her out. She was afraid to know what he would think of her body, was trying to put off the inevitable. Unabashedly, he removed his boxers and let her drink in the sight of him. Swallowing, she allowed her eyes to rest on the part of him that she had wondered about so many times. He did not disappoint, was in fact, exquisitely beautiful, his sex springing long and turgid from a thatch of brown gold hair, his narrow hips complimented by his flat, hard abdomen and powerful looking thighs.

His steps were slow and measured. He approached the sofa and instantly lowered himself to his knees in front of her. His hands were rough and warm sliding up the inside of her thighs, plying them apart, inch by inch.

She blushed, could feel her cheeks warming up like a virgin's. He began placing open mouth kisses to the tender skin revealed by his hands, and she knew he intended to pleasure her with his lips and tongue.

It was something that she wanted, but feared. It had been so long since she had shared her body in such a way and Jim had never understood how to please her. She anticipated being disappointed, and could not bear the thought of feigning anything with Will McGomery. This experience could not be ruined by her inability to express her needs. She would not take the chance of marring their time—possibly one time—together.

She pushed him back, her fingers pressing firmly into his shoulders. "No."

"No?" His eyes dropped to the flower of her exposed sex and he smiled sensuously. He undoubtedly could see that she was ready for him.

She caught his hand, tan and rugged over the fairer skin of her thigh. "I don't expect you to understand, but not that. Just let me please you. That's all I want for now."

He sobered immediately. "What's wrong?"

Of course he wouldn't understand, and how could he? She blinked at him, watched him swallow, the way his Adam's apple bobbed up and down, and felt her heart catch. He did not want damaged goods, was afraid that she was exactly that, and would pull away if he thought...

She planted her hands on his shoulders again, splayed her fingers and pushed him back until she could slip off the sofa and slowly lower herself upon him. They gasped at the same time as her body gloved him. He looked into her eyes and sucked in another breath as she shifted, adjusting to the size of him.

"Goddamn, Madison." He brushed her hair back, seemed to recognize the uncertainty in her eyes. "You're tight. Easy does it."

"I'm okay," she said, embarrassed.

Threading long fingers through her auburn curls, he dipped

his head and trailed kisses along her neck. His other hand found her breast and he tweaked the aroused bud of her nipple between his thumb and index finger.

She began to tremble, her body tightening around him already. Inconceivably, the very pressure of him was going to be her undoing. His name escaped her breathless lips, and he raised his head from the swell of her breast where he had just begun to suckle.

His rugged face lit up. "Ahh, God, Maddie. Yes. Yes."

Nearby, something clanged, then crashed, sending Clovis into a barking frenzy. Freezing up, Madison swiveled her head toward the stone hearth a couple of yards away. An array of fireplace implements, as well as the metal rack that had housed them, lay strewn across the floor. It was like someone had stumbled right into them, causing them to topple over.

Confused, she looked from them to Will. He tried to defuse the situation, shook his head, and then nuzzled her beneath her jaw line.

"She can't do anything if you refuse to let her. Ignore it. Don't feed into it."

"What?" She pushed back from him, her fingertips biting into his pectoral muscles. "Who am I ignoring? Sarah Chambers?"

He sighed. "Madison, please. Focus on us. Feel me inside—"

"Will." She framed his face in her hands, probed his eyes with her own. Taking a tremulous breath, she then closed them. "Why is she here?"

"Look at me," he said, holding her hips firmly so that she wouldn't try to move off of him. "Please, look at me."

She did. His eyes were dark with desire. He smiled just slightly and cupped her behind, pulling himself deeper into her body.

"You won't talk about her," she said, bracing against the tiny tremors of need that threatened to engulf her. "Why won't you tell me why she's haunting you?"

He slid his tongue along the rim of her lower lip. "Not the time for talk."

After another moment of fighting to keep her desire at bay, she struggled off his lap. "Sarah just caused that thing to career across the floor and it's not the time to talk about her? Last night I saw her in your window." She glanced at Clovis, still barking. "And so did he."

Will's eyes were on his aroused cock, his expression one of discomfort. She cast the scattered objects by the fireplace another look, and came cautiously to her feet. In seconds, she had almost all of her clothes back on, and what she didn't have on, she was trying to get on. She made sure she never looked Will's way, though through her peripheral vision, she discerned he had moved from the floor to the sofa.

"I can't believe you're going to leave because of a damn shovel, broom, and poker," he said testily, causing her to at once abandon her decision to avoid looking at him.

He was sprawled over the sofa cushion, one arm thrown over the back of the couch, and his erection as apparent as ever. If it had flagged at all, she couldn't tell.

"It's not that and you know it," she replied. "It's the fact you won't talk to me about her. You just want me to pretend nothing's going on." Their eyes did battle and she sighed. "And besides that, there's my sister, the things she told me. I can't…I don't…God, I don't even know you."

"Madison, come on." He leaned forward. "We're getting to know one another. Give me a chance."

"Talk to me," she said.

He just looked at her. He looked at her for a very long time and said nothing.

She nodded and swallowed the lump in her throat. With another glance at the fireplace, she turned and left his cabin.

Left his barking dog and his insistent poltergeist.

But she did not take her heart with her.

# CHAPTER ELEVEN

Will threw back the covers and swung his legs over the side of the bed. He shouldn't be thinking of Madison Owens, and yet he was. He couldn't get to sleep for thinking about her. And the really worrisome part was that he wasn't sweating over the last thing she had said to him, couldn't even focus on the fact she had been right.

She didn't know him at all.

For days now, since that night she had left him painfully aroused and just as confused, he had been thinking only about how attracted he was to her. The scent of her hair, the sound of her voice—his memory of each drove him to distraction.

Sarah's voice haunted him nightly in dreams that continued to bring him to the trap in the woods, and yet, when awake, all he could manage to contemplate was how he might get Marshy's youngest daughter to come back up on the ridge. In the trap dream, Madison begged for him to help her. In reality he should try to run her off, but so far he had done a hell of a shitty job of that.

He didn't want to and was miserable for it, his mind filled with the memory of her—the way her small body hugged his cock, the taste and feel of her mouth.

He stood from the bed and started for the bathroom, halted when he heard a knock on the cabin's front door and Clovis's ensuing, excited barks. He didn't think. He moved for the gun safe in the corner of the room, Sarah's whisper like fingertips trailing over his thoughts.

*The time has come.*

He couldn't take a chance and assume this was Madison. Her last visit had been in false bravado and she wouldn't come back, especially after the fireplace incident. It was just after midnight and anybody could be at his door. She would not be back.

He thought of Aubrey as he removed the weapon of choice from his safe. Then, he considered the possibility that Madison had been talking about her visits up on the ridge, talking just to spite him, and cringed at the thought of some fanatical preacher type coming to rain fire and brimstone on him for daring to mingle with society again.

He exited the cabin from the rear and stealthily maneuvered around the side to the front. The night air was humid and as still as molasses in a jar. He held the 9millimeter close to his chest. Easing his head out from the end of the house, he stared at the vehicle parked on his graveled drive.

It wasn't Madison's Jeep, but rather a midsize sedan that glimmered dully in the weak light from a crescent moon. He leaned out farther and looked at the porch, just making out the shadowy figure waiting within the gloom. Another rapping of knuckles on the door, and then a petulant voice.

"McGomery, open the door. I want to talk to you."

He hung his head for a moment, debated the wisdom of talking to Lorna Owens. He stepped out from the shadows and stormed the front yard, approaching the porch so fast, she jumped back from the door and clutched her chest.

"What the fuck are you doing here?" he said, holding the gun by his thigh.

She couldn't seem to get her breath, reached for the doorjamb and braced herself against it. "You scared the living shit out of me, McGomery! Why are you lurking in the dark like some vampire?"

From inside the house, Clovis continued to bark frantically and she lifted a hand to her temple. "Can we go inside so the mutt will shut up?"

"No." He felt her eyes scouring him in the darkness and wished he'd taken the time to put his overalls on. As if reading his mind, she smiled, her teeth appearing blue-white in the grim of the night.

"Barefoot, in his boxers, and toting a gun. My visit must have startled the hell out of you, Slick Willie."

"I figured it was trouble and looks like I was right."

Her smile dimmed. "Why are you messing around with my sister, Will?"

"I'm not going to play this game with you, Lorna," he said. "Get out of here and leave me alone."

She stepped forward, trailed a fingertip through his chest hair, seemingly oblivious to Clovis now. "You've been screwing around with my sister and it's got you paranoid. Why else would you think you were about to be ambushed?"

"You smell like a brewery," he said. "Are you drunk?"

"No, and what does that have to do with the price of eggs in China?" Her finger traveled down and plucked lightly at the waistband of his boxers. When he pushed her hand away, she glowered at him.

"The crazies will come after you if you continue this romance with Maddie. I'll see to it, Will. I'll plant a bug in all the right places, have all the good, church going people in the community fearing you for the reprobate you are. They'll be afraid to let their teenaged daughters leave their houses by the time I'm finished."

He smiled, but felt like wrapping his hands around her throat. "You'd like that, wouldn't you? To strip me of what little peace I have up here."

"You broke my heart, and I won't allow you to do the same to my sister." She eyed the Ruger in his hand. "I told her what a waste of time you are, and I told her that you're the one who drowned Sarah. It's true, isn't it? She was carrying your bastard. What else could you do to save face with your dear little Molly?"

He lifted the gun, held it between them without aiming it at her. "I could shoot you, Lorna, and tell them I thought you were a vandal."

"Like they would believe someone like you," she scoffed.

She took a step back anyway, her eyes glittering seductively as they played between his face and the gun. "Just wait until your cousin catches wind of your relations with our sweet, erstwhile Maddie. You think he's gonna let it slide, you having a woman after you killed his Sarah?"

She moved for the steps and he was relieved because part of him really wanted to make her pay for threatening him, and their close proximity had caused that urge to be almost overwhelming. She was a bitch, a woman he wished he'd had a chance to avoid, and one he regretted not leaving alone.

"What's the matter, Will?" Her smile was a simper. "You look a little green around the gills, even in the dark."

That was it. She wasn't going to taunt him this way. He sprung forward, startling her. She pitched backward and he caught her behind the neck before she stumbled down the steps. Pulling her roughly against him, he brought the gun to her face, trailing the barrel down her cheek.

"You sure you want to cross me, Lorna? Because I can tell you right now, it would be a mistake."

She didn't angle her face away from his. Instead, she emitted a whimper and slid her tongue out, running the tip of it along the parted seam of his lips. He recoiled and as he released her, her eyes glittered with tears.

"Please, Will. I love you," she said. "I want to be with you. I won't say a thing to Aubrey. Just give me a chance, give us a chance. Stop being so mad all the time and just let…"

Her voice trailed off and then extending her hands toward him, she finished brokenly. "Just let me take care of you, baby."

"Leave." He stepped back before her hungry fingers could make contact. Her eyes were like transparent jewels shimmering in the diluted moonlight. A part of him, a very remote part, did not want to humiliate her, understood she was to be pitied.

Then her expression hardened and his empathy dissipated. "Leave or I'll call your Pap, tell him you're up to your old tricks again. You want to be degraded like that, Lorna?"

"Aubrey knows you killed Sarah and I'm going to help him prove it," she said, spilling down the porch steps backward and glaring up at him. "You're going to regret this, Slick Willie."

He watched her cross the short expanse of yard and get into her Volvo. Then, he came down the steps, eager to retrace his steps to the back of the cabin and assuage his dog's anxiety.

He waited until Lorna was a good distance across the field and then he started back around the house to the unlocked door, his thoughts already returning to Madison Owens like busy bees to honey.

****

Madison sensed the stares of the half dozen men gathered around the back corner of the Russell County Fair sound stage.

Most of them, she suspected, were tobacco users because an oppressive cloud of smoke blanketed this part of the fairgrounds where a breeze had a minimal chance of dipping between the rolling fields of pastureland. It hung like a creeping ghost over the spectators milling around the stage, appeared milky white beneath the dark canopy of night sky.

She was obviously one of very few people not smoking, judging by the amount of it. Of those who weren't smoking, she figured a high percentage had a wad of Red Man or the equivalent packed in their jaw.

She penetrated the posse toward the back of the stage, and made her way over to Dow McGomery, who stood on the fringe. He was one of the individuals contributing to the air pollution with a cigarette pinched between his lips and the tip glowing red as he took a long drag from it. His eyes were trained on hers and she found it difficult to keep her smile intact.

Why had she even come? She had no reason to believe Will McGomery would be here—he certainly hadn't seemed intrigued by his uncle's invitation. Neither did she know what to say to Dow upon approaching him. She had a few questions mapped out in her mind but now they seemed too personal, intrusive even.

The etched lines in his face testified to years of difficulty, heartbreak. Suffering. In his weary but pointed gaze lurked wariness. She made him uncomfortable, had undoubtedly made him uncomfortable that day she'd gone up on the ridge to see McGomery.

She ignored the weight of his band members' curious stares and widened her smile. "I enjoyed the show, Dow. Was glad I could make it."

She thought his smile was at least as brittle as the rubber of a blown tire. He surveyed her face another moment then seemed to relax some. "Appreciate that. It's, uh, Madison, isn't it?"

"You can call me Maddie," she said. She glanced around. "Can we talk, Dow? I need to speak to you about your nephew and Sarah Chambers."

At this point he couldn't disguise his discomfiture and shifted on his feet. She guessed he had gone into the fight or flight mode, and she wondered which it would be. He gave his cigarette a flick and tugged on his bedraggled looking beard.

"I reckon we could talk, but I ain't sure what I could tell you about them that you don't already know." He looked beyond her shoulder. "Hey, Earl, don't let Jenkins get out of here. I gotta talk to him."

She pivoted to see a man with enough facial hair and gut to play Santa at the local mall. His eyes narrowing over her, he spat a stream of tobacco juice at the ground, and nodded.

"Will do, Hoss."

Dow's shambling walk as he led her behind the stage to where his Ford was parked made her wonder if he'd been drinking. He propped himself against the truck bed, and went about lighting another cigarette, his hunched position making him appear even more troll-like.

"What exactly's on your mind, Maddie?"

She braced herself. "Will McGomery has implied to me that there was more to the Sarah Chambers' case than meets the eye, that, in fact, there may have been a cover up. I know

Aubrey is your son. Do you think he was framed?"

"Will said that to you, said that there was a cover up?"

The heat in his faded blue eyes was potent and she resisted the urge to glance away from it, knowing that if she were to figure out why Sarah haunted Will, she had to be determined. "Not in as many words. He did say that Tritt Davidson's son was involved with Sarah at the time of her murder though."

"I know he was." He stared hard at her for a long moment then offered an insouciant shrug. "But I learned a long time ago not to ask questions about the sheriff's son."

"What do you mean you learned?"

He smiled blandly, sucked on his cigarette, and sent a stream of smoke into the haze above their heads. "I learned just as you will."

"Are you saying if I ask questions, I will meet with some kind of foul play? What was done to you for asking questions about the sheriff's son?"

He didn't say anything, just continued to smoke and gaze idly at her. She reached up, slid a curl behind her ear.

"So there was a cover up. Your son was tried for a murder he didn't commit. Will tried to warn me because he knows if I start poking around, I'll encounter trouble of some kind."

"It didn't much matter who killed that girl," he said, dropping his cigarette and crushing the butt beneath his boot heel. "What mattered was that Jake Davidson didn't get caught with his pants down. That being said, I hope you'll leave this alone. Sarah Chambers ain't no one you ought to be asking questions about."

How could he be so indifferent to that poor girl? A knot of anger formed in her chest, threatening to rise and constrict her throat. "Do you think Sarah was pregnant with Will's child?"

"What does it matter what I think?"

"Did he tell you that he was having an affair with her?"

"That's none of your business."

Stalemate.

She rolled her lips inward, considered her options, finally decided that she should push a little harder.

"While coins were being tossed over the drowning death of Sarah Chambers—heads, Aubrey McGomery, tails Molly McGomery—the real killer was allowed to slip completely under the radar. My sister calls Aubrey a friend. I think I have a right to know if he is also a killer. If he was the father of that baby then he had a reason for wanting Sarah dead, and I..."

She stopped, didn't know how to finish.

He frowned. "And you?"

"Nothing." Flummoxed, she glanced down and then her head shot upward at his whispered exclamation.

"Well I'll be digging up clams in a cotton field."

She followed his eyes, ultimately looking over her shoulder, and spotted Will McGomery a few yards away talking to a man with a fiddle. Her heart leapt at the sight of him, and then a twinge of anxiety surfaced. The memory of their last encounter remained fresh in her mind. She could only imagine that it was still vivid in his as well, and it was likely that he was sore with her for leaving him the way she had.

Will smiled at the guy he was conversing with, his angular face catching the miasma of lights emanating from the stage. When he leaned in to take a look at the instrument, she whipped her head back around and pinned Dow with a stare.

"You're surprised he's here?"

The old man's scowl was fierce. "The last time him and Swirly Elkins swapped brags about fiddle playing was when I drove Swirly up on the ridge five years ago. Course, I'm surprised. Pickers go to Willie if they want to play music with him or talk shop, not the other way around."

She experienced a tiny rush. Had McGomery come here thinking she might be in attendance? Was he simply taking Dow up on his invite to play music or was he actually still interested in seeing her again after the fiasco that had been their lovemaking? She glanced in his direction again. One thing was for certain; she was about to find out.

He shared a lengthy stare with Dow as he approached, and then turned a cold gaze onto her, his eyes taking in her camouflage Capri's. "What are you up to, Private Benjamin?"

"Not a lot," she said, sensing immediately his unhappiness over her being there. "And you?"

His blue eyes torch hot, he continued to look down at her. "I think she wants me to believe she's minding her own business. What do you say, Dow?"

Dow McGomery fumbled for another cigarette. "I say you might want to watch out for this one. She don't know the first thing about minding her own business."

She didn't miss the wry smile tugging at the corners of Dow's lips. Glancing back at Will, she tried to keep her frustration at bay but, in the end, failed.

"If you must know, I was asking him what he knew about Sarah Chambers, since you mostly refuse to acknowledge she is still a part of your—"

"You exhaust me, Owens, with all this horseshit about ghosts," he said, cutting her off as effectively as he would a vine with a pair of sharp pruning shears.

She glared at him. "I beg your pardon?"

He winked at Dow McGomery, fixed her with a challenging stare. "You heard me. Come on, it's been a hundred years since I rode a Ferris wheel. Humor me. Join me on that one at the top of the hill."

Was he serious? "I don't do Ferris wheels, I'm not fond of heights."

"So Private Benjamin in her camouflage is a chicken shit."

Dow laughed and, shaking his head, started back across to the group of men he'd abandoned. She watched him go and then turned withering eyes to Will.

"Lead the way, hillbilly."

# CHAPTER TWELVE

Madison took the bottle of spring water from Will's fingers as he sat down across from her at the picnic table.

The Ferris wheel had been a ridiculous venture. The ride had lasted approximately three minutes and they had spoken few words. She didn't know why she had even conceded, except she felt she had something to prove to him after the way she had left him that night.

The girl who had destroyed his marriage was haunting him. He wouldn't talk about the past. He wouldn't talk about Lorna. She wanted to know the truth and would ride a dozen Ferris Wheels if it brought her closer to the truth.

He looked at her as if he knew what she was thinking and she averted her eyes to take in their surroundings.

Under different circumstances she would have loved being there. It had been years since she'd been to a county fair and being there evoked memories from her youth. Horse manure, funnel cakes, the eager fair mongers; she would have been game had she not been so caught up in talking to Dow McGomery, and getting herself caught.

Will popped opened his Mountain Dew and she brought her eyes back to his face. She watched his throat work as he swallowed, the way his Adam's apple moved. An artery pulsed beneath the solid line of his jaw in tune with her heart, it seemed, and she imagined sliding her lips and her tongue over his neck, over the heated skin and corded muscles.

Memories of their erotic exchange on the floor next to his sofa assaulted her, caused her cheeks to flush and her body to tingle all over. She wanted to move to his side of the picnic table, taste that throbbing place that beckoned, and say to hell with his past and his involvement with Lorna.

She fiddled with the fleece jacket she had tied around her

waist. She could tell he was thinking about speaking and folded her hands over the table diplomatically. Afraid he had correctly judged her line of thinking, she decided to beat him to the draw, set the stage for conversation. And the farther she set it away from what had happened between them, the better.

"Dow says that you haven't seen Swirly Elkins in five years."

"Yeah, no skin off my teeth. Elkins is a motor mouth."

She studied his face, the way his thick, dark brows pulled down into a scowl, and decided that he was definitely sore with her. "Why don't you ever get out, Will? Dow says the only time—"

"I wager you've never had your house torched," he cut in, his mouth a hard line. "Or been excommunicated by your church, your neighbors, people you thought were above reproach."

Her fingers clutched the bottle of water on the table. She twisted off the cap and took a drink, buying as much time as she could. He stared at her so hard though, that finally, she felt she must say something.

"You're angry with me because I want some answers."

"No," he said and his voice was low, almost a whisper. "I'm irritated that you would ask such a stupid question. I know your mother told you all about the way people treated me, and yet you would ask me why I'm a recluse. You want the dirty facts? I'll give them to you. I was a deacon in my church, people looked up to me. They thought Molly and I were the perfect couple and when I fell, I fell hard in their eyes. I went face down into a pile of shit they thought I deserved to wallow in, and they were not about to help me out. Not a chance. Instead, they asked me to stay the hell away."

She touched the tip of her tongue to the corner of her mouth, not allowing herself to wince. "My mother didn't tell me that you and Molly were members of a church, that you were banished."

For several seconds, he kept his eyes trained on what she thought was the agriculture building a few meters away, then he looked at her, reached across the table and offered her his hand.

"Feel the tips of my fingers," he said.

"What?"

"Touch them." He splayed his fingers across one of the wooden planks in the table and waited for her to comply. After she did and placed both of her hands in her lap, he frowned at her.

"Well?"

"Calluses," she said and felt her cheeks suffuse with color. "I've felt them before. They're from your fiddle, right?"

His expression serious, he nodded. "Surprisingly, it doesn't take all that long to acquire them."

"Your point being?"

"To every cause there is an effect." He watched her reach for her water and take another drink. "You keep turning over stones and sooner or later you're going to find a snake, Madison Owens. Don't be asking my uncle questions about Sarah. Leave it alone."

He filled his hand with the Mountain Dew he'd placed on the table, stared into the near distance again. The sound of revving engines from the upcoming demolition derby filled the air and set Madison's nerves on edge.

"She clearly needs help. Do you not care about her at all?"

"Help?" He laughed. "She's dead."

"And haunting you."

"Says who?"

She tapped her nails over the table's course surface. "Why didn't you tell the sheriff about his son's involvement with Sarah?"

"Don't do this," he said, their eyes locking now. "Don't appoint yourself my judge because I didn't involve myself in that investigation."

"I just want to know why you didn't."

"My wife hung herself in our barn not even a week after Sarah's drowning," he interjected loudly, seemingly oblivious to the fair enthusiasts around them. "I was the one who found her. Do you have any inkling how Goddamned difficult that was? Her eyes looked like eggs pushing out of her head, Owens, boiled eggs. She shit herself. I smelled it for days. The last thing I cared about was Sarah Chambers and now it's too late to care. I don't want to care."

She chewed on her lower lip, shifted her eyes toward the group of people sitting to the left of them at another picnic table.

"It wasn't my intention to trivialize what happened to your wife, Will. I'm sorry."

He finished his soda and crushed the can in his fist. Tossing it into the barrel situated between their table and the next, he glanced at the four elderly people staring at him and made a face at them that said 'what?'.

"Why did you come here tonight?" She speared him with a look. "Were you hoping I'd be here?"

"Yes and no," he said, and his eyes turned dark with virulent emotion. "Sure to hell wasn't hoping to find you drilling Dow like some little hard-nosed investigator."

"I wouldn't put it that way." She straightened somewhat, knowing her eyes conveyed her hurt all to well. "Is it really so wrong for me to want to know a little about what went on with you and that girl?"

"You want to talk about the past?" he asked. "Fine. Let's talk about yours. Why were you so afraid to let me pleasure you the other night? What's up with that?"

She glanced around. "Would you keep your voice down?"

His eyes dropped to her mouth and his brow furrowed for a moment as though he was conflicted about something. "Let's get out of here. I hate being stared at by geriatrics."

"And where do you propose we go?" Her heart stuttered at the thought of being alone with him. "Up on the ridge so Sarah can make another futile attempt to get your attention?"

"I had somewhere else in mind."

"Where?"

He waited a beat. "Where she drowned. Would you like to see the pond?"

Was he intentionally trying to set a Wes Craven mood? "In the dark? Where is it?"

"In a pasture near Big A Mountain...on what used to be my land." He glanced at the watch on his wrist. "We could make it back before the fairgrounds close for the night."

She willed her heart to be still. It pounded with a type of exhilaration that was fueled by adrenaline. "I know where your house was. When it burned, Daddy rode Mama and me out to see the smoldering remains. For an eleven-year-old, it was a big deal. I remember asking why it caught on fire and him saying that it was because Slick Willie liked to tempt God and God was giving him his due."

A flicker of something passed through his eyes, maybe regrets, perhaps wounded pride, or a blend of both.

"The pond is less than half a mile from the house site, just beyond a clustering of trees. It's posted, but the guy I sold the land to leases it for cattle. He won't be around, and besides you're a pro at trespassing, aren't you, Owens?"

She had ventured onto his land covertly one time. A single isolated case and it was so that she could see the spring, get a glimpse of his cabin. "Why?" She looked at him again. "Why do you want to go the pond?"

He spent several moments staring into her eyes. "I believe you're afraid of me, Maddie."

She thought that she was a little now. "Of course I'm not afraid of you."

"Liar."

She lifted both hands, tucked her hair behind her ears. "Let's go. I'll follow you." He watched quietly as she untied the jacket from her waist and put it on over her tank top. Then, resting his elbows on the table, he leaned forward, instantly snagging her attention.

"Well now that's too bad."

"What is?"

His gaze slid to her chest. "Fall is in the air. It's brought your nipples up beneath that tank top and now I can't see them. I want to see them. In fact I want to bite them."

A bastion of warring emotions assailed her—frustration, distrust, and pure, raw need. "Are we going or not?"

"Not."

She crossed her arms over her chest, watched as he stood from the table. "Then what are we doing?"

"You're going to go to home to your Mama and I'm going to follow you to make sure you arrive safely."

"And the pond was what? Your idea of a joke?"

He smiled. "A way to gauge your naiveté. You're pretty gullible, Owens, and have proven yourself fully capable of getting in over your head." He gestured for her to stand up. "Come on, ladies first."

Bracing her hands on the table, she pushed up and glared at him. "Don't patronize me, Will McGomery."

"Where are you parked?"

Suddenly furious with him, she started up the hill without him. "Screw yourself."

He caught up to her, gripping her upper arm firmly and pulling her around to face him. A gaggle of teens went careening down the hill near them, the girls squealing like jubilant toddlers. Her would-be captor seemed not to notice at all.

"You're a threat to my peace of mind," he said between clenched teeth. "You will afford me this and not say one word about it."

"Why should I afford you anything? I don't need an escort, especially not one of your caliber. Let go of me, you hedonistic brute."

"You think I derive pleasure from having to watch your back?" He released her so abruptly she almost lost her balance.

His eyes bore into hers like icy drill bits. "All I wanted was to be left alone, but no, you just had to disrupt my life, start with this shit, this poking your nose into things that could get you…"

She massaged her arm as his voice dropped off, beheld him mistrustfully.

He drove his fingers into his long hair and stalked away, leaving her to wonder if the conclusion to his tirade would have ended with the word 'killed'.

# CHAPTER THIRTEEN

Madison scrambled into her Jeep and fumbled to answer her cell phone, the kaleidoscope of lights from the carnival rides blurring with her angry tears.

"What are you doing?" Lorna's voice filled her ear, causing her to wilt in the seat.

She recalled the heat in McGomery's eyes when he'd told her she was a threat to him. "Nothing."

"Where are you?"

She cringed. "At the fair...thought I'd check out the local musicians."

"On a date?"

"Lor, can we talk later? I was just leaving and I don't like to chat while driving."

"You seen Will McGomery lately?"

Everything in her went dead still. "Why?"

"I'll take that as a yes." She sighed in Madison's ear. "Whatever, but you need to know something. I went up there to talk to him couple nights ago and he put a gun to my head. He's crazy."

"He did what?"

Silence and then, "Maddie, I've wrestled with this now for two days. I didn't want to tell you because, frankly, I'm embarrassed. I knew better than to go up there, but I just wanted to see him again, talk to him."

"And he held you at gunpoint? Why?"

"I'm thinking about going to the police about it."

Madison pinched the bridge of her nose. "What was his reason? There had to have been a reason he would go that far."

"Same reason he drowned Sarah Chambers. He thought I was going to be a problem for him. Luckily, I talked my way out of it and got the hell out of dodge."

"If he's so crazy, then why can't you just leave him alone?" Lorna snorted. "Why can't you?"

The question caught Madison off guard. "My curiosity has been appeased. I'm not seeking him out."

"Are you sure about that?"

"I can take care of myself, Lorna."

Her sister laughed. "You clearly don't know what you're dealing with, Little Sissa."

"Well, thanks for the warning. Really."

"What if he'd killed me when I went up there? My boys...what would they do without their mother?"

"Where were your boys when you threw caution to the wind and visited McGomery?"

"Darius is plenty old enough to watch Chaz for a short period of time."

Madison shook her head. "God, Lorna."

"You don't understand. I had to see him, had to try to make him understand how much he hurt me. He fucking broke my heart, Maddie."

She wanted to hold her head. What the hell was going on with her sister and Will McGomery? "He says it didn't happen, Lor, that he's never been with you."

"Then he's a liar!"

"He also says you approached him before you and Bobby ever split up."

What could have been a sob filled Madison's ear. "Me and Bobby were fighting constantly. I'm human...let McGomery's flirting get to me. He was so seductive, Maddie. At first he was irresistible and yes, I fell prey to his charms."

Lorna's voice became shrill. "I'm not lying to you. I swear to God. I confessed to going up there, didn't I? I've been honest about my affair with him. He's the one lying. He lied about being with Sarah and now he's lying about being with me. It's what he does. He'll probably kill me, and you won't even care."

"Fine, he's a liar." Madison disconnected and then sat

trembling as she remembered the way Will had denied leaving the photo in his bathroom. Either he was a liar, or Sarah Chambers had left her a message. She just didn't know what to believe at this point.

She made a swipe at her eyes. Through the Jeep's flimsy canvas top, she could just make out the song the current band was playing. It was a cover of an old Hank Williams' number. The singer was giving a poor rendition but succeeding, in any case, to entertain the crowd. She could hear claps and whistles.

She squirmed in her seat until she wrestled her keys from her pants pocket. A moment later, she drove across the cow pasture parking lot and left Hank and his fans behind.

What she didn't leave behind was her deep unease about Will McGomery and her sister.

****

Lorna spotted Dwight Wray's 84 Camaro parked just behind Aubrey's similarly rusted Mustang, and considered the possibilities.

The only visible light in Aubrey's trailer was in the bedroom-slash-makeshift garage at the end, and that was a good indication that he was tinkering on his bike. A Confederate flag served as a curtain to the room's one window, barring her from seeing in, and she hoped they didn't have women with them.

Depending on how much alcohol the two had consumed that night, Aubrey would be either extremely difficult to get along with or extremely easy.

She crossed her fingers for easy.

She parked her Volvo in the grass alongside the Camaro and walked around it, listened for the telltale ticking sounds that would indicate Wray's ride hadn't been parked long, and heard nothing. She touched the hood, finding the surface cool to the touch. Dew had settled over the paint and she wiped her hand on the seat of her low-riding jeans to dry the pads of her fingers.

Good. Dwight had been there awhile and he'd probably brought plenty of beer.

She crossed the unkempt yard, cursing the dirt-encrusted grass, which was currently slimy with moisture and sullying the suede of her designer boots.

*Dammit.*

She couldn't afford to shell out the money to have the things professionally cleaned. That's what working as a bank teller got you: unable to clean your expensive leather after crossing your redneck boyfriend's pathetic excuse of a yard.

It was abominable, just like Aubrey staying all the way out here in the middle of nowhere and renting this hellhole of a sardine tin. It was amazing that Cecilia had ever agreed to come out here for their little rendezvous with him.

The ramp he'd built onto the end of the trailer led to a wide metal door he'd installed for his bike. She knocked tentatively, felt his eyeball on her as she waited for him to open the door, and smirked at the peephole.

*Come on, asshole*, it conveyed, *open the door.*

When it did open, Aubrey McGomery leaned indolently against the jamb. His narrowed eyes raked over her, and with his jaw set, his face took on a hawkish appearance. She glanced beyond his lean, chiseled physique and saw a just as fit male specimen sprawled on a dingy couch. Dwight Wray might have been dozing if not for inebriated smile on his face.

Aubrey's Harley was parked in the center of the room and an array of tools and mechanical whatnots were spread across the grimy carpet.

"You and that stupid bike," she said, flipping her hair.

He clutched her sleeve and drew her inside. His touch was rougher than necessary, but not because he wasn't attracted to her. She knew it was the opposite, in fact. He pushed her up against the door, crushing the white denim of her jacket beneath his shirtless chest, and buried his grease-smeared face in her hair.

"You smell good enough to eat, Lorna Mae."

He released her when she began to squirm and watched

with languid sky-blue eyes as she attempted to smooth her hair.

She glanced again at Wray. The man leaned forward and tied a strip of something around his long, sinewy arm. Her eyes honed in on the needle resting on the couch cushion beside of him.

"He's been partying all night," Aubrey supplied, moving back over to the motorcycle. He straddled it, his corded back vying for her attention. "Dumb motherfuck. That stuff's gonna rot the teeth right out of his head."

His head shot to the side and he laughed at Dwight, who was now injecting what Lorna suspected was methamphetamine into his arm. At Dwight's fantastic grimace, Aubrey squinted, licked his lips like a wolf. "That's right, your brother's latest batch is some potent shit, ain't it?"

Dwight released the makeshift tourniquet and then pressed himself into the back of the couch. His smoke colored eyes rolled back into his head, and he muttered something that ended with the words, "my ever-loving dick".

"I can't stay, Aub." Lorna said pointedly. "My boys are home alone."

"Good for them." Aubrey said, his mouth tightening. "What do you want with me?"

She touched the tip of her tongue to the peak of her full upper lip, and then crossed her arms over her chest. "You're pissed about something. What is it?"

Aubrey got off the bike and faced her. "Your little gal pal called the sheriff and told him I've been harassing her. He says he better not catch me down at the gym again. He paid me a visit at the body shop today, and now my boss wants to know if he's got something to worry about. You tell that cunt she better keep her trap shut. She gets me fired, me and Dwight here are gonna work her over real good."

She felt her face flush red. "She did what?"

"What the hell happened between the two of you?" he asked. "Why she getting all uppity with me like this?"

"I broke it off with her," she said. "She was getting jealous of you."

"Of me?" He shook his head and chuckled. "Lesbians. You're all the same."

"I'm not a lesbian, Aubrey."

"Sure you're not," Dwight said, his head back and eyes closed.

She shot him a look. "Not talking to you, you dick."

Aubrey crouched next to the bike. "You give her my message, Lorna Mae."

She couldn't wait to give Cecilia his message, but for now, she had bigger fish to fry. "Aubrey, I've got a problem."

He didn't look at her. "With what?"

"My sister has developed a little crush on your cousin, it seems." She licked her lips. "I'm worried sick about her."

Aubrey came to his booted feet slowly and gave her a look. "The hell you say. Your sister and Will?"

"Not Rachel," she said. "My younger sister who moved back from Ohio. She started going up on the ridge, says it's over now, but I don't believe her. You've got to do something to stop this. I'm afraid he'll…God, you know what I'm afraid of."

Dwight sat up and gaped at her, his long brown hair falling over his shoulders and meshing with the thick carpet that was on his chest. "That he'll drown the bitch?"

"Mind your own business, Wray," Aubrey said, moving over to her and caressing her cheek with a greasy thumb. "What do you want me to do, baby?"

"Scare her off. Make her believe what I can't."

He looked at her shrewdly. "Make her believe that they framed me when they had the real killer right under their goddamned noses?"

She nodded. "He'll end up killing her too. I know he will."

"Hmm, but what if he's really in love this time? You know like the fairytale stuff, like Beauty and the fucking Beast. Or is your sister even pretty? Aw, I bet she is. And I bet she's got small little titties just like her sis. I bet Slick up there is licking all over them right about now."

"Shut up." She batted his hand away and rubbed impatiently at her cheek. "Will's incapable of loving anyone. I want you to stop this thing between them. Please."

"With a cherry on top?"

Her eyes jerked over to Dwight Wray, who had uttered the question. Good looking as he was in a derelict sort of way, he looked ridiculous with that vacant smile on his face. He resembled a ventriloquist's puppet.

The smile stretched wider. "Oh, that's right. You've not had a cherry for eons, have you, Lorna?"

"You going to let him get away with that?" she asked, glancing back at Aubrey. In response, he wrapped a large, grimy hand around her throat and she swallowed convulsively.

"Forget Dwight," he said. "I want to know something."

She didn't allow her eyes to wander from his, was afraid to look away. She nodded and he smiled encouragingly.

"You in love with my cousin, Lorna Mae?"

"No," she choked. "Not anymore."

His pale irises remained on her face for several seconds and then he eased the pressure off of her larynx. He turned to Dwight and grinned. "Me and Lorna's going to my room now."

Dwight's eyes moved from his and roved over her. "Yeah, right. Whatever you say."

Lorna thought about Darius. When Chastin cried, he got uneasy. She could smooth it over later. It wasn't a big deal. The brat needed to learn about responsibility sometime, didn't he?

She sauntered over to Aubrey and slid her hand down the front of his t-shirt. Her eyes still on Dwight, she ran her tongue up the corded length of Aubrey's neck and made a purring sound of pleasure. Let the wise-ass junkie get a hard on for her. She hoped he got so hard it caused him all kinds of discomfort.

He groaned in response to the erotic show and Aubrey laughed at him. Kissing her savagely, he pulled her toward the door leading to other parts of the trailer. Her blood coursed through her veins, rampant and hot. Darius and Chastin were instantly forgotten, thoughts of them vaporizing like beads of water on a hot stove eye.

She felt Aubrey's hand fumbling to unfasten her jeans, felt his dirty fingers as they attempted to gain access to the moist wonderland beneath the satin barrier of her panties. A fleeting image of Maddie with her huge brown eyes and pouting mouth assaulted her.

Her sister was flirting with the pick of the litter, while she had to settle for a greasy mechanic with lank blond hair and a rap sheet.

It wasn't fair.

She shoved Aubrey away from her and glared at him. "You touch me after you take a shower, lover."

# CHAPTER FOURTEEN

Her Manolo Blahnik, resurrected from a storage box in her parents' garage, didn't clear the step and Madison pitched forward violently, her cell phone flying from her hand like a tiny missile.

She righted herself, smoothed a hand over her skirt, and snatched the Motorola up off the porch, inspecting it for damage.

Then she gave her shoe a cursory examination and winced when she saw the damaged leather on the toe.

It was to be expected. She should have changed into something more practical for the trip up the ridge. What had been appropriate attire for lunch with her sister Rachael at The Tavern in Abingdon now seemed ridiculous overkill.

She just hadn't wanted to take the time to change, was desperate to get to the bottom of this thing with her sister and Will.

Selecting one of the rocking chairs on the porch, she sat down; content to wait for him to return from wherever he'd gone that afternoon. She crossed her legs and smoothed her thumb over the scuffed place on her shoe.

So what the hell had happened up here with her sister? Had Will really pulled a gun on her? And if he had, didn't that mean that she was courting danger herself?

Oh, God, yes. She was. She was becoming hopelessly intrigued with this community outcast, this man who had proven to her, time and again, just how unpredictable he could be.

No.

She couldn't rely on what Lorna had told her. Perhaps he'd brandished a gun, but there had to have been some provocation on her sister's part. He wouldn't just pull a gun on Lorna for the thrill of scaring her.

Would he?

The way he had come after her at the fair, nagged at her. The look on his face had been volatile. Frightening.

*You will afford me this and not say one word about it.* She shivered at the memory of his words and then leaned forward when she felt something cold and moist on her leg.

Will had left Clovis to hold down the fort apparently, and he was currently sniffing her calf. She stroked his head and he upended his nose to lick her palm. His eyes landed on her face and they were earnest, trusting.

She smiled as she studied the pale, marbled depths of them. Then her head jerked up at the sound of a vehicle clearing the woods. It barreled across the field, dust billowing into clouds that rose up from the old wagon trail like mud swirls into water.

It was Dow McGomery and he seemed to be in a hurry to close in the space between the woods and the cabin. When he succeeded, he brought the Ford to a lurching stop right behind her Jeep.

When she saw his face, she instantly stiffened because it wasn't his face.

A much younger man, bearing a faint resemblance to Will, hopped out of the truck and bounded up onto the porch, gawking at her as if she might be that day's featured item on the lunch menu.

She knew that it was Aubrey McGomery the way someone knows they're about to get hit from behind by a speeding car—immediately but then too late all the same.

Brushing an errant curl out of her eye, she swallowed tightly. Of all the things she might have considered, Will's cousin wasn't one of them.

With his shoulder-length blond hair and angular face, he might have passed for Will's brother, but his pale gaze was menacing, and she wondered what the hell she had gotten herself into. She rose from the rocker, smiled tentatively. "Aubrey, right?"

He sported a couple days worth of reddish beard on his face, had the disheveled look of someone who had been on a bender. Those Alaskan Husky eyes were bloodshot, his shirt and jeans unkempt. It was the way he stared at her, though, caused bells and whistles to go off in her head.

That look was decidedly predatory.

Her chest ached with fear, her heart an adrenaline pump wheezing beneath her breastbone.

Aubrey stepped forward and snatched her phone out of her hand. His movement was so quick, so unexpected, that she hardly reacted at all. He smiled at her. They might have been in seventh grade at that moment, only the challenge in his curved lips was scarcely playful.

"He went to get shit for his clocks, didn't he?"

She opened her mouth, hesitated, and then said, "I don't have a clue. I was hoping you could tell me."

His eyes dropped to the lacy shell she wore, making her wish fervently that she had put on something less feminine that day.

"What's a woman like you doing up here?" he asked, his voice a slither of malcontent. "You in your pretty high heels and rich bitch outfit. Don't you know whose porch you've been sitting on?"

"Why don't you tell me?" She hated that her voice sounded so strained, so full of her terror.

The way his gaze glimmered like sterling silver under a blue light unnerved her. His voice was no less chilling.

"You been lounging on a killer's porch," he said. "Not just the ill-tempered country bumpkin kind either, but the kind of cold bastard who would drown the life out of a helpless pregnant girl."

"I'm not sure I buy that," she told him hesitantly.

He slanted her a smile. "The kind who would fuck my girlfriend and then throw her in a cow pond."

"What do you want with him? Why are you here, Aubrey?"

"It ain't him I want to see," he said. "I came to see about you."

"I don't understand. How did you know I was here?" She wanted to make a grab for her phone, didn't dare.

"Your sister," he said. "She called me a while ago from the bank and said she'd just got off the phone with your Mama. Seems mommy dearest was sure you had ridden up here, was fretting over it. Being as I keep tabs on Willie, I know what day he ventures out to do his business in town. I told Lorna I'd ride up and check on you. Truth is I was dying for the opportunity to have a one on one with the gal who's crushing on my cuz."

Her throat constricted. "Lorna told you that?"

"Sure she did." He tapped her phone against his palm, then lifted his hand and crossed long, grease stained fingers in front of her face. "Me and Lorna, we're like this, see. She tells me everything, and she's told me that she's real worried about her little headstrong sister. You up here screwing around with the likes of Slick Willie. Who wouldn't be worried?"

"Does my mother know you came up here?"

He shrugged. "Not unless Lorna called her back and told her. Why? You think me being with you would scare her? More than having my cousin's blood-stained hands on you?"

"Yes," she said. "I think as far as she's concerned, you're the one who killed that girl."

His stare chilled her blood. "Well, I know how people think. That's why I borrowed Daddy's truck. Your folks are used to him coming up here. See, no one has to be afraid for Lorna's pretty little sis in her fancy-schmancy clothes. It's just dumb ol' Dow coming up here to pay his shut-in nephew a visit."

"Dow," she said, convinced she needed to keep him talking. "What did you tell him about using his truck? He probably wouldn't be okay with you coming up here."

He snorted. "You're right about that. The old fart would shit a brick. I told him that since I'm off work today, I was gonna drive up to Laurel Bed Lake and fish awhile. See how easy it is to spare people all the fuss and worry? You just feed 'em lies." He stepped closer. "You ever tell lies?"

This was bad.

Not good. Not good. Not good.

She glanced at Clovis. The dog was sprawled between her and Aubrey McGomery, thoroughly absorbed in the business of licking his privates. She felt her heart rate kick up another notch. She might as well be trying to navigate a desert in a John boat as far as funny eyes was concerned. The dog was useless to her.

And Aubrey was definitely a threat that neither she nor Clovis had anticipated.

He flipped open her phone, studied it for a moment, and then tossed it far across the yard.

"Sometimes, like today for instance, it pays to be charitable," he said. "I score points with your big sis and get to be up close and personal with you too. You're damn fine, I might add. And I bet you're tight as the eye of a needle, huh?"

She folded her arms around her middle, coaching herself to be smart, to buy more time. "I guess Lorna knows first hand about how dangerous Will is. What's their story, Aubrey?" Her smile felt impossibly wrong on her lips, exceedingly fragile. "Indulge me. What's the history between Lorna and Will?"

His resulting laughter was thoroughly unsettling, like funhouse giggles in the dark when you're eight years old. "What's to tell? She had the hots for him. He used her, used her like he always uses women."

The smile on her face fell to nothing. It felt like invisible fingers pulling down the corners of her mouth. "And you're what, salvaging what's left of my sister?"

"I didn't come here to talk about her," he said without hesitation. "I came here to find out what you're up to."

"What do you think I'm up to?"

A muscle in his jaw ticked. "Well, I know what Willie's up to. He's just like his Daddy, always sticking his dick in places it don't belong. He doesn't deserve to have pussy nice as yours. You're a cut above his wife Molly. Cut above Sarah too. Doesn't make sense an uppity bitch like you paying him attention. What are you after? Lorna says you're a writer. You gonna do a tell-all about him? Because if you are, you better tell it like it is. He drowned my girl, put his greasy little monkey in her belly, and then drowned her like an unwanted litter of kittens."

As if he anticipated Madison entering the cabin, Clovis stood and ambled toward the door, casting her a hopeful backward glance. She looked sadly at him. He wasn't the only one wishing for a change of scenery.

"My only business with Will McGomery is to get him off my land." She had to swallow back the unsavory lump of fear that had formed in her throat. "This was supposed to be mine, the land, the cabin he dismantled…everything."

He took a step toward her. She lost her breath, made an attempt to move beyond him. He blocked her with amazing speed. Catching her against his chest, he forced her back until he had her pinioned between his body and the front of the cabin.

In the commotion, his snakeskin boot came down hard on the bewildered Clovis. The dog yelped in pain and fright, and high tailed it across the yard in the direction of the chicken coop.

"No!" she said between clenched teeth, her voice a guttural sound. Her limbs trembled like reed thin branches in his grip. The distant sky seemed too bright, a callous, faceless witness, and the porch suddenly deep with shadows, like it had been consumed in hungry vines. "Let go of me!"

Her body bucked against him, but in the end, he was simply too strong to shake off. She shrank against the house, wishing it would swallow her whole. She managed a couple of ragged breaths only to have him wheel her around and press the front of her body into the rustic logs. All of the air was squeezed out of her lungs and she felt panic seize her like jaws of ice-cold steel.

"Don't talk," he said, exhaling hotly into her hair. "I want you to open up those goddamned ears of yours and listen. That's all. Just listen."

His hand found the swell of her buttock through the slinky fabric of her skirt and squeezed. Tears sprang into her eyes. The hard length of him pressed into her backside so that she felt his erection. She slammed her eyes shut.

He situated his mouth over her ear. "Much as I'd like a piece of your tight little ass, I ain't come here to force myself on you. Leave him alone, sugar beet. There's things going on here that you don't no part of. He ain't what he seems, our Willie. He'll rip your heart out, feed it to that damn dog there."

Fueled by adrenaline, she brought up her hands and shoved against the house, managing to break free of the pressure of his body.

He caught her around the waist before she could clear the porch, and savagely pulled her around. He brought her up against him hard, and this time, her nails raked his cheek.

"You fucking bitch!" he spat.

He backhanded her, knocking her off balance. She stumbled and then, slowly, she touched trembling fingertips to her lips and came away with blood, lifted her eyes and beheld him with hatred and horror.

"You're an animal. What does my sister see in you?"

"Rule number one," he said, ignoring the question. "No bitch in heat writer gets to call the shots with me. You understand?"

His hands were balled into fists, his eyes as cold as cave water. After a moment, she nodded reluctantly, knew she had little choice but to try to pacify him.

"Good," he said. He shook out the tension in his arms and flexed his fingers. "You think that hurt, me smacking you around a little? Wait until he's through with you. You're a damn fool if you think he won't cause you a world of pain."

She glared at him and he raised a hand to blot gently at the blood on her split lip. Licking it off his knuckle and making a fairly big production out of the action by smacking his lips, he grinned lasciviously. "Yeah, you're just asking to be hurt, aren't you?"

"Leave me alone."

"Don't say I didn't warn you about him." Turning and moving down the steps, he slid his fingers through his long hair and spit in the grass.

She watched him get into Dow's truck and spin it around in the yard, throwing scatterings of grass toward the porch. Once he was out of sight, only the rumble of the engine sounding in the distance, she came slowly down the steps and crossed the yard to retrieve her phone.

She felt weighted down and yet impossibly light on her feet, and she decided to just sit down on the grass until she regained her equilibrium. Her eyes welled with fresh tears. She stared through them and watched numbly as the dust slowly began to settle over the meadow.

Somewhere in the distance, a Morning Dove let out a sorrowful call and she glanced toward the spread of Poplars encompassing the spring. Clovis hunkered by the chicken coop. His butt tucked and his head cocked sideways, he watched her with his pale eyes.

He looked pitiful. Whipped. Totally defeated.

Like her.

She struggled to her feet, wobbling unsteadily in her designer pumps. Wanting to curse the expensive confections, at the same time she wished she'd planted the heel of one of them through Aubrey McGomery's booted foot.

Ambling toward her Jeep, she knew precisely what she had to do. Information was power; she had to obtain more of it.

# CHAPTER FIFTEEN

Tritt Davidson entered his office. Madison straightened from the chair, both relieved that the wait was over and intimidated by the fact the sheriff looked like a drill sergeant.

He was approximately the same age as her father, and like her father, had shoulders like a quarterback, a buzz cut the color of steel wool, and a square, unyielding jaw. A portly clerk, whose gum snapping had been as disconcerting as her platinum hair and penciled-on brows, had gruffly pointed her into the his office ten minutes earlier. Those minutes had proven to be adequate time in which to second-guess her decision to come to town, and beneath the man's penetrating stare, her apprehension escalated.

She turned and extended him her hand anyway, conscious of the fact her lip was swollen and wearing a fresh and shiny scab. "I was looking at your photos, sheriff."

She gestured toward the hunting pictures on the wall behind him, which featured several seasons' worth of slain white tail deer. "Didn't see anything less than an eight point."

Davidson smiled without showing his teeth and extended a hand that looked a lot like a cured ham. Her fingers were swallowed in a firm shake and she rushed to introduce herself before he could speak.

"Madison Owens," she said. "I recently moved back from Ohio and I'm staying with my parents, Marshall and Hannah Owens. You might know them?"

He stared pensively at a point just to the side of her face. "Doesn't ring a bell. They live here in town?"

"Over Swords Creek way," she said, tipping her chin at the photos again. "That your grandson?"

"Yep, but you're supposed to guess that he's my son because I look so young and handsome." He moved his rangy body around his battered desk and sat down, his eyes lingering on her breasts for several seconds before sliding back up to her face.

"You here to tell me the story behind that lip of yours? Looks like someone popped you a good one recently."

She considered the things Aubrey McGomery could have done to her that afternoon, but hadn't. Had Aubrey simply been doing Lorna's bidding? What had he meant when he'd said there were things going on that she didn't want to be a part of?

Giving herself a mental shake, she returned her attention to the sheriff's question. "I'm here to tell you if you're interested in hearing."

He looked at her through the fringe of his thick brows. "Course I'm interested, sugar. I'm sitting here behind this desk because I believe in helping people. Now what'd you come down here to tell me?"

"Ask," she corrected. "Sorry, I should've clarified. I came here to ask you what your thoughts are on Aubrey and Will McGomery."

Not moving at all, not even blinking, he tilted his large head imperceptibly. "My thoughts?"

"Yes," she said. "Aubrey showed up today on Will's property while I was awaiting Will's return from town, hinted to me that he'd been falsely accused in the Chambers' case."

Davidson sat there another moment as unflinching as Mount Rushmore, then straightened in the large swivel chair, his storm colored eyes pinning on her lip. "Aubrey have anything to do with you looking like you lost a boxing match?"

She lowered into the chair she'd recently abandoned. "We had words and he struck me...but only after I drew first blood. I thought his intention was to rape me and I clawed his face. For my daring, I got a slap and a split lip. Then he told me that I should leave Will McGomery alone, suggested that his cousin was Sarah Chambers' killer. After that, he left."

"If you'd called 911, an officer would've corralled him and

brought him in," he said, raising his huge hands into the air as if to say she'd blown things and he didn't know how to help her. "You could have pressed charges, still can if you want to, of course." His speculative gaze raked over her once more. "You want to hold him accountable for this or what?"

She considered the condescending tone of his voice, knew she would not be able to keep the reproof out of her own. "I'm familiar with the Chambers case. After being charged with that girl's death his cousin's house was torched. Aubrey's not someone I want to cross if I can at all help it. I just think you should know that he's trespassing onto private property."

"And you're not?" He scowled at her. "You said you were waiting for Will McGomery to return."

The sheriff was fishing for information. She tucked her hair behind her ear and gazed at him as calmly as her erratic heartbeat would allow, saying nothing.

His eyes played over her, lingering too long on her crossed legs. "I see. You and Will McGomery are romantically involved. Well, well." He shook his head. "Last I heard, he bought some land way out on Horton's Ridge and was living up there like Grizzly Adams. How in the hell does a gal like you happen upon someone like him?"

"That land on Horton's Ridge is—" She almost said it, almost called the land hers. "It was sold to Will by my father. I've been talking to him about selling it, am hoping that he will ultimately accept an offer from me."

"Hermit like him?" he said with a small grin. "He's been holed up on that ridge for some time now. He ain't about to sell. Invited you to come back and discuss it further, though, did he?"

"I'm compelled to say that's none of your business." She uncrossed her legs and leaned forward. "This is about Aubrey McGomery being where he doesn't belong—near my family. It's not about Will McGomery being a hermit or my intention to purchase his property."

He appeared embarrassed instead of angered by the

chastising. "Would you care to file a report on Aubrey, Miss Owens? From what I can tell, his parole officer has had him on a loose leash for some time now, but this would make a nice start in changing that. Truth be told, I've been waiting to nail his ass on something, knew it would only be a matter of time."

"I'm not here to file a report," she said. "I'm here because my father gave Will McGomery a right of way across his property, and if there's going to be trouble, it's going to drive right by my parent's house just like it did today. I don't want trouble for them, sheriff."

"You don't want a report filed over something that actually took place, but you want me to get up in arms over something you think might happen?" He shook his head, laughed abruptly.

"I want to know what I'm dealing with when it comes to these men," she said, knowing she had reached the heart of why she'd come to see him. "If one of them is going to continue living just up the ridge from my parents, then I should know what kind of trouble he's capable of attracting."

His animated expression slid off his face like melting snow on glass. "Seems the only trouble William McGomery has attracted lately is you."

He rolled his leather swivel back, got up and closed the door. When he returned to his desk, he sat down with the gravity of a man who was about to say something he didn't relish.

He reached across his barrel of a chest and massaged his massive shoulder. "Look, the best advice I can give you is to mind your own business, Ms. Owens. Don't be going up and visiting William McGomery. Nobody lives the way he does and has all his marbles in place. He's a social outcast, could be dangerous."

He took a moment to consult his blunt fingernails. "Aubrey, on the other hand, is flat out crazy; a mean spirited son of a gun who knows exactly who drowned that girl because he did it himself. Roughing you up is just his way of letting his cousin know that he hasn't forgotten the betrayal that led to that drowning." He skewered her with a hard look. "Leave them boys alone."

"Will McGomery lives the way he does because his whole world was taken from him," she argued without thinking. "Being lonely doesn't make him dangerous."

Davidson looked at her sagely and she inwardly groaned. He was so onto her, knew that she had feelings for Will, knew that she had come with one thing in mind—to learn whatever she could about his past.

One side of his mouth twitched. "I get the feeling you don't really believe he's safe at all, and you know as well as I do that he tossed his world aside, is a reckless, two-faced Judas. Listen, sweet pea. Take it from an old man who knows all about these guys. You're dealing with someone who doesn't have a lot to lose these days. Be wise, don't contest what's his, and don't be the one to resurrect a history no one wants to remember."

"Why wasn't he a suspect in Sarah Chambers' drowning?" she asked, knowing she had come too far to turn back now. "Nothing I've read indicates he was ever more than a person of interest."

"He had an alibi, that's why," he said, almost eagerly. "Bill Hudgen, the coroner, estimated that Sarah Chambers had been in the water just a few hours when her Daddy found her, and that she had been breathing when she went in. Will was in West Virginia at the time of her death. In fact, he'd been there for almost a week and didn't return until after I drove up there and talked to him."

She stared at him, praying that he wasn't lying to her to cover his own ass in regard to the Chambers' case. "West Virginia?"

"Visiting his terminally ill mother," he said. "Several of his mother's people vouched for his whereabouts that week." His chiseled face took on a reflective expression. "I imagine he sustained quite a shock when he returned and found his wife hanging from a barn rafter. Guess that was his defining moment, the moment he realized just how much he'd failed his pretty little wife."

"So you believe she hung herself because he was having an affair with Sarah Chambers?"

"Water under the bridge," he said brusquely. "All of it. You just need to keep your distance from the McGomerys. Been peaceful around here a long time and I'd hate to see that end because you refuse to leave well enough alone."

He stood, passed a hand over his steely buzz cut, and hitched up his brown regulation trousers. He extended one of his monstrous hands across the desk. "I have your word, Miss Owens?"

She remained seated, considered his large, yellow-tinged fingers. "You want me to say yes and then shake on it, like we're children making a pact?"

When he smiled and tilted his head to one side, she arched her brows at him. "Will McGomery has done nothing to make me think he's mentally unstable."

He dropped his arm. "Then it appears my hands are tied. You put out the cheese and expect me to dissuade the rats? Look, I don't know what you want from me, Miss Owens."

"I don't know what I expected from you either, to be honest," she said. "Sorry I wasted your time."

She rose from the chair. She had obtained more information from Davidson than she thought he's give. It was time to leave, time to get out of there before he saw just how shook up she was by her encounter with him. "Good day, sheriff."

She was at the door when he spoke, his voice like a smirk on the face of a teenaged bully. "Aubrey must have thought he'd met himself a real fashion icon up there today. I bet he won't soon forget you."

She knew the look on her face conveyed her discomfiture. She opened the door and left, saying nothing.

In her mind, however, she wondered how it was that she had become so determined to solve the riddle that was Will

McGomery.

# CHAPTER SIXTEEN

Tritt Davidson took a stabilizing breath as he watched Madison Owens pass through the lobby's glass door.

Damn it all to hell.

The last thing he needed was another of Marshall Owens' daughters taking an interest in Will McGomery. The first one was trouble enough, like a bad termite infestation, constantly eating away at the foundation of his patience.

He certainly didn't have the patience required to deal with twice the drama. Something told him this latest sister had already gotten in too deep, and there would be no extracting her.

Messy.

Will McGomery had been a convenient and needful distraction during the Chambers murder investigation. Because of his alleged weakness for that girl, he had snagged the gossips' attention and drew their scrutiny completely away from another man—a boy really.

*His* boy.

Thanks to Aubrey McGomery's steadfast belief in his cousin's betrayal, no one ever doubted that the baby in Chambers' belly was Will McGomery's. In truth, it had stood more than a reasonable chance of being Jake's. Because of that, Tritt had worked tirelessly to prove that McGomery was the cause and Aubrey the effect—a love triangle that had ended in murder—and his strategy had been a success in spite of a hung jury.

Ancient history did not need to get mixed in with what he knew was going on now, and this Madison woman's poking around posed a definite risk.

Could get very, very messy.

He wished he hadn't recently found out certain things about the Chambers case. Ignorance was oftentimes a blessing.

As things stood now, Madison Owens couldn't have chosen a less convenient time to stir things up. She was a problematic ingredient and one he had no idea how to neutralize.

What had been set in motion could not be recalled or aborted, and she was smack dab in the middle of the plans now. She needed to make herself scarce, and pronto, but he had no faith that she would.

She was the stubborn type; he could see it in those sultry, brown eyes. And that unfortunate characteristic had placed her in imminent danger. Of that he had no doubt. To become romantically involved with a McGomery was the equivalent of a SWAT team making a bust without bulletproof vests.

Both of Marshall Owens' daughters were extremely vulnerable. The one with her head up Aubrey's ass was a given. But she'd proven herself cunning and tough, not someone he spent a lot of time feeling sorry for.

This latest one, though...this one he didn't know about.

This one wore hurt in her expression like an abused kid wore bruises on the skin, and he'd suffered a twinge of guilt just looking into that guileless face. She had come back to Virginia in search of something—he could sense that acutely—and he was afraid that something had manifested in the form of the reclusive and murderous Will McGomery.

He closed the door to his office and crossed back over to his desk. Once there, he dialed his son's cell number and waited impatiently for him to pick up. Figuring he was either in surgery or in the middle of a consult, he disconnected before the voice mail kicked on then tried Jake's office.

It was imperative that his boy not be the confused young man he'd been just a few short years ago. He needed to have a normal, mundane conversation with him. He would invite him, Gail, and the munchkin over to dinner.

That would be good. He could inquire about his son's day and listen to him prattle about that week's successful gastric bypass procedures. He could take comfort in knowing that when it came to internal medicine, his son was the county's golden boy.

The sound of the receptionist's voice was a pleasant caress to his ear. A distraction he needed. "Tammy," he said. "Tritt here. Jake's tied up, ain't he? Yeah, I figured. Well, have him call me here at the office or on my cell soon as he gets an opening, will you? Thanks, sweetheart."

He moved back to the window in his office, poked a finger into the blinds, parting them so that he could stare into the patch of sky visible from his office. Clouds were building, but rain was not forecasted until the weekend. The arthritis in his knee would no doubt flare up right along with the weather, bringing him a great deal of pain.

Regrettably, his arthritis was the least of his worries.

****

Will wasn't watching her.

Her eyes moving over him eagerly as he picked at the horse's shoe, Madison allowed herself this time to appreciate just how wonderful he looked.

Even bent at the waist, with the horse's front hoof propped over his knee, she could ascertain how tall he was. He had long, muscular legs to match an impressively lean and fit torso.

With the sleeves of his button down shirt rolled to his elbows, she could see, and studied at length, his tanned forearms. The evening sun, a blaze caught between banks of bruised looking clouds, caught the hairs on them, burnishing them gold.

She closed in on him and finished her perusal with a glance to his faded overalls. She had grown fond of them in the short time she'd known him.

A bit too fond of them, perhaps. Lately all she could seem to think about was the way he had looked when he'd yanked them open at his waist and let them fall. She'd never seen anything so sexy, would never, ever think of denim overalls in the way same again.

Tongue lolling, Clovis did a little dance about his master's booted feet and she was struck by the enthusiastic greeting. She had half expected him to cower in distrust after the injury brought upon him by her earlier visit.

Will suddenly abandoned what he was doing and turned his attention to her. His expression was guarded and she wondered just how bent out of shape he still was over their skirmish at the fair.

"What's his name...your horse?"

He adjusted his floppy hat, his eyes submersed in shadow and almost violet in the hazy sunlight.

"Molly named him Cornflower but I call him Blue." His brows drew down in consternation at her smirk. "Cornflowers are blue, are they not?"

"And Blue sounds more befitting since the horse is a stud," she said.

To this he shrugged. "What happened to your lip?"

She fiddled with the hem of her tee, unwilling to answer the question until she got some answers of her own. "What happened between you and my sister the other night?"

He brushed off the knee of his overalls and stepped closer to her. He extended a callused hand and rubbed her hair between his fingertips. "How in God's name am I supposed to deal with you, Madison Owens?"

"Don't," she said, brushing his hand aside. His propensity to demolish her defenses was amazing. One touch from him and she had a belly full of gossamer wings, fluttering wildly. "Lorna said you held her at gun point."

He stared thoughtfully across the sun-drenched meadow. "Let's go for a ride on Blue. Sunsets are magnificent up here and I know just the place where we can—"

"You don't think I'm smart enough to know you're trying to distract me?" She glowered at him. "Just stop it, Will."

"Someone was up here while I was out today," he volunteered. "They tore up my yard with their vehicle. You gonna tell me what you know about that?"

She thought about Aubrey spinning Dow's truck around in front of the cabin. He'd done a lot more than tear up his cousin's grass, but until Will offered an explanation about Lorna, she wasn't saying anything. "Appears we are at a stand off."

"Sure to hell looks that way," he said, his lips thinning.

"Oh, for crying out loud." She exhaled loudly through her nose. "I don't have to answer to you, Will, about something that has nothing to do with me."

"Nothing to do with you?" He hooked his index finger under her chin and tipped her face up. His eyes were like homing devices, roaming over hers, seeking out the truth. "Madison, tell me what's going on. What happened to you today?"

She stepped back, fearing what his reaction would be to the truth. Not certain what she should believe about him after her encounter with Aubrey, she stalled. "I don't have to tell you anything, McGomery."

"Don't be childish." His eyes now scoured hers. "Talk to me."

"That's all I'm asking you to do," she said. "But you refuse."

"We're going for that ride on Blue." He moved toward the barn; she guessed to retrieve a saddle and bridle.

Lord.

On a horse with her breasts flattened against his back? Desire, like warm molasses, spread through her at the thought, but she was angry.

She should say no. No horse. No ride.

No physical intimacy between herself and Will McGomery.

She spotted his mule plucking hay from the trough attached to the barn, slid her eyes to Clovis, digging urgently at a molehill.

What to do? What to do?

She strolled over to where the horse had wandered, slid her

hands over the animal's sateen side. Will approached and immediately set about situating a saddle over his back. She noticed that his jaw was set.

Her eyes narrowed over his face. "Don't be this way. Don't be angry because I want to know what's going on with you and my sister."

"What the hell does it matter what's going on? You don't need to know." He continued to work with the saddle, grunted with the exertion. "Shit."

"You need to calm down."

"No, what I need is to have my head examined."

She felt her throat seizing up. "What do you mean by that?"

"I mean for putting up with you. You don't have the sense of that jackass over there."

"I'm sure I don't know what the hell you're talking about."

His hands stilled on the saddle and he stared at her over the horse. "Owens, you wear disillusion like a turban around your head. You think this is not dangerous, this game you're playing? You got hurt today because of me." He jabbed at his shirt in the vicinity of his chest. "Me."

Taken by surprise, she stood motionless, her eyes fixed on his. Then her hands flew to her face, and her fingers pushed strands of hair behind her ears. The tears popped unwanted into her eyes, hot and blinding.

"I don't want to ride your idiotic horse," she said. "I want you to tell me you didn't pull a gun on Lorna."

He broke eye contact with her. Looking pensively at the ground, he shook his head. "Liar. You came up here because, like me, you want to finish what we started."

She watched him remove the saddle from the horse and experienced a rush of panic because she did want to feel her breasts mashed against him, the heat of his body pulsating through her.

Again. Longer this time. Until he spent himself on her.

"All right, forget Lorna," she said. "Deny what everyone

says about you. Deny you were having an affair with Sarah Chambers."

He tugged at the saddle and then angrily heaved it toward the barn, startling Clovis and causing him to run in the direction of the cabin. Dust plumed around where the saddle lay. The horse nickered. Madison's mouth went dry.

"You want a saint? That what you're looking for?" He sneered. "Well, you're looking in the wrong place, sweetheart."

Suddenly he was standing right in front of her. Behind him, the horse lowered his broad head to munch grass.

Snip-crunch. Snip-crunch.

Somewhere, Clovis watched from a distance. She felt his peculiar, forlorn eyes on them.

Jesus. Did she really need two ugly confrontations with McGomerys in one day? Was Will going to grab her, shake her, what? And if he did get rough with her, how would she stop that from breaking her heart?

He brought his face down close to hers. "If it's a reprobate you're after, though, then you've hit pay dirt."

"I'm not after anything," she said, her tongue like a dusty towel in her mouth. "And I had a reprobate for a husband, don't need another."

His smirk was cold. "The one you had didn't even know how to please you in bed. Trust me, you won't find me lacking in that department."

"And I dare say Lorna didn't find you lacking? Or Sarah Chambers?" She regretted the reckless words the moment they left her lips, wished she could retract them.

Will sprang to his full height, his whole body going rigid. A sudden breeze swept the field, almost taking his hat. He crammed a hand over his head and continued to glare mistrustfully at her, chest heaving, shoulders hunched.

"Lorna has no fucking idea what it's like to be with me."

Through tendrils of her hair, she held his gaze, fought to keep the tears still brimming in her eyes from sliding down her face. "I have no idea why I believe you but I do, Will. I do."

Stepping into her space, his body relaxed slightly and he slowly gathered her into his arms, buried his face in her hair, causing his hat to tumble to the ground. His hands claimed what was immediately available to them, one splaying over her lower back, and one over her bottom. His long fingers curling hungrily into her left buttock, he exhaled raggedly near her ear.

"Let me prove that it wasn't you."

She stiffened marginally. "What wasn't me?"

"The problem in your marital bed," he whispered gruffly against the sticky heat of her temple. He cocked his head and ever so lightly grazed her mouth with his, just barely skimming her injured lip with a kiss. Unable to bear the tantalizing treatment, she felt her womb contract as she slid her tongue over her lips nervously and came into contact with his.

His hands came between them as their kiss deepened, his fingers working at the pair of buttons on the front of her denim shorts.

"We can't," she mumbled plaintively against his lips, but he either did not hear her feeble protest, or simply wasn't interested in heeding it. She heard the rasp of a zipper, felt her shorts loosen at her waist and hips, felt him deftly slide his fingers down the back of her panties and over her tingling skin.

He clutched her bottom firmly, and pulled her tightly against him, then slid his mouth over her neck, over one breast and down, until he was on one knee and placing warm kisses to the exposed skin above her panties. The silky garment was tugged down along with her shorts, and then gently shoved past her calves. He nuzzled the short strip of hair covering her mound, executed small, moist kisses to the tight curls.

"I want to wake up tomorrow morning knowing what you taste like," he murmured against her.

She sifted her fingertips through his locks of sun-gilded hair and closed her eyes. "We can't, Will. I can't."

"You can," he growled, taking firm hold of her ankle and

pulling her foot clear of the clothing pooled around it.

Gripping his shoulders for balance, she made a small sound, a cry of surprise. He situated her sandaled foot over his raised knee and immediately set about exploring her with his lips and tongue.

Liquid desire filled her veins, licked into the plush heat of her labia. His mouth was hot and exquisitely familiar with the landscape of her anatomy. He kissed her, nipped lightly with his teeth, and stroked her with his tongue. She gasped, clutched his head, and bit into her lower lip.

He wouldn't stop finessing the tight bud he'd found within her sensitive folds until she shuddered uncontrollably and cried out.

When it was over and she stood trembling before him, he continued to kiss her moist curls, pressed his cheek against them and breathed deeply in as though he wanted to commit the scent of her to his memory.

"Thank you," he said softly, shifting his head and rubbing his lips back and forth over her lower belly. "I've been wanting to do that since that day you stood at my sink washing dishes."

She swallowed the lump of emotion that had gathered in her throat. "I...I can't...believe..."

"That I made you come?" He kissed her thigh, lowered her foot to the ground and then struggled to his feet, wincing as he straightened. "You weren't leaving here until I did."

When he showed no sign of wanting the same for himself, she immediately felt awkward, and set about putting her clothes back on. She felt him watching her. When she'd buttoned her shorts, she looked at him, and found that she desperately wanted to bring him the kind of pleasure he had brought to her.

"Don't look at me like that, Maddie," he said tersely. "You know and I know that this isn't going to work between us. As much as I want it to, this shouldn't go any further."

She shrugged, unable to glance away from him. "You can't tell me the truth about you, about the past. Is that it?"

"You're right. I don't talk about the past," he admitted. "But the reason this won't work is because you're too naïve. You don't know what you're getting yourself into and I'm not about to play these guessing games with you. I won't abide you keeping secrets when they could get you hurt, more so than what you've been already."

Her heart kicked. "I have nothing to hide."

Turning, he started walking toward the cabin. "You shouldn't come back up here. We've dabbled in this enough. Nothing good will come of it."

"Dabbled?" She stood there completely immobilized, watched dumbfounded as he put space between them. "Why did you just…do that to me if you knew nothing good would come of it?"

He pivoted, anger making his eyes like blue flash cards. "I did it because you needed to know that nothing is wrong with you. And I did it because I don't want to spend the rest of my life wondering what I'd missed."

She shook her head, threw up her hands and started across the yard toward the cabin and her Jeep. His voice drew her up short.

"You said you have nothing to hide."

Her eyes hooking with his, she lifted her shoulders. "I don't."

"Tell me about that lip," he said.

Walking away, she didn't speak. She was still afraid to tell him.

# CHAPTER SEVENTEEN

He imagined the cursed stillness that descended as a prelude to his seizures was like being on a darkened stage awaiting curtain call.

Will didn't know what horror awaited him on the other side of this curtain, but knew he had to be ready to face it. When the velvet wall parted, it was time to lock and load, no bowing out.

An audience would never laud his appearance; he knew this. No crowd of spectators existed, only a stage, and scenes from the realm of the dead.

Only the dead themselves.

He was merely the observer.

Reaching out to brace himself against the wall, he thought of Madison. He had wanted to stop her from leaving, but as she'd cut across the backyard toward the front of the cabin, her hair flaming like a halo around her head in the burnt red of the sinking sun, he had sensed the change in him. An eerie quiet had closed in, clasped him like a slumbering lover, and he'd made his way quickly to the house.

His fingertips curled into the painted sheet rock along the hallway. It felt insubstantial, like he'd pushed his fingers into a huge belly, but when he focused on the wall, he saw that his mind was playing tricks on him. It wasn't yielding to the trembling pressure of his fingers at all.

He withdrew his hand, pressed his back to the wall and slid down to the floor. The roaring had started in his ears now. Like the surf, and yet it wasn't. It was the racket of his erratic brain waves, a sound that would ratchet up in its intensity before fading to a dull hum.

He pinched his eyelids together, but there was no commitment in the delicate muscles that would keep them closed and they drifted back open. In that second while he'd been submerged in the complete darkness of the stage behind closed eyes, it had happened. The curtain had split, invisible ghost hands raising the veil of his subconscious with zealous fervor.

He was about to take in act two, or three…or five hundred. He simply knew it was a familiar scene, one in which he was a silent watcher, an unwilling witness with eyes that could not look away.

Molly stood in their bedroom within the house that no longer existed, the house that had burned to the ground years ago. On the bed was a book, an ancient looking thing with faded gold lettering across the front.

The letters, though worn, were exquisitely rendered, tall and slanted like ornate etchings in an Egyptian tomb.

*Bequeathed.*

His vision acute, he saw the word plainly from where he sat. He would not be able to see his own hands if he was to raise them to his face, but he saw those seven letters with laser clarity. A lump formed in his throat because he knew what came next.

Molly crossed to the bed and snatched the book up, flipped through it frantically. Her fingers faltered and she almost dropped it.

Her fear was like a bat caught in her throat, squeaking, shrilling.

Christ.

It was awful. He wanted it to stop. He wanted to tell her it was okay. He would fix it. He would take it back, this deed that had compelled her to end her life.

He knew, however, that it was impossible to take anything back.

"*My name*," she said, fingers crumpling the pages as they savagely turned them one after another after another. "*It's never here. My name isn't here. Where's my name?*"

Something was behind him, always behind him in this room. He could hear it breathing now, above the dissonant roar, a moist guttural wheezing. He couldn't turn to see what it was, though. He could only see what was before him, understood that this was, in part, because he was locked in a seizure, for all purposes dead to the tangible, the drifting lost.

He tried to speak but his tongue was a frightened soldier hiding behind the wall of his teeth. Molly hurled the book across the room and instantly, her image dissipated like delicate sand moldings in water.

But instead of his own astral departure from the room, he remained.

This was something different. This felt totally wrong and very ominous.

The book skidded on its spine, falling open at the spot where his feet would be if he were in his body. Among lines and lines of names on the revealed page, one stood out to him; it shone an ethereal blue, like the sky in spring.

Sarah Chambers.

She was in the book, but not his wife, not his beautiful, confused Molly.

And something was behind him, still behind him and ripe with decay. He must do whatever was necessary to stop his dreams, these aberrations of his mind. Do whatever it took to assuage this guilt that breathed upon his neck like a vampire.

In his mind, he felt a stirring, the caress of a soft, familiar whisper, like pale flowers imprinted upon the wallpaper of his mind.

*The time fast approaches.*

A rustling noise came from behind him, and he strained to turn around, this time succeeding. It was a cloud of black mist, nothing else. As if by turning to face this blight, this awful apparition, he had caused the entity to vaporize into tiny black molecules. They seeped into the wall and floor, and were gone.

He turned back to the bed, hoping to see Molly, but seeing someone else instead. It was another familiar scene, only this one overlapped with the prior vision. He stood in what had once been both his and Molly's bedroom, and the one that had belonged to Sarah Chambers' mother, Veronica. He stood in them at the same time.

Veronica lay sprawled across an antique sleigh bed that he recognized from his earlier visions, her eyes open but milky. Corpse eyes.

An empty prescription bottle rested on the rumpled quilt beside her.

As though she was a puppet and someone had pulled an invisible string attached to her head, she bolted upward. It was an unanimated movement, stiff and unnatural, and though he'd seen it all before, he still recoiled at the sight of her.

She laughed and it was a blend of many voices, a grim cacophony of sound that reminded him of a story about a man possessed with legions of devils.

He had gone to church with this woman and her husband Joshua. They had been devout Christians—his neighbors—and then Sarah had drowned and Joshua had started drinking, Veronica pill popping.

The woman's bloated face, as though coated in old paint, had split in several places. Black beetles spilled out of the peeling crevices, and a gurgling sound emanated from her throat. A sludgy liquid oozed out of the corner of her mouth, and in it he could see tiny white worms moving about.

Maggots. So many maggots. The scene never varied.

Only this time, Veronica rose from the bed. She came toward him, each step a disjointed effort. Her limbs were like the spindly, twisted branches of a Sassafras tree. Her rotted teeth like boards teeming with the cadaver eaters, the larvae and beetles.

*Shall we go to the pond and set things right? Oh, but we will. We must.*

The voice, filled with his impending death, was the most horrifying aspect of the scene. She was going to wrap him in her earthy arms and take him down into that water, where Sarah waited. This was the seizure that would kill him.

"No, not yet," he said, his voice echoing throughout the stage in his mind like it would echo through a vast canyon. The aching, hollow sound of it terrified him. He envisioned Madison Owens, tried to bring her into focus.

If he could place her beautiful visage over the one seeking to damn him, maybe it wouldn't be so bad. Maybe he could face death if, when it embraced him, it was Madison's countenance that was before him.

The thing that had once been Veronica Chambers laughed again, her breath a putrid waft from the grave in which her embalmed corpse slowly decomposed. She reached for him before exploding into the black molecules he'd seen moments before.

The mist blinded him, burned like arsenic in his lungs. He stumbled back from it and encountered something damp and soft—another body. Hands, cold like driftwood floating in wintry water, slid up the back of his neck, the fingers parting his hair and slipping over his temples to cover his eyes.

His eyes.

He saw nothing but darkness and felt nothing but cold. It was Sarah. She had emerged from the water and found him, found him in this seizure, vulnerable and at her complete mercy.

A breath in his ear, cool and dank, filled his ailing brain. She would take him with her. He had run out of time and she would fill his lungs with pond water, snuff out his life. His name would join hers in the book and Molly would never know peace.

Never.

*"The time has come,"* the voice whispered, *"for sacrifice."*

\*\*\*\*

All that remained of the sun was a streak of solar blood low across the western horizon. Locusts already thickened the air with their peculiar white noise and Madison was struck by how much louder they were up on the ridge.

She wanted to be here, didn't want to leave and didn't plan

to.

Slipping down out of her Jeep, she clenched her jaw, bracing herself for another intimidating encounter. Her thoughts swirled around the angry words her father had showered her with, just minutes ago.

'*You have lost your God damned mind, going up there to play that bastard's girlfriend. Do you not care at all about your reputation? First Lorna, now you. Rachel's the only one of you that has any sense.*'

She had anticipated his wrath at some point over her involvement with Will but hadn't been prepared to deal with it that night.

Nor with her mother's stricken expression.

Her delicate sandals sticky on her feet, she felt the grass, damp with the setting dew, on her toes as she started for the porch. She jumped when Will's voice reached out to her from the porch like a rough grasp.

"See Clovis on your way up?"

Forcing her hand down from her chest, where her heart was thrashing out a chaotic rhythm against her breastbone, she shook her head back and forth. She could just make out Will's form where he leaned against a porch post.

"You decide to come clean about your lip?" he asked.

Her duffel bag of clothes was in her Jeep. What was he going to say about her plans to stay with him? "I came because I'd rather be up here with you and on my land than be heckled to death by my parents."

"They're giving you a hard time about me."

She made a snuffling sound. "That's putting it mildly. Lorna's got a hand in it. She's been calling and talking to them about us, saying God knows what."

"And you're surprised?" he said flatly. "Now you want to make matters worse, camp out up here with public enemy number one. Brilliant."

Saying nothing, she wrapped her arms around herself and

stared into the shadows of his face. He was right. It was crazy to think this was going to solve her problems. She had a feeling it was going to be the beginning of a whole new set.

"Before we talk about that, I'd like to address what my cousin did to you," he stated, and she thought the calmness in his voice was deceptive.

Her stomach dropped. "How do you know about him?"

"Come inside."

She hesitated for only a moment before closing in on the porch. He pushed off the post and crossed to the door, opening it and flipping a switch on the wall. The living room was, at once, illuminated and as she passed by him into the cabin, she noticed that he seemed to be sensitive to the light.

He ducked his head, moved beyond her to turn on a table lamp. "Would you mind turning off the overhead?"

Stepping over to the wall, she flipped it off then watched as he sat down in the winged back near the bookcase.

"Are you all right?" she said, moving for the rocker and slowly sitting down.

Will said nothing for a moment, and then smiled dismally. "You saw the medicine I take, you know I'm an epileptic. What you don't know is that the drugs only half work."

"You had a seizure after I left awhile ago?"

A deep breath, then he moved his eyes from her face to her hands, which she realized were knotted in her lap. She pulled them apart and slid her palms up and down her thighs.

"I'm not Frankenstein, just prone to seizures," he said, his voice was gently chiding.

"I'm sorry to hear that the meds don't prevent them. I hope it wasn't bad."

His gaze dropped to the floor and after a moment, he leaned over and picked up something that was lying in front of the bookshelf. As he lifted it, she saw that it was the photo she had come across in his bathroom, the one of the two women. He appeared startled by it, reached over and hastily slid it between two books.

"What was that?" She heard the trepidation in her voice and hated it.

He shrugged. "Nothing. Does it repel you to know I have these episodes?"

Her mind was stuck on the photograph, but she wasn't comfortable with the idea of pressing him for more information. Not at the moment anyway.

"How did you find out about Aubrey?"

"It's a small fucking world, or haven't you figured that out yet?" Wincing, he massaged his temples then looked at her. "I ran into the sheriff this afternoon at the post office."

She was assaulted by a memory of the cumbersome man— his nicotine stained fingers and hard, gunmetal eyes. "What did he say exactly?"

"Among other things?" He flashed a self-deprecating smile. "He asked me if I really think I have a chance with a woman whose outfit was probably worth more than my truck."

Her heart was awash with sudden empathy for him. Davidson was a real bastard to cut a man down who had already been reduced to hiding on a ridge. If she'd disliked him before, she truly detested him now.

Will stared intensely at her. "What the hell were you wearing today and where did it go to?"

The clothes had been disposed of immediately upon her return from the sheriff's office. She hadn't been able to stand the thought of wearing them one second longer, had felt as though they had been contaminated by Aubrey's hands and by Davidson's penetrating stare. She shrugged and said nothing.

Will rested his head against the back of the chair, closed his eyes. "I wish you would've told me about Aubrey."

She moved her gaze from him to the nearby window, caught the room's reflection in it and glanced away from that as well, afraid that she would see the girl again. "I guess I was embarrassed by the whole thing."

His head came up and his stare grabbed her, held firm. "Davidson said you thought Aubrey was going to rape you. He could have. Easily. Now you see why this can't go any further between us? My life isn't anything you should want to get involved in."

"Allow me to make that decision."

"He hit you and you weren't even going to tell me about it."

"I wasn't ready to talk to you about it."

His jaw tensed. "Maybe you're not ready for a lot of things."

"What is that supposed to mean?" she asked, her heart thumping painfully.

"We don't belong together, Maddie. I know what I'm talking about here."

Their eyes did battle. Her pulse rapid and leaving her breathless, she gripped the wooden arms of the rocker. "I agree. But I do belong up here and you're just going to have to deal with me. Deal with me or sell me a tract of this land."

"You stay here with me, both our lives get complicated," he said. "When we're together, I can't keep my hands or my mouth off of you. That's not a good thing. You're vulnerable, not anywhere near to being over what's his name, your dickhead husband. I can't promise that I won't take advantage of you in every possible physical way. Is that what you want? To be Slick Willie's next sexual conquest? That's all you can be to me, Madison. I'm not capable of offering anything more than what I gave you today."

Her voice had dried up, leaving her throat a desert corridor while another place much lower blossomed with arousal despite her best efforts to hinder it.

In the dim corner of the room, his eyes were like deep cups of indigo dye as they held hers captive. Without blinking, he leaned forward.

"Stay and you'll be hurt, Owens, not by Aubrey, but by

me."

# CHAPTER EIGHTEEN

Without another word, Will rose from the chair and made his way toward the back of the house, disappearing down the short hallway. Madison heard him shaking pills out of a bottle in the bathroom. When he reemerged, he went into the kitchen, and her eyes followed his movements as he set about pouring them some coffee from a carafe on the counter.

"You like cream or sugar in your brew?" he asked, glancing at her over the half wall dividing them.

"I don't want any coffee." Her eyes cut to the bookcase. She knew which books he'd slid the photo between and was anxious for an opportunity to retrieve it and study it at length.

She wished she could rid herself of the need to get her hands on it again. Wished also that she felt more prepared to deal with whatever paranormal activity was to be in store. "What was Aubrey talking about when he said there were things going on with you?"

He brought her a mug of coffee and grinned a little when she eagerly reached for it. Taking his to the wingback, he lowered himself into the chair and took a sip, watched her do the same. "Why the hell didn't you ask him, being as he's the one who made the statement?"

"I would have except he backhanded me. I kind of lost my focus after that."

The low burn in his eyes intensified. "I'll fucking kill him when I get my hands on him."

"He held back," she said, "and I think it was because he fears you."

"Only thing that bastard ever feared was the wrath of my Pap and that was years ago."

She set her coffee on the table next to the rocking chair. Appealing to him with her eyes, she leaned forward. "His only intent seemed to be to warn me away from you."

"Only it didn't work. You're sitting in my living room."

"Tritt Davidson issued a warning as well, claims you might be dangerous."

He laughed softly. "Not even Tritt wants to see a pretty little thing like you get your heart broken."

"The sheriff isn't that noble," she said, her coffee momentarily forgotten.

He pondered the contents of his mug, and then treated her to a long-suffering sigh. "You're right, he's not. You shouldn't have gone to see him. He's corrupt. He framed Aubrey for the fire that burned my house because he wanted to make sure that no one doubted my cousin's malicious streak, and he's not going to like the fact that you're stirring things up."

She assimilated this for a few moments. "He framed Aubrey? The sheriff kept the attention on your cousin to ensure that his son slipped under the radar. Christ."

His expression remained bland. "People do a lot of things in the name of love."

"How do you know that he framed Aubrey?" She stood from the rocker, placed her hands on her hips. "How could you possibly know?"

He stood, crossed to the counter and placed his mug on it. Then he approached her, tucked an errant strand of her hair behind her ear. "You wouldn't believe me if I told you."

Her lips compressed. She lowered her eyes to a button on his shirt, shrugged. "I never thought I'd believe in ghosts, but I do. Sarah Chambers is with you and I want to know why."

"The thing with Sarah is complicated," he said, absently taking hold of the drawstrings at her neck and tugging on her jacket. Moving away from her, he went to the door, opened it, and called for Clovis. When the dog still hadn't appeared after a sharp whistle, he pulled his head back inside. Leaning his back against the door, he moved his eyes over her slowly.

"Complicated," she said, crossing her arms over her chest,

and feeling suddenly wary about the subject of the drowned girl.

"I wasn't a good guy back then," he supplied. "And I can't change that."

"You cheated on your wife."

He was silent. She felt her heart canonize. "You were afraid she was going to find out about you and Sarah, about the pregnancy."

He pushed away from the door, and with amazing stealth, moved back into her personal space. He bent his head and put his face close to hers, his breath a husky pressure on her skin.

"No, I wasn't afraid of her finding out. That was the least of my fears. You don't want to know what kind of fears I had to deal with." He lifted his hands, made to cup her face, then thought better of it and dropped them to his sides.

"Please, leave here and don't look back, Madison. I'm a piece of shit who will bring you nothing but heartache."

She lifted a hand and caressed his rough cheek. "You have feelings for me, Will, and I don't believe for one second that you intend to hurt me."

His eyes narrowed over hers. Then, they grew moist with tears, and he wheeled around, putting his back to her. Stepping over to the half wall, he spread his arms and braced his hands on the counter, took several deep breaths.

He sniffed and turned back around, glaring at her through red eyes. "I didn't want to cheat on my wife, Madison, but I did. Stay and you become a part of that and something even worse."

"You mean the haunting, Sarah haunting you."

"No," he said and his expression was suddenly haggard. "Look, the pills I took a minute ago are going to knock me on my ass. I have to sleep this off."

She shrugged. "Fine. We'll talk in the morning. I'll just go get my things out of the Jeep and take them to your guest bedroom."

"Madison," he said, as she moved for the front door. She turned to look at him and he cleared his throat. "Why? Why are you so determined to ruin your perfect life? Staying here will ruin it."

"Perfect?" She laughed at him. "And you think I'm disillusioned."

He said nothing else, but when she returned with her duffel bag, he had retreated to his bedroom and shut the door.

It was just as well.

# CHAPTER NINETEEN

An hour passed before she emerged from the guest bedroom. When she did, she slipped across the hallway and into the bathroom, which adjoined Will's bedroom. Pressing her ear to the door, she heard him breathing, slow and deep, the rhythmic breaths of someone buried in the soft layers of sleep.

She made her way into the dark living room by feeling with her hands, and located the lamp on the table next to the rocker. She switched it on and walked directly to the bookcase, sliding out a volume and sticking her fingers into the vacant space.

The photo was not there.

Her hands fumbled through four more books before accepting the fact Will had retrieved it while she'd gone to get her duffel bag.

"Fabulous," she whispered, returning the books to their rightful position on the shelf and sighing in frustration. She spent a moment scanning the various titles spread out before her, but was too distracted to take an interest.

Perhaps Will hadn't taken the photo at all. Why had it been in the floor in the first place?

She stood there thinking.

He had said that he hadn't wanted to cheat on Molly McGomery. Of course, what philandering husband wouldn't say that? The fact remained that he had cheated on his wife and Sarah Chambers was dead. Haunting him.

A slight creak came from somewhere in the cabin and she jerked her head in the direction of his bedroom, certain she would see him standing in the hallway.

She saw nothing, but felt something.

Attributing the noise to the house settling around her, she chafed her arms and decided that she was not so ready to think about all the things that staying there entailed.

She turned off the lamp and quietly set about getting ready for bed, debated taking a shower, and decided that it could wait until morning. By the time she had finished brushing her teeth, she was filled with unease and could hardly wait to get into her room and shut the door.

When she lay in the bed, beneath Will McGomery's sheets, she closed her eyes to the darkness and wondered if every night in his cabin would feel so forlorn, so queer.

So...*wrong*.

No, not if she were in his arms, their bodies entwined and heartbeats in sync.

Lord. She couldn't afford to think about that.

But, in the end, she could think of nothing else.

****

Madison didn't know what actually pulled her from the foggy trenches of her slumber. She only knew that she was suddenly very aware of the room she was in, and that it was not her old room in her parents' house.

She flipped back the sheet and quilt, and reached for the lamp beside the bed. The same golden light as before filled the space but it was no longer comforting. Something was wrong, very wrong.

Oblivious to the fact she wore nothing but an oversized t-shirt, she left the room, was immediately drawn to the light that emanated from the kitchen. She could see the room from where she stood in the hallway and it was empty.

What time was it?

"Will?" Filled with dread, she inched down the hallway. "Will?"

"Here," he said, his voice uncharacteristically thick.

She propelled herself along the wall, everything a blur and yet in slow motion. She drew to an abrupt halt when she saw him standing rigid at the opened front door.

His back rippled with muscles that were taut, seemingly ready for combat. His shoulders heaved with every breath he took.

"What is it?" She gripped the counter, came around it slowly, feeling dizzy with fear.

When she saw the brown fur, and the blood, her hand came up, her palm pressing into her injured lip and bringing about a bright flower of pain. Forcing her hand down, she shook her head. "What happened to him?"

He turned partially and fixed her with a look. "Someone shot him. He's dying."

Her eyes moved from his face to the porch, where the familiar mottled hair had become a shoulder and a leg—tremulous, racked with spasms. She looked away only when the man blocking her view moved toward her.

"I have to put him down," he said, rounding the half wall and disappearing into his bedroom.

She shot another look toward the porch and felt her stomach lurch. Most of Clovis's head was unrecognizable. How the animal had managed to make it onto the porch, she couldn't fathom. She turned away and prayed she wouldn't hear some piteous sound that would attest to his suffering.

Wrapping her arms around her middle, she hugged herself, raising her hands to her cheeks when Will suddenly reentered the kitchen, a gun in his hand.

"Get out of here, Owens. Go back in the bedroom and shut the door."

The last thing she wanted to see was Will McGomery shooting his dog. Shooting Funny eyes. Horrified, she turned, started moving away from the living room.

The hallway was as far as she ventured though, and in the dimness, with her forehead pressed to the wall, she braced herself for what was coming. It turned out to be McGomery's voice, raw like an abrasion, and low.

"Goddamn it to hell."

Then came the gun's shattering discharge and she shuddered violently. The silence that followed was deafening.

She wiped at the tears on her cheeks, jumped when Will appeared at the end of the short hallway.

"I'm going to bury him, and then clean off the porch."

She sniffed. "I'll help you."

"No," he said, shaking his head. "I don't need your help."

He was shaking. She saw it, noticed also the gun still gripped in his hand. Was he afraid for her to go outside with him? Afraid that whoever had done this was watching, waiting? An image of him pressing the gun to her sister's head played through her mind. Was he capable of using that thing to kill the person responsible for this horrific act of animal cruelty?

Yes, he probably was, and the realization made her feel squeamish all over again.

"You want me to use my cell phone to call the police?"

Looking at her as if she had just sprouted wings, he laughed harshly. "Why, so Davidson can gloat about how he told me so? Hell no. I wouldn't put it past that son-of-a-bitch to be the one behind it."

He walked away, leaving her to sort through the debris of her fear and confusion.

## CHAPTER TWENTY

Madison brought the coffee Will had fixed her earlier from the living room, and cast the photo on the kitchen table a wary glance.

She rinsed the mug, left it in the sink, and leaned against the counter, her eyes trained on the hallway. She hoped when McGomery finished showering, he would come in search of her and they could talk. Talk about what had happened to his dog. Or about the two women in the photo that continued to crop up mysteriously.

Stepping over to the table, she plucked up the troublesome picture, convinced she was looking at the images of McGomery's wife and her friend.

It was the blonde that she had seen in the window. She was sure of it, but which of them had been blonde? She couldn't help but to think Sarah. Sarah had been the one with the Aster blue eyes and white-blond hair.

She heard the distant sound of a door opening and knew Will had exited the bathroom by the door leading to his bedroom. Immediately, she glided through the kitchen and approached the other door to his room, knocking tentatively.

"You decent?"

The door opened. He had put on his denim overalls but was shirtless. Her eyes flitting over him, she saw that he was also barefoot. It was not a time to be impressed with his feet, but she was, and embarrassed with how her attention was fixed on his strong, tan toes, she cleared her throat. She held the photo in her hand. She lifted it, handed it to him.

"You were looking at this around the time you went to check on Clovis?"

He frowned at the photo, immediately taking it over to the nightstand and depositing it into the drawer. "Where was it this time?"

Stepping back over to where she stood, he studied her face and she felt her cheeks warm beneath his scrutiny. "On your bed. I glanced in, spotted it. I was curious."

"It's almost two in the morning," he said. "Be curious tomorrow."

"You honestly expect me to be able to sleep after what happened to Clovis?"

This seemed to mollify him. "If it's any consolation, I doubt I'll be able to either."

She leaned against the doorframe, her eyes burning suddenly. "This happened because I'm here."

He pushed by her, moved into the kitchen. "I don't want you to feel sorry for me. Go if you're not willing to put up with the harassment, but don't pity me. Christ, I'd rather you hate me."

"What if this isn't the last of it? What if there's more to come?" She retraced her steps and joined him in the kitchen, watched him put on a fresh pot of coffee. Blinking, and causing the wall of tears in her eyes to cascade down her cheeks, she swept her fingers across the wet tracks left behind.

His hand grabbed a chair at the table and yanked it out. "Sit down. I'll pour you some coffee when it's ready. After you finish, I'll follow you to your Pap's, make sure you get there safely."

She came forward but didn't sit down. Her eyes sought his. "I'd rather face this with you than be treated to a dressing down by him. I'm serious, Will. I feel like I belong here. We...we got ourselves into this, and I won't leave you to face it alone."

"I'm used to facing things alone. I don't need you."

His thoughtless words caused her to shudder. She found she couldn't even acknowledge them. "Maybe this isn't what it seems. Maybe Clovis wandered off and someone who doesn't even know you is responsible."

"He didn't get back to the porch on his own," he said,

giving her a look as he pulled the chair he'd offered her further out and sat down. "He was put there."

She stepped back, leaned against the counter. "Are you certain?"

Eyes on his hands, he swallowed. "I would lay money on it."

"Who, then? Aubrey? Davidson? Who would be callous enough to do that to an animal, leave him out there in that shape?"

"Either or." He put his elbows on the table and slid his fingers into his damp hair. He stared unseeingly at the table and though he said nothing to give away his thoughts, she suspected he was, like her, thinking about what might be coming next.

"How likely is it that it was someone outside of those two?"

He pushed up violently, stalked over to the cabinet and pulled down two mugs. "Owens, leave me alone."

Stunned, she watched him pour coffee into one of the mugs. His hand was trembling.

"Why don't you sit down? Let me pour the coffee."

He placed the carafe back on the warmer and picked up the mug that he hadn't filled. For a moment, he stared at it in his hand and then he flung it across the half wall. It collided with the rocking chair in the living room, setting it in motion, and then rolled across the large floor rug. His eyes dazzling with the fervor of his temper, he glared at her.

"I said get out of my sight."

"What's wrong?" she said, almost choking on the words and prompting him to toss up his hands.

"What's wrong?" he shouted. "What's wrong? I had to kill my dog, wash his blood and brains off my front porch."

She hugged herself. "I know you're upset but you don't have—"

"To take it out on you?" He took a step toward her. Just one, but it brought him within a couple feet and she cowered against the half wall.

"Maybe I do have to take it out on you," he said. "You've brought nothing but more trouble into my life."

"Stop," she whispered. "Don't say something you'll regret later."

Backing up, he stared at her. Then he rounded the table and disappeared into his bedroom, slamming the door with so much force it sounded like it would fly off the hinges.

She stumbled over to the chair he'd vacated and lowered into it. He was right, of course. She had, indeed, brought trouble back into his life. By simply being here, being curious, being consumed with desire for him, she had opened some deep, dark, ugly chasm.

Someone out there had yet to forgive him his part in the scandal that had involved Sarah Chambers—whatever that part had been. Or maybe they just wanted to remind him that he was not the one calling the shots when it came to the truth about Sarah's murder, and he better tread carefully.

In any case, there was someone who apparently didn't want her thrown in the mix.

Someone who had killed McGomery's dog, may have killed Sarah Chambers, and could very likely kill again.

# CHAPTER TWENTY-ONE

Madison looked into her twelve-year-old nephew's face, and knew instantly that he was one of the proverbial latchkey kids. It was in the way he'd only half met her eyes, the tightness around his mouth—a boy who had been made into a man against his will.

She was glad she'd come.

It wasn't as if she was wanted up on the ridge. Will had been practically mute since their words the night before. All that day he had played the avoidance game with her. Had spent most of his time in the building where he did his woodworking.

She had left him a vague note about going shopping after she had eaten a can of soup alone that evening, and then wondered why she hadn't been honest about where she'd been headed.

Had he bought her assertion that she was going shopping? Did he even care?

Despite her deception and the guilt it inspired, she smiled brightly at Lorna's eldest son. To him, she was Aunt Maddie, just dropping in to say hello, not a worried sister. Not a woman whose mind was still churning with turbulent thoughts about what had happened to a sweet-natured mongrel named Clovis.

"Hi, Darius. Where's your mom?"

Darius Boardwine stood there, already a head taller than she was, and for a moment, he said nothing as he stared despondently at her from the doorway. Then he shrugged. "The gym maybe. Said she'd be back in a bit, for me to watch Chaz."

The younger of Lorna's sons, as if on cue, began screaming in the background, screaming as though his two-year old body had been doused in gasoline and set afire. She grimaced, stepped inside and immediately headed in the direction of the ear-piercing shrieks.

"Did she tell you to take the phone off the hook?" she directed over her shoulder. "I've been trying to call for a long time, Dare."

Close behind her, the boy's voice, uneven with puberty, came sheepishly. "She doesn't like people to know she's not here with us."

*Latchkey.*

She entered the modular home's living room and absently noticed the disarray as she scooped the now-bellowing Chastin Boardwine from the floor.

"You have to know this isn't fair to you, Darius. Call your Dad, tell him she's left you guys here."

He shook his head back and forth. "She'll lose her right to see us."

She used her thumb to whisk away the tears that had made the toddler's plump, red cheeks shiny and slick. His wispy, blond hair stood on end in places, and in other areas was clumped to his perfect round skull as though plastered down with spit.

This was truly horrible. Heart punching sad. Lorna was even more screwed up than she had guessed. What the hell was the matter with her, strapping Darius with a very young child like this and with such guilt? Lorna would lose her right?

She had forfeited her right.

Over Chastin's tapering sobs, she met the older boy's worried eyes and spoke gently. "She isn't seeing you anyway, baby."

He looked at the floor. "I don't mind. Really, Mad, I don't. It's just a little hard when Chaz gets all cranked up. I thought I had got him to stop, but then you showed up and I had to leave the room. I think he's cutting a tooth or something and he's got a rash on his butt...a bad one. Dad always puts A&D ointment on him and I found some under the bathroom sink, but I think it's old."

Her lips found Chastin's ear and she whispered something

that she didn't even think about, but something that sounded like a lie when it left her lips.

*I'm here now?*

Like she could fix anything.

Chaz burrowed his head against her neck, smearing wet snot across her skin. She felt sticky and tired, and precariously close to tears herself, but for the sake of the older boy looking at her, she would not allow herself the luxury of crying.

Darius' gaze dropped and snagged on her cut off shorts. He appeared genuinely confused by the sight of them. "What's that?"

She shifted on her feet, angling her head away from Chastin to follow the direction of Darius' gaze. Spotting the blue ribbon half in her pocket, half out, she frowned. Hoisting the child on her hip, she used the fingers on one hand to pull it out. It was a bookmark, the kind she remembered from various summer Vacation Bible-Schools growing up. In contrasting white were the words: *Surely goodness and mercy will follow me all the days of my life.*

A Bible verse.

Where had this come from?

She pushed it back into her pocket and touched Chastin's cheek. "This staying here alone stuff ends here and now." Her eyes locked with Darius Boardwine's. "Okay, Dare?"

The boy nodded. He looked both scared and relieved at the same time.

\*\*\*\*

Lorna sized up the present situation in her kitchen and decided it boded nothing good.

"What are you doing here, Maddie? If you'd just held your horses, I would've called you back. I was getting ready to, in fact, when my mobile's battery went dead." She watched Madison's eyes crawl up to the clock positioned above the stove, and gave her a cold once over.

Her younger sister had a wholesome, natural kind of

beauty. Lorna hated her for it, hated how good she looked in those ratty cut-offs and faded tank top. She could not look as beautiful as Maddie if she had a thousand bucks to put toward her appearance. When Maddie actually wore her coveted Gucci and fixed her hair, she was almost too difficult to look at.

"You put the kids to bed or something?" she asked hesitantly, moving her eyes from her sister's high, round breasts to her face.

"It's nearly eleven o'clock," Madison said. "I'm sure they're sleeping, but not under this roof. Bobby came and got them. After I phoned him, of course."

Lorna actually felt her face drain of color. It was probably turning the same opaque shade as her kitchen linoleum.

*Take a deep breath.*

She needed to wade into this, to take her time. It was just Maddie. She could deal with Maddie. And she could deal with Bobby. He would do nothing more than what he always did; he'd pitch a royal fit and then pretend he didn't have time for her. Treat her like some awful nightmare that he'd woken up from and didn't want to remember.

"Well, I guess after this, any chance at me getting visitation will be nil." She moved to the table, flung her purse across the scarred surface of it, and collapsed into a chair across from Madison.

"You actually did me a huge favor," she said with a one-shoulder shrug. "I couldn't have kept this up much longer anyway. That judge is a hard ass, Mad. Every time I have to go to court over those kids, I'm sick with nerves a whole two days prior. He's horrible, detests women. None of this is fair to me, or the boys. They're better off with one parent and you know who that one parent is by now."

"I don't understand why you couldn't just be here for them," Madison said. "You get them one week a month. One week, Lorna."

Tension pulled at Lorna's shoulders. Maddie was one to

lecture her about kids. She didn't have any, had put her writing career first. Now she had snagged the attention of the one man Lorna couldn't generate an ounce of interest from.

"You don't understand." Lorna folded her hands over the table and hoped the disdain she felt for her sister was evident in her eyes. "It's not easy being me," she said. "Unlike you, I haven't made a fortune selling books. I don't have enough money to make ends meet. I have a dead end job, parents who worry more about their baby's infatuation with a hillbilly than they do about me, and on top of that, my love life sucks. I'm sleeping with a masochistic asshole these days."

Madison's eyes rebuked her. "You mean Aubrey McGomery."

"Oh, I mentioned it to you?" Sometimes Madison really got on her nerves. This was one of those times.

Sanctimonious bitch.

Apparently unaffected by the drop-dead look she was being treated to, Madison continued. "He told me when he came up on the ridge to do your dirty work. Did he mention that busting my lip was a little bonus he threw in?"

She wanted to reach across the table and smack Maddie herself. Of course, he'd mentioned it. He'd still been steaming mad when she saw him, had called Maddie everything under the sun.

She had wanted to clap, to jump and down with excitement over the fact Will McGomery would not be getting what he wanted. But then their mother had phoned her in tears to say that Maddie had packed a bag and driven back up there.

"Oh, don't be such a baby," she said to Maddie now, spitting the words at her. "If you'd just listened to what he'd said instead of trying to claw his eyes out, that wouldn't have happened. Do you know how difficult that was for me in the first place, sending him up there? I didn't want to stoop to that level, but scaring you seemed like the only way to put some sense into your—"

"Don't try to justify it," Madison interrupted. "What you did was outrageous. Do you hate me, Lor? Is that it?"

Lorna gazed at her for several seconds, her lips pursed to one side. "Aubrey thinks Will got Sarah Chambers pregnant and killed her, and he intends to make him pay for it. If you want to place yourself in a position where you get to be a witness, maybe get hurt yourself, that's your decision. I just think it's foolish, and I was trying to spare you a broken heart, Maddie, or worse."

"Last night someone shot Will's dog and left him at the front door of his cabin." Madison paused and Lorna gauged her expression carefully, wondering just how invested her younger sister had become in Will McGomery's plight.

"You see?" she said, raising her hands and smirking at Madison. "I told you some bad shit was about to happen, and that won't be the end of it, either. You can count on it."

Madison stared at her, the wall of defense apparently down for the moment. "I saw what was done to Clovis. His head was horribly mangled but he was still alive. It must have been a shotgun, there was a lot of external damage." Her eyes clouded. "Did Aubrey do this? Do you know?"

"I saw him tonight and he told me nothing," she said, filled with jealousy at the thought of her sister spending the night up on the ridge.

And the incident with the dog hadn't driven her away. Their mother had unknowingly given that away that morning when she'd called her and asked if Maddie had come to her senses.

She had no idea if Aubrey had killed the dog or not, but she had a gut feeling that he or Dwight had done the deed.

"Did you tell Mama and Daddy about it?" she asked Madison cautiously.

"And have them go completely off the deep end? Mama's already giving Daddy grief over him selling the land to a whoremonger. Will has transformed from their perfect neighbor into a nasty leper, thanks to you. Every time Mama calls you, you fill her head with garbage. I know you do."

"I fill her head with the truth." She squeezed her hands into fists and glared at Madison. "It's not like she doesn't know anyway. She knows how badly he hurt me, and knows that you're next. Now, after this dog incident, she's going to know that you walked into a veritable landmine."

"Don't tell her what happened with the dog, Lorna. Do not involve her."

Lorna scraped back from the table. Crossing her arms over her chest tightly, she turned her back to Madison. "I don't want to talk to you anymore, Maddie. It does no good. Go back to your murderous lover. You'll get your just rewards. I promise you."

After she heard Madison slam out the front door, she turned back around. Their chairs were as they'd left them—cock-eyed on either side of the table—evidence that they had not been able to find neutral ground.

And as long as Maddie remained moon-faced over Will McGomery, they never would.

# CHAPTER TWENTY-TWO

Will wasn't home when she returned from Lorna's. Still, Madison continued to stare at the darkened cabin through the windshield of her Jeep, telling herself that he could have parked his truck in the barn.

A full moon had made its trek halfway across the night sky, was directly overhead now and swaddling the landscape in its luminous curtain of light. It caught on the ridges of the cabin's corrugated steel roof, casting the lower portion of the structure into stark relief.

Absent from the landscape were McGomery's livestock and his battered ride. The animals were likely in the barn. But the whereabouts of the old Ford pick-up, she couldn't fathom.

Maybe he had gone in search of her? Would he? Or maybe, and this seemed even less feasible, he was paying her back for taking off on him the way she had.

*Jeez, she needed to get over herself.*

He didn't care one whit about where she was and there was no telling where he'd gone himself. No telling why he hadn't returned.

She made the decision to wait him out and shifted in her seat, removing the bookmarker from her pocket and staring at the ghostly white scripture while her disturbing thoughts about her sister continued to plague her.

Anger was like a hard kernel lodged in her solar plexus. Why was Lorna involved with a man like Aubrey McGomery? Just to spite Will for rejecting her?

That would be childish and vindictive. She didn't want to think it, but she just couldn't escape the feeling that there was more to what Will had said in regard to her sister. He claimed that he hadn't been involved with her, but it was painfully clear that he had done something to hurt Lorna, something beyond a simple brush off.

His words about Sarah Chambers came back to her. His involvement with her had been complicated. Complicated in the same way as his relations with Lorna?

Besieged by confusion, she laid aside the bookmarker and dug her cell phone out of the drink holder in the console. She dialed Lorna's home number. The way they had parted bothered her tremendously and she wanted to get to the bottom of the discontent that she sensed in her sister's life.

She needed to ask her the hard questions about McGomery. Even though she greatly feared the truth, and feared as much the possibility of being lied to, she had to try to get to the source of Lorna's hatred for the man. If nothing else, she could present Will with whatever Lorna said, and give him an opportunity to defend himself.

Maybe if she and Lorna talked again, they would find some safe territory, find the unconditional bond of sisterhood they had lost over the years and miles between them. When her sister's answering machine kicked on, she feared that the lines for communication were closed, perhaps for good.

"Lor, please call my cell when you get this message," she said into her phone. "I realize that McGomery must have hurt you and I'm sorry. It's not my intention to do the same. I don't know what to think anymore about this thing that happened with the two of you, but I do feel that Aubrey McGomery is the dangerous one here. Please be careful around him. Just call me...okay?"

She disconnected, listened to the wind flirting with the Jeep's canvas top. She considered calling her other sister and then decided that Rachel would have heard too much from their mother by now and would be compelled to drill her about her intentions to stay with Will.

The absolute truth of the matter was that she was chastising herself over the decision already. She thought she was losing her mind in addition to her heart and all for a man who could offer her nothing but an impossible future—a future full of enigmatic clues, and possible visits, from the dead.

With moon's silver sheen casting everything outside in a funereal glow, and the rustle of the wind sending a sense of foreboding through her, she looked at the bookmark lying in the passenger seat until the vague white words seemed to bounce before her eyes. She would wait for Will to return while submersed in the cocoon of her uneasy thoughts.

Unfortunately, there were plenty of them in there to keep her busy.

****

Will pulled alongside her Jeep, the moon a giant sphere now balanced on the cusp of the horizon amid storm clouds scudding in from the west.

Madison climbed out of the stale environment of her worries and into the dew-laden air of predawn, and experienced the familiar rush that came upon sight of him. In the incandescent light of the driveway, his long hair was run through with fine filaments of silver, and the frayed places on his overalls shone an ethereal white.

Next to the solid moon-rimmed lines of his rusty old truck, he was an apparition, a study of light and dark and mystery, and suddenly, irrevocably, she knew she would write about him one day.

His keys in hand, he moved toward the porch. "I've been thinking and I want you to find somewhere else to stay. This thing with Clovis worries me. You may not be safe, especially up here by yourself."

"Where have you been?" she said, falling in suit. "I thought you didn't go out much."

He withdrew something from the inside of his denim jacket and it glinted once in the moonlight before it was swallowed by the deep shadows of the porch. She realized it was a gun and she halted on the bottom step, her heart performing a drum roll in her chest.

He unlocked the door, and stepped inside the cabin, weapon brandished. Then the living room lit up and, feeling vulnerable in the dark, she climbed the steps and followed him into the house.

After he'd swept the entire place, flipping lights on along the way, he returned to the living room where she stood on the rug, her fingers fidgeting with the hem of her hooded jacket. She watched him slide the safety and then place the gun on the counter.

"Oh, I see, this is something else you won't talk about," she said. "Where you go in the middle of the night."

He sighed. "I couldn't sleep, so I decided to go for a drive and wound up at the pond."

"The pond?" Why in hell had he gone out there? It made her question whether his invitation to visit the tragic area the night of the fair had been only half in jest. Clearly, he was preoccupied with the place, as well as with Sarah Chambers.

"After what happened last night?" she asked. "Alone?"

"I had my 9millimeter," he said, drawing a hand over his jaw tiredly.

She went over to the couch and collapsed onto the cushion. Her eyes found him staring intensely at her and she resisted the urge to glance away. "I imagine it was beautiful out there tonight. The moon being so bri—"

"Sarah is drawing strength from you...from us," he said, cutting off her words. He walked slowly across the room and sat down on the couch, leaving considerable space between them.

She wanted to reach out to him, touch him, but was riveted by what he had said and was afraid to move. "You implied that if we ignored what was going on, it wouldn't escalate."

"Well, obviously that was wishful thinking." He turned his head and looked at her, his eyes full of sadness. "She whispers things to me, Madison. She's relentless. Sometimes I go to the pond because I think I will see her there, and I'll have an image to go with the voice. Then I can convince myself that I really am a full blown lunatic."

He swallowed causing Madison's eyes to move to his throat. "But I never do. I never see her, not even in my dreams or during my seizures. The places I go, I only see the images and ghosts of other people. It's...absurd."

"Your seizures?" She leaned forward, twining her fingers together between her knees. "What are you saying, Will, that during those episodes you are actually leaving your body? Like some kind of astral travel?"

He stood abruptly, moved toward the hallway. "We'll talk later. Right now, I've got to get some sleep."

She watched him go, chilled to the marrow and yet all the more intrigued.

## CHAPTER TWENTY-THREE

She hadn't thought it possible that she could sleep, but when Madison woke with a start after six hours, she glanced around the small bedroom in wonderment.

The distant buzz of a band saw had most likely been her alarm clock. She yawned and twisted up in bed. The window in the room revealed a sky thick with lead-colored clouds. Outside, the sagebrush in the field swayed like waves in a white gold sea.

It would be raining soon—an ideal time in which to curl up with a book. Only the book that she wanted to curl up with was in the form of a man. A man whose seizures were maybe not seizures at all, and whose secrets were deeply buried in a story she almost feared to know.

She slipped out of bed and retrieved her pair of camouflage Capri's and a tee from the chest of drawers. Soon, she would have to return to her parents' for more clothes and she hoped that when she did, they would not make it into a big deal.

Crazy as it seemed, even to herself, she had made up her mind to tough this out with Will, to see where this path would lead them. Whatever his past held, they shared a common thread. They were each in search of a fresh start, a new beginning.

She dressed and grabbed her hairbrush. She heard him enter the house through the front door. After a moment, his footsteps came closer and then they halted outside her room. He knocked and she consulted her reflection in the mirror. Feeling self-conscious, she set aside the brush and opened the door.

His smile was abrupt and small. "Morning."

"Good morning." Her eyes moved over him shyly, and she sensed the tension in his body. It was in the way he stood there, hands shoved deep into the pockets of his overalls, shoulders hunched like he was bracing against a stiff and biting wind.

"I heard you working," she said. "Have you eaten yet?"

He nodded. "Oatmeal, early. Didn't want to wake you. I just came in to tell you to make yourself at home. I'm going out for a few minutes."

She knew it was hardly any of her business where he was going, but she found she couldn't resist making the inquiry. "Are you going to the store? Because if you are, I could ride along. We could talk?"

"I'm going down to see your Pap," he said.

She placed her hand over the corner of the chest of drawers, leaned her weight into it. "Why?"

"About three months ago, he made a joke when I brought down some eggs," he said. "He told me he was going to get me to make him a clock for his study, that he'd tried to parlay your Mama's but she was adamant that the one I gave them remain on the mantle. I'm going to take him one."

She glanced down. "I see. A peace offering. You don't have to do this, Will. You don't have to try and make things right with them."

"Do you think it could make a difference?" He removed a hand from his pocket, massaged his chin. "Your parents have always been nice to me up 'til now, accepted me. Even after the ordeal with your sister, when she started coming up here and I basically had to be a prick to get her to leave."

He reached out his hand, lifted a piece of her hair from her shoulder and then let it fall. "They seemed to understand that Lorna was the aggressor, but with you, I don't know. I think they're afraid that I might be your worst nightmare come true."

"They might." She smiled a little. "But I don't see the harm in making an effort to change their thinking. I think the clock is a great idea. I think you should shave, put on your Sunday best—in your case, a newer pair of overalls—and round up some extra eggs."

The corners of his mouth turned up. "Maybe a whole lot of extra eggs, huh?"

She laughed softly. "And telling them you plan to become an ordained minister wouldn't hurt."

A smile still curving his lips, he stepped back from the door, unhooking his overalls at his chest. He removed his shirt as he maneuvered into the bathroom and refastened the straps. Transfixed, she unthinkingly edged into the hallway so she could watch him prepare to shave.

"I've been experimenting with a new design," he said, glancing at her as he blotted one side of his face with a damp washcloth. "For my clocks."

She nodded, stepped up to the door and leaned against the jamb. The water from the tap was steaming now. He gingerly placed the washcloth into the stream and then shut it off.

"I've made three so far by this new pattern and this last one I perfected...I'd like it to be the one I present to your father." He pressed the hot cloth to his chin and then reached for the shaving cream.

She stood perfectly still, overwhelmed by this intimate visage of him. With his chest exposed, and the deep brown hair covering it damp and curly with the moisture now encompassing them both, he was simply magnificent. She wanted to press her face into that delta of male warmth and safety. Wanted it so much she trembled.

He had turned away from her after that last steamy encounter though, and she couldn't afford to go through that again.

She watched as he slathered his face with white foam, and froze when he turned and looked at her. Their eyes locked. Seconds ticked by. Silent words of longing were exchanged between them. She reached up and tucked her hair behind her ears and broke the spell.

"Would you mind if I went on out to see it?"

"I won't be but just a few minutes," he said, his voice husky. "I'm going to jump in the shower and then I'll take you out there."

She nodded, wondered if he didn't want her to go by herself because of what happened to Clovis. Forcing herself to move, she pushed off the doorframe and smiled at him.

"Very well. I'll just get myself some breakfast."

And when she escaped to the kitchen, she took long, deep breaths to calm her jumping senses, but still found she was dizzy with desire.

****

His new clocks were even more remarkable than the one on the mantle at her parents' house, and Madison was furious that her father had refused to accept one as a gift.

She sat down across from Will at the kitchen table, wishing he would talk to her. He stared stone-faced at the salt-and-pepper shakers, saying nothing.

"That's all he said?" she asked. "That they wouldn't be accepting anything more from you?"

His gaze lifted from the table, pinning hers in a hostile stare. "No, but I'd rather not get into the particulars of the rest."

"But I have a right to know." She swallowed, but the sudden lump in her throat didn't budge. "What did he say to you?"

"He said no one would have touched my dog had I not overstepped my boundaries...like I'm not even supposed to speak to a woman."

She bit her lip, moved her hands from the surface of the table to her lap where she clenched them together like someone who had just learned of a death. "Lorna told them about Clovis even though I begged her not to."

"Oh, you think?" he said, his voice rising. "Apparently you went to see her and then she reported everything that was said back to them. You wrote on that piece of paper that you were going shopping. I knew better than to trust you."

"What was I supposed to do?" Her hands beneath the table sprang apart, lifted to her head. She pushed her fingers through her hair and stared at him haplessly. "You wouldn't even talk to me, spent the whole day avoiding me. I had to get out of here and I thought that maybe she would know something, or that Aubrey might have bragged to her about shooting Clovis."

He ground his fingertips into his eyes, sighed wearily. "I'm not up to this. I swear to God, I'm not. You're more trouble than you're worth and right now, I'd like to throttle the living daylights out of you."

"For what?" She brought her palms down onto the table hard. "For what?"

His lips thinned. "Talking to your sister will only make things worse for me. Don't you get that by now?"

"No, I guess I'm stupid," she said.

His eyes condemning, he shrugged. "Maybe you are."

"Maybe I'll just go be stupid somewhere else then. How's that?" She shot up from the table but never made it passed him. He clutched her hand, held firm.

"I'm sorry." He pressed her fingers against his lips, took a ragged breath. She felt the intake of air being pulled through her knuckles. He kissed them, raised blue eyes that were rimmed with tears.

"I'm sorry I lashed out at you," he whispered. "It's the last thing I want to do."

She gazed down at him, completely speechless. He rubbed his lips back and forth over her fingers, closed his eyes.

"You were shaking, Madison, when you watched me in the bathroom. I could see your shirt, the way it quivered over your breasts." He made a low sound in his throat, an agonized sound. "I can't take this. I don't think it's a good idea for us to be together, but all I can think about is how much I want to fuck you."

She swayed a little in the face of his crude, yet incredibly arousing, statement, her own eyes drifting closed for a brief moment. Her breath was lost, gone like a fleeting spirit passed on to some other place, and then it was back, an intrepid force in her lungs that caused them to ache.

"Will…you have to tell me the truth about the past."

He pulled himself up from the table, placed her hand over his chest in the vicinity of his heart. His voice was a deep anchor lodging in trappings of her soul.

"It's not a nice story. You will hate me."

She looked up into his face, so beautiful but haunted, and shook her head back and forth slightly. "I don't believe I could do that if I tried."

# CHAPTER TWENTY-FOUR

Will grazed her fingertips with his lips. With her free hand, Madison explored a strand of his hair, reveled in how it felt pressed between her fingertips.

He didn't look into her eyes. He seemed content to study her neck, his voice quiet like a church. "If you want to know about the past, then I'll tell you. But first you have to tell me something."

"All right." Her voice felt as delicate as a petal slipping through her vocal chords. Her eyes flitted over his face in rapid little quests to memorize what they saw.

He smiled, laved the tip of her index finger with his tongue. "How did you get hooked up with such a bastard, this husband of yours? I can tell that he did a number on you."

She gently pulled her hand from his warm, callused grasp, and averted her eyes. "Jim wasn't always...he loved me very much, I think, but he was weak." Her heartbeat in her ears, she hugged herself. "We...I had a miscarriage and became very depressed. Afterward, I withdrew from him. There was this woman at the university, one of his students." She couldn't continue, pressed her lips together.

"That stupid fuck," he said, tipping her chin up and capturing her eyes. He smiled tenderly, moved his thumb across the delicate area below her eye where a tear had strayed.

She stiffened. "Tell me about your wife's friend."

He slid his hands down her arms, interlacing his fingers with hers. He backed toward his bedroom, pulling her along with him. Once there, he abandoned her to retrieve the photo from the nightstand drawer.

Stepping up to her, he extended it, pointed to the image of the brunette. "Molly. One year before we married."

"And the other is Sarah Chambers?" Her eyes moved to the

gamine faced blond in the photo and then to his face.

He nodded. "Molly always called her Pix. You know, short for pixie."

"I thought you lost everything in the fire. Where did this come from?"

"Dow came across it in Aubrey's stuff while Aubrey was pulling his stint at Wallens' Ridge and thought I might like to have it."

"Was Sarah pregnant with your child when she died?" she asked, swallowing tightly.

Fingers steeped beneath his chin, he searched her eyes, for what she wasn't sure. Forgiveness? Acceptance? She wasn't certain she could offer him either at that moment. He dropped his hands, took a deep breath.

"There was a distinct possibility."

She stared not at Sarah Chambers' face in the photo, but at Molly's. Stared at it until it blurred with her tears. Molly had been in the same situation as herself. She had been the jilted bride, Will McGomery's jilted bride.

"How could you do that?

"Give me the photo," he said, plucking it from her fingers unexpectedly and returning it to the nightstand. "I should destroy the damned thing."

He came back, stood before her, but kept his gaze leveled at the floor.

"Almost from day one of our marriage, Molly aspired to become pregnant," he said quietly. "She conceived within two months and we were very happy, very excited until she miscarried. She wanted to try again and we did. She made it twenty-two weeks and went into premature labor. The baby didn't make it, his lungs weren't developed enough."

He lifted his head and impaled her with his eyes. She instantly looked away, confused by his words and not willing yet to feel sorry for him. Clearing his voice, he continued.

"Molly almost didn't make it herself. For some reason, she

began hemorrhaging and the only way they could stop her from bleeding out was to do an emergency hysterectomy."

She dared a glance at him and saw that a muscle in his jaw had begun to tick. He pinched the bridge of his nose and continued. "She was devastated, and before long completely obsessed with the fact we couldn't have children. When Sarah turned up pregnant and asking us for help, she was hit with an idea. Long story short, she hatched a plan where Sarah would live with us and when the baby was born, we'd adopt it."

He shrugged. "It was crazy. The baby was the result of Sarah's cousin forcing himself on her. I knew there was a possibility that Aubrey wouldn't believe Sarah's story and would make her life a living hell. There were her parents to worry about, too, and Molly's fragile emotional state…but when Sarah agreed to the scheme, agreed to give us her baby, I found I couldn't tell Molly no. This baby had become her sole reason for living."

"But Sarah miscarried," she said, remembering what he had told her before.

He averted his eyes from hers, his expression pained. "The baby spontaneously aborted around three months. Molly was inconsolable all over again."

She winced, remembering what she had gone through herself when she'd lost her baby at twelve weeks.

He shoved his hands into his overall pockets. "I don't know. She just came unglued. It took both of us, Sarah and me, to hold her together. I know it couldn't have been easy for Sarah. She had just gone through an ordeal herself, and here she was trying to console my wife."

He took a deep breath, gazed at the ceiling. "I told Molly that we could adopt another baby and she immediately wanted Sarah to play surrogate again, got on her knees and, as pathetic as this sounds, begged her to have another baby for us."

He let the words hang and after a moment, she understood where he was heading.

"She wanted Sarah to become pregnant with your child?" she asked.

As though a weight had been lifted from his shoulders, he straightened marginally. Evident in his face though, was his pain, his features drawn tight, like those of a man who is shackled to the ugly elements of the world and knows he will never escape them.

"It was the only thing that seemed to make sense to her," he said. "No matter how much I argued with her about it, she said it was the only way she would ever get to be a mother to my child. She said she trusted Sarah, would never have to worry about her telling the kid the truth. I told her she was out of her mind."

"But in the end you agreed to it."

He turned and moved to the window, placed his hands on either side of it and stared out into the gloom. It had begun to rain and a dense fog had settled over the mountain, leaving the cabin's interior cloaked in shadows.

His voice came to her like a tendril of fog, melancholy and cold. "I was foolish, just wanted Molly to be okay again, would've done anything to make her better again."

"After being raped and miscarrying a baby, Sarah was willing to do this for her?" She found the young woman's devotion to her best friend astounding.

He nodded without turning to look at her. "More than willing. She and Molly approached the whole thing like it was nothing, had both sets of their parents over to dinner and told them their intentions."

"It was ludicrous," he continued. "Joshua Chambers completely lost it, no doubt thinking we were insane. Even though I told him I was opposed to the idea, he called me a polygamist and tried to start a fight with me. Molly and Sarah came to my defense like they were both my wives, turning the whole thing into a surreal nightmare. Joshua stormed out, the other three of them on his heels, and Molly shut herself in our bedroom for two days, utterly crushed, like she had really expected them to be thrilled with her idea."

He hung his head. "She couldn't be made to see reason. I told her I wouldn't go through with it, that I thought it was wrong, and at the very least, something that had the potential to destroy us."

"She clammed up, didn't mention it for days and I thought she had come to her senses. Then I came in from the field one day and she and Sarah were waiting for me. They had simply been waiting until Sarah was ovulating again. Molly told me that timing was crucial as though she expected me to perform upon command."

"Which you did." Her voice was barely a whisper.

"Yeah," he said, turning slowly and looking at her. "At first I balked, attempted to leave. Molly fell on me. She begged me to stay and I remember looking at Sarah, her mouthing the words, *please, just do it.*"

His eyes full of his pain, he held her gaze. "When I told you that they were like Ruth and Naomi, I wasn't lying. I just had it backward. It wasn't Molly always looking up to Sarah. It was Sarah always looking up to Molly. Molly lost sight of that after I consummated what she and Sarah had planned. If she hadn't become so disillusioned...if Sarah hadn't been murdered...I don't know. Maybe we could have pulled the whole thing off. I look at that photo and can't help wondering."

"She coerced you into sleeping with Sarah, and then turned against you both," she said.

He closed his eyes and shook his head. "Oh no, it wasn't coercion. It was lust. I was fed up with all the baby crap but the more Molly pushed Sarah at me, the easier it was to channel my frustration into thoughts of being with her."

At this point, the muscles in his neck were pronounced, straining with his pent-up emotion. "You saw her picture. Sarah was beautiful. My God, she'd been a fixture in my life for years. She was my grandparents' neighbor, always around...a sweet kid turned alluring blond, someone I probably would have started seeing had she not introduced me to her best friend and me and Molly not clicked so well."

She took a faltering step toward him. "Molly set the stage for what ultimately happened. She wore you down, made it impossible for you to—"

"I didn't tell you any of this so you could try to make me feel better about it," he warned. "I ordered my wife to get in the car and go for a ride so I could fuck her best friend. Just so we're clear on this, there's no feeling better about that. Ever."

Her eyes shifted to the bed. She moved to the side of it and sat down, sliding her hands between her thighs and looking at him again. "How long before it happened, before she got jealous?"

"A few days," he said after a long pause. "She started asking me questions, stupid, pointless questions. How did she compare with Sarah in bed? Did Sarah and I engage in foreplay? Take all our clothes off or just the necessary ones? No matter how I answered, I answered wrong, and if I tried to deflect the questions then I was hiding something."

His sigh was shallow, like his grief was fresh instead of layered in years. "When she discovered that Sarah was pregnant, it got worse. She started ridiculing Sarah, saying Sarah was going to steal her baby, and try to steal me. And when she discovered that Sarah had been seeing Jacob Davidson, she totally freaked out, had it in her head that Jacob would claim the baby as his and she would never get to be a mother."

"Was she unstable to the point she could have killed Sarah?"

The question seemed to knock the air out of him. "No, God no. My wife was a threat only to herself."

"That's not really true," she said. "She went to Aubrey and told him Sarah was pregnant when she could have told him the truth, told him that she had manipulated Sarah into being your lover because she could not bear the thought of being childless. Because of her jealousy, Sarah and her unborn child died.

Whoever killed Sarah, it was due to Molly's skewed version of the truth."

"You're making a judgment call on someone you didn't even know," he said, his voice laced with bitterness. "My wife."

"Fair enough," she said. "It's not for me to say whether Molly was aware of what she was doing or not. And yet it is completely safe for me to say that you are the one being harassed for something that was her doing. You are the one hiding on this ridge and living with all the guilt."

He shrugged. "I can't change that. I am guilty. I'm guilty of taking Sarah Chambers to my bed when deep inside I think I knew what it would do to my wife, and to our marriage."

"She was already in your bed," she cried. "Molly put her there." She pushed her hair back in frustration. "Maybe this sounds a little over the top to you, but you were like a lamb to the slaughter, Will. I don't know that any man could have withstood what your wife presented you with. Sarah was beautiful and not only that, she was willing. You were stressed and desperate to restore Molly's happiness and made a bad decision, but that doesn't make you a hideous person, undeserving of happiness or a future."

She slid her hands up and down her thighs, suddenly knowing what she wanted to do. "Will, I should talk to my parents. If they know the true story behind you and Sarah, they will see you in a different light. I want them to know what I've always sensed, that you are a good man. Telling them the truth is better than letting them think you wantonly strayed from your vows, that you were some skirt-chasing lowlife. My sister feeds them crap and I have an opportunity here to do some damage control."

"Damage control," he said without inflection, and then laughed abruptly. "You must believe in miracles."

"What...I'm supposed to just willingly sit on this truth and let the world think you're scum when really you're a victim of some very sad circumstances?"

He came toward her. "Molly and Sarah's parents sat on the truth. Why shouldn't you? The truth doesn't redeem me."

"Doesn't redeem you?" She stood from the bed. "It might in Aubrey's eyes. Right now, when he could very well be concocting another stunt like Clovis, you refuse to tell him the truth. You're a glutton for punishment."

He made a dismissive gesture. "Tell your parents whatever you like. They'll think it's a bunch of bullshit."

"And Aubrey?" she said in a hostile voice. "I guess you're going to be a pessimist about telling him?"

"He knows the truth!" he shouted, his sudden anger causing her to flinch. His voice thunderous, he glared at her. "He knows that I got his girlfriend pregnant. To him the reason doesn't matter. To him it is black and white. And how the hell is it that you're so sure it was him that shot Clovis anyway? That seems to be all you know how to do, pass judgment. Who made you God, Madison Owens? Because you're a writer, you think you have the right to psychoanalyze everybody?"

"Don't yell at me," she said, lunging off the bed and moving hastily toward the door. She hesitated at the threshold, stared at him incredulously, then turned and headed toward the kitchen. "I'm leaving. I can't stand you talking to me like that."

"Great!" he yelled. "And just so you know, I don't care what your parents have to say about the truth. I'm through with this. Don't bother coming back up here."

"Fine," she said between clenched teeth. But on the inside, it wasn't fine.

It was anything but fine.

And, in her heart, nowhere close to being goodbye.

# CHAPTER TWENTY-FIVE

Bolstered by the sight of the Jeep Wrangler parked in Marshy Owens' drive, Will eased the Ford across the cattle guard.

He felt lower than low, knew that losing his temper had probably cost him dearly with Madison. She had not berated him for his relations with Sarah Chambers—hell, she'd made excuses for him—so why had he blown up on her?

Every time he turned around he was blowing his top. Aside from her benign acceptance of what he'd told her earlier that morning, she had been keeping him in a constant state of turmoil with her questions and probing. And it seemed that if she wasn't saying something that didn't sit right with him, then she was tearing him up with those big, hurt eyes of hers.

He wanted to put an end to her curiosity and confusion about him. He wanted to shut her up, and damnably, he wanted to do that with his mouth.

He was crazy about her, could think of nothing else except being with her. More than anything, he wanted her gaze to be filled with love for him, but because he was aware of the fact it would soon be filled with hatred, he was acting like a total jackass: mad at the world, mad at himself, just plain mad.

And yet here he was, prepared to face Marshall Owens again, just for a few more sparring sessions with her. He needed her in his life and could not stop hoping that they had a chance somehow. Despite the heated arguments. Despite what Sarah whispered. Despite whatever sacrifice would be required of him.

He parked behind the Jeep and sprinted across the yard in the rain. Marshy waited for him at the door, stepped out onto the porch and glowered at him.

"Get back in that truck, McGomery," he said around his pipe. "Ain't nothing here for you."

He was wrong about that. His heart was here, and would be wherever Madison resided. Pathetic, he acknowledged, but true.

"I just want to talk to her," he said, hearing the desperation in his voice. "At least tell her I'm here. If she refuses to see me then I'll leave."

White smoke trailed up from the compact bowl inches from Marshy's lips as he puffed on the pipe. "You really expect us to believe that cockamamie story about your wife wanting you to get that Chambers girl pregnant?"

So they did think it was bullshit.

He took a step back, clenched his fists. "I don't expect anything from you. This isn't about you."

"Oh, I believe I know what it's about." Marshy stepped over to the porch railing and tapped the contents of his pipe into a rain-saturated flowerbed. "This is about you wanting to look like a victim in my daughter's eyes."

"That's not true," he said, wanting fervently to call him a son of a bitch. "I care about Madison. You can't see it because of your other daughter. Lorna has painted me into a corner, hasn't she? And you're not about to let me out of it."

"I'm not a fool when it comes to Lorna," Marshy retorted. "I know she chased the pants off you and that you can't stand her. I know she's vindictive and selfish. All the same, she isn't the one I listen to. I listen to my other daughter who tells me you're epileptic and full of remorse and in dire need of a second chance. Boy, you sure poured it on thick with Maddie, didn't you?"

Will's body tensed. He turned abruptly and left the porch, knowing he was dangerously close to pummeling the other man, sinking his fists into the ruddy face of Madison's father like a raging maniac incapable of controlling himself.

Behind him he heard the older man's parting words, "If you care about my girl, McGomery, you'll stay the hell away from her," and the fight went out of him. He sagged, walked slowly across the yard to his truck, the rain drenching him.

Marshy Owens was a biased old fart, but capable of uttering some very wise words. And that left him feeling, among other things, like a very big, very selfish, fool.

****

Madison forced the last box of her things into her Jeep and ducked in behind the wheel, shaking the rain from her mane of hair. Tears ran down her face and she wiped them away impatiently with the back of her hand.

At Will's cabin, she spent a moment just sitting in the dark, trying to mentally shake off her father's awful words. They were like ugly zits on the face of her thoughts—pustules that throbbed and ached with infectious emotion.

She grabbed a few belongings from the Jeep and darted through the sheeting rain and onto the porch.

The door opened just as she raised her hand to knock, and she frowned at the way Will used his body as a barrier between her and the interior of the house.

"When I said don't bother, I meant it," he said.

She slumped. How much more could she take today? It was inconceivable that the man she'd so stubbornly defended to her father was now refusing to let her in his house.

"All my stuff is in my Jeep. I don't have the energy to take it back down there and listen to them."

His brows drew lower over his eyes and then it seemed to register with him that she was shaking from the wet, night air. Reluctantly, he turned and moved into the living room.

"You can go get your stuff out of the bedroom but then I want you gone. And I don't want to discuss it."

She came inside, closed the door behind her and found that her throat burned as though she had swallowed a tarnished piece of piano wire. "You don't understand, McGomery. I cannot go back down there. I can't allow that man I'm ashamed to call my father to do that to me again."

He had paced over to the bookcase but now turned his head to look at her. "What are you talking about?"

"He called me your whore." She made a quick pass over her cheek with her hand. "He was angry because I dared to defy him."

"Don't defy him," he said. "Go back and tell him and your Mama that you've come to your senses. Or don't go back. Just return to where you came from…Ohio…wherever. Just stay the hell away from here. It's for your own good, and besides I want nothing to do with you. Whatever I thought I felt is gone, over."

She pushed her hair behind her ears and stared incredulously at him, chewed on her lip. After several seconds passed, she turned and made her way to the bedroom where she threw belongings into the duffel bag she'd retrieved from the closet.

When she returned, she found him still standing at the bookcase, bracing his hands on either side of it. His jaw looked exceedingly tight, like he was standing on the precipice of some canyon and bracing himself to jump. His eyes were squeezed closed, his body rigid.

"Are you okay?" she asked, her heart tripping when he swept the contents of one of the shelves before him onto the floor.

The books tumbled noisily across the polished wood planks and she stared at them in speechless wonder. Then she jumped backward at the explosion that was his voice.

"I told you they wouldn't believe you!"

She cringed. "I thought it was worth a sh—"

"Then you thought wrong." Now his voice was flat, devoid of emotion. Her heart recoiled.

"If I'd known my father would act like a stubborn ass, I wouldn't have wasted my time. I thought they might be able to see beyond their fear, but they can't. They speak in ignorance when it comes to you."

"I don't care if they're speaking Pig Latin. I'm used to being the cad, the lowlife fornicator. Stop trying to be my champion, God damn it."

"How did you know they wouldn't listen to me?" she said, her voice failing her. More words came out on a breathless whisper. "You came down there?"

He kicked books out of his way, closed the distance between them. Towering over her, he treated her to a scathing stare.

"Yes, I came down there. I felt bad about losing my temper, wanted to apologize to you. I need a foot in the ass for thinking it even mattered, though. You don't belong here. We don't belong here."

"No matter what they think, I feel better for saying what I did," she said, trying to swallow her dread. "You gave me permission to come to your defense and I did. Does it not mean anything to you that I would want to do that?"

"I warned you that they wouldn't listen. Just get out of here. Go on. I don't want to look at you anymore."

"You're lying, Will." She inched back from him so that he was not bearing directly down on her. "And furthermore, you're scared. You're scared of letting anyone know your secrets because your secrets would depict your wife in a less than respectable light. It's time to let go. I'm sorry, but the fact is she's dead and you have a right to go on living."

He surged forward, seizing her by the upper arms. "Do I look scared to you?"

She shook her head, winced at the biting pressure of his fingers. "You're hurting me."

"Get out of my house, Owens," he said between his teeth, pushing her away from him.

He pivoted and stalked across the living room. After a moment, he turned back around and she thought perhaps tears glistened in his eyes as he looked at her. Or maybe it was just a trick of the light.

"You are nothing to me," he said. "And I want you gone."

Gripping the duffel bag to her side, she choked back a sob, tore across the rug to get to the door.

He was right behind her, prevented her from opening the door by placing his palms to it on either side of her shoulders. She froze. He pressed his weight into the length of her, buried his face in her hair near her ear.

"I didn't mean it." It was a hoarse whisper, then his lungs emptied heavily into her hair. A sob.

She shuddered and dropped the duffel bag. "How did I not know you were at their house today? I wish I'd…"

He groaned, and the sound was anguished, tormented even. Her words faded into nothing. He placed his hands over her shoulders and pulled her around. Then those hands, warm and strong, slid over her back, pressing her into the solid length of his body.

His mouth was a hot brand on her lips, his tongue a welcome pressure inside her mouth. Fluid warmth spread through her, fast and sweet, causing a blossom of need in her womb and making her feel impossibly weak, as weak as a mewling kitten, but as vital as the rain descending upon on the trees outside.

She opened herself to him, gripped handfuls of his shirt and accepted what he seemed so desperate to give her. Their tongues made playful war, darting about, chasing and encountering the curious and powerful texture of rampant desire. She found it amazing, this pressure behind his kiss and this raging desire for him swelling deep within her. She found it a brand new love, raw and aching.

Her hands let go of his shirt. She slid all ten fingers into his tousled hair and his hands moved, hungry and eager, up her rib cage. His thumbs made dragging passes over her breasts, coaxing her nipples up beneath the thin barrier of her shirt and bra.

"If you leave I might as well die." It was mumbled against her teeth. He shifted his head the other way and kissed her with an urgency that fueled her own raging need.

Then, abruptly lifting his head, he stared down into her

face, his fingers sliding up her cheeks, into her hair and over her scalp. Clasping her head lightly, he searched her eyes.

"Say it again," she whispered.

His resulting smile brought heat into his eyes; they radiated with it. Without saying a word, he bent his head and began a new assault with his lips.

# CHAPTER TWENTY-SIX

They stumbled, feet over feet and hands everywhere, finally making it to Will's bedroom. His overall straps had come unfastened—he wasn't exactly sure if her fingers or his had won out on that one—and now it was a race to see who could get his shirt off.

He opted to let her work on the buttons so he could put his hands up her own. His fingers found her warm skin to be supple like a baby's and smooth as silk. He couldn't touch enough of it, wanted more and more and finally knocked her hands out of his way so he could whisk her shirt over her head.

Her bra was something incredibly, fantastically provocative, and the complete opposite of the camouflage pants she had on. He trailed his fingertips over the delicate cups, coaxing her nipples up, and bent his head quickly to draw one of them into the hungry heat of his mouth.

He played with her through the confection of white lace, using both his tongue and his teeth, and she threw her head back, murmuring his name, which somehow rocked him to the core.

Lifting his head and putting his palm where his mouth had been, he placed random kisses to her face. "I like that. Immensely."

Bewilderment clouded her eyes as she pulled back to look at him, and he chuckled as he fondled her damp breast with his fingers. "The sound of my name on your lips, when we're doing this."

Her hands trembled as they found a button still fastened midway down his torso. Her fingers worked on it while her mouth opened to accept his tongue again. His breath caught when his shirt fell all the way open and her fingers slid over his exposed chest hair and skin. He looked into her eyes, delighted by the fact they were dazed with passion.

"Will." She drew it out this time, his name like a purr emanating from her throat. She took hold of his hand at her breast and guided it down to the button on her pants.

He stared into her eyes, recognized the urgent light in them despite the dimness of the room, and immediately unfastened it. He tugged down the zipper and slipped his fingers inside her panties. The lips here were as swollen as the ones he'd just plundered with his kisses, his cock instantly aching hard at the discovery.

"I want to be inside you," he said, kissing her, kissing her again and sweeping his tongue through her mouth, claiming it as his own and savoring the nectar of it.

"Yes," she mumbled against his lips, and he shifted so that he could nudge her legs farther apart.

He penetrated her with his fingers, pushing two inside of her slowly and applying the pad of his thumb to the part of her he'd recently made love to with his mouth. She made little sounds in her throat, cried out as he finessed the tight little kernel with small, rapid motions. She sought his lips with hers and he kissed her tenderly, exploring her teeth and the silky lining of her mouth with his tongue as she trembled against him and he moved in and out of her with a gentle motion of his arm.

"That night," he said, between gentle nips at her lower lip. "When you slid off the couch and straddled me. I've never felt anything like that. It blew me away."

"I want you to feel it again," she said, the whispered words caressing his lips along with her sweet breath. She reached for him, gently pressing her fingers against his erection. "I want you to feel my body tightening around this."

His jaw clenching, he tugged her pants down, her panties with them, and then worked desperately to free her of her strappy sandals. Once he removed the shoes, she stepped out of her clothes, and he rid himself of his. Naked, he pressed her across the width of his bed, his body covering hers and his hand pushing her knee out of his way.

He entered her in one streamline thrust, heard her small cry as he buried himself to the hilt. Feeling her fingers curling into his ass and drawing him deeper, he moved against her roughly. He was unable to control the primal need to claim her completely and was spurred along by her choppy pants, which felt hot and wonderful on the skin of his neck.

It took precious few seconds to get to the brink of orgasm. Lifted above her and pressing both of her knees toward her chest, he brought his thrusts to a fevered rhythm, and then pushed his body very deep into the snug glove, tucking his face in the crook of her fragrant neck. His body tensed for the sweetness of release, his lips mumbling endearments against her damp skin.

Wanting his eyes on hers when he filled her with his seed, wanting to see Madison's face as she flushed with her own climax, he pulled his head back and saw, not her face, but Sarah's—her accusing blue eyes and matted blond curls.

He blinked, tried to refocus, and then stifled a scream when the image didn't recede. He abruptly pulled away from Madison and rolled to the side, burying his face in the mattress while he struggled to catch his breath. Shaking, he forced himself to look at the woman now propped beside him, and saw Madison, her face perplexed, even fearful.

"I'm sorry, Maddie," he groaned, "I don't....I can't..."

Her huge eyes stared at him with a mixture of confusion and unsatisfied desire. "What happened, Will?"

He turned his head and stared vacantly at the nightstand where he'd put the photo. Breathing unevenly, he closed his eyes. "She doesn't want me to forget...her...what happened." His throat closed over his next words. He couldn't bring himself to tell her what he'd seen. How could she possibly understand something like that, no matter how forgiving she'd been up to this point?

"You're starting to scare me, Will. Tell me who doesn't want you to forget. Is it Sarah?"

"It wasn't me that killed her, if that's what you're thinking," he said roughly. Struggling up, he stumbled to the bathroom, shut the door and tried to get his wits about him.

His hands trembling hard as he stood over the sink, he knew that his days with Madison were numbered. In his head, he heard Sarah whisper. It was a ghastly sound that scared the hell out of him.

*Sacrifice.*

\*\*\*\*

By tacit understanding, Madison didn't attempt to talk to Will after he emerged from the bathroom. She sat Indian style in his bed with the sheet pulled around her and waited for his cue.

He told her she could stay in his room if she wanted, that he needed some time alone to think, was going to go out to his wood working shop for awhile.

She let him go without a word and then padded to the guest bedroom, where she pressed her face into the pillow and cried for several long minutes. She told herself she wasn't angry with him, but with Sarah who was seemingly determined to come between them, and who had somehow managed to interrupt their passion once more.

Deep down though, she was deeply upset that he had shut her out, had chose to leave her alone with her confusion and fear.

After a while, she slipped beneath the sheets, tucked her arm beneath her pillow and was able to somehow shut it all out. She fell asleep only to wake when he returned to the cabin. Listening to the soft sounds he made as he moved through the house to his room, she felt the tears choking off her throat again.

The next morning, after sporadic and restless sleep, they yet again cropped up when she heard him banging around in the kitchen.

She decided to face him, got dressed and pulled a brush through her long hair before leaving her room. In the kitchen she glanced away from his direct gaze.

"I was just coming to see about you," he said, contritely. "I was disappointed when I came back last night and you weren't in my room. Although, I do understand why you left."

She gave him a look and he moved over to the refrigerator. As he perused the shelves silently, she waited for him to acknowledge what had happened the night before and when he didn't, she moved into the living room and performed an inventory of his bookcase. She lifted a hand and began to twirl a piece of her hair.

"You're a huge fan of the paranormal."

He closed the refrigerator door and straightened to his full height, angled her a look. "I wouldn't call myself a fan, exactly. In fact, when I went to clean all those books off the floor this morning, I thought about trashing them."

"Electronic Voice Phenomena?" She tilted her head toward the shelf in front of her. "I've counted three books on that alone."

"Yeah, well." He moved to the table but didn't sit down, just fingered the back of a chair.

"Well, what?" she asked. "You've experimented with that stuff?"

"I told you she whispers to me."

"And I assumed you meant telepathically."

"Are you hungry?" he asked wearily. "I could fix—"

"No." She indicated the room just beyond the kitchen, his bedroom. "I want to talk about what happened in there."

He pulled out the chair, sat down heavily. "I'm sorry, Maddie. I saw something that wasn't there and I freaked out. I thought maybe a seizure was coming on and didn't want you to see it."

She crossed over into the kitchen and retrieved eggs and butter from the refrigerator. "I'll fix you some eggs. Scrambled or fried?"

"Madison, I think you should get the hell of this ridge, not fix me breakfast."

"Scrambled or fried? And what about bacon? I'll fix some bacon and toast."

He was silent. She set the eggs on the counter, the tub of butter next to them. "Do you want bacon?"

His eyes were staring sightlessly out the kitchen window, and he had such a lost look on his face that she couldn't do anything but stand there, her heart twisting painfully.

"You have sawdust in your hair," she said quietly.

He looked at her sharply. "Sorry to offend. I'll take a shower after I eat."

"I wasn't registering a complaint, Will."

His eyes penetrated her. "What would you say if I told you I've caught a few EVP's on tape over the years, and that I believe them to be Sarah Chambers?"

Her expression guarded, she shrugged. "I'd think you should let me hear them."

Smirking, he picked at the edge of the table. "Right. I can see that happening."

"You're being difficult on purpose," she said.

The familiar tightness returned to his mouth. "Last night..."

Suddenly, she didn't want to hear what he had to say, was afraid to hear it. "You didn't have to leave the way you did."

"I told you, I thought that maybe I'd had a seizure." He blew air out through his lips. "Damn it, it scared the fucking hell out of me. I was afraid to touch you after that."

"What does Sarah say in these EVPs?" she asked.

"Just drop it. I wish I hadn't said anything about them."

She snatched up the eggs and returned them to the refrigerator. "Fine."

"What did your sister say to you when you asked her about Clovis?" His expression went flat. "Did she let on that it was Aubrey?"

"She said if he did it, he wasn't bragging about it," she said. "Not to her anyway."

"She probably did it herself."

"Talk about me passing judgment."

"I'm not basing my suspicion on gossip," he told her, his voice rising. "I know Lorna, and I'm fully aware of how much she would like to hurt me."

"Yeah, you know her."

They stared at one another and then he pushed up from the table, walked over to stand right in front of her. She shook her head, the simple gesture intended to convey she did not want to hear whatever he was about to say.

She sidestepped him and started for the hallway, but he reached out and caught her by the waistband of her pants. He gave her chinos a jerk and spun her around, catching her to him when she was knocked off balance.

"I could have your sister any day of the week and not lose a minute of sleep over using her," he said in a fierce whisper against her lips. "But I don't want her. I think it's pretty apparent that you're the one I can't resist."

"Get off me, Will," she said between clenched teeth, the heels of her palms jammed against his chest. Her voice was full of contempt, but she knew her eyes shone with something else.

It was not enough to counter her words, however. He released her abruptly and moved away. "I'm going to take a shower now."

When he came into the bathroom a moment later, she was there, standing in front of the shower stall. Her hands plastered to the front of her thighs, fingers splayed, she held his gaze. "Will you lose sleep over using me?"

He seemed to deflate. Approaching her, he cupped her cheek in his palm. "You don't get it, do you? You're like the very air that I take into my lungs, Maddie. How could I regret breathing?"

A loaded silence passed between them and Madison's heart ached with her love for him.

He bent his head and aligned his mouth with hers. Her lips parted. Their tongues melded. Hands groped, then fumbled to remove the articles of clothing between them.

She tossed his shirt to the floor where hers was pooled already, and he stepped out of his overalls. When they were both stripped to the skin, he reached in and turned on the shower. He backed into the stall, bringing her with him.

The spray of cool water hit her and she gasped. He placed his open mouth over her breast, drew on her until she whimpered and arched against him.

Then, he was upright again and ravaging her mouth, his tongue pushing against hers and his muscles straining into the pliant curves of her body. He hoisted her up and against the back of the stall, entering her in increments until he was deeply ensconced. Growling his pleasure and sliding his mouth and tongue over the throbbing pulse in her neck, he ground his hips against hers.

Steam crowded the air as the water and their bodies heated the small space. Their hair became thick with the moisture of it.

"I don't care what happened last night. I want you in my bed tonight." He breathed the words against her damp skin. "I want you there every night."

She pressed her teeth into the swell of his biceps, stifled a cry against the tensed muscle.

He drove into her as she climaxed, began to shake like a man on the brink of dying, and trembling herself, she prayed he would never let her go.

# CHAPTER TWENTY-SEVEN

Lorna noticed Cecilia Onate heading in her direction and jabbed a button on the treadmill to slow her pace.

Lord, what did she want now?

The woman stopped in front of the treadmill and handed Lorna a towel. "*Hola, chica.* Wow, you look done in."

"Do I?" Lorna snatched the towel from Cecilia's hand and blotted her face with it as she walked. "Well, I've just jogged five miles."

"I guessed four," Cecilia said. "You do not hit it like this usually, I take it you are working off some steam, no? Bad day at work?"

Lorna thought it was no one's business, and yet she couldn't quite resist the temptation to vent.

"No, my sister is headed up the shit creek without a paddle," she said, blowing air out of her mouth.

"The shit creek?"

She placed the towel over her shoulder and knocked the machine down another point. "It's Will McGomery. I told you about her being up there. She's falling for him and I can't stand it. She's going to get hurt if I don't figure out how to get her to leave."

"That is no problem," Cecilia said. "I know someone who can get her to leave for the right price. You looking to scare *tu hermana*, just shake her up enough she will not want to hang around?"

What the hell kind of crazy Mexican family was this woman a part of?

Gripping the sidebars, Lorna didn't look into Cecilia's fathomless, glittery eyes. Instead, she glanced at the teenager jogging on the treadmill next to her. The girl had a MP3 player attached to her hip and headphones on.

"Forget that. I want to talk about you calling the sheriff on Aubrey."

Cecilia shrugged. "I worry about him. That is all."

"You worry about him?" She laughed and the other woman frowned.

"*Sí, mi preocupo…*I worry."

Lorna smirked. "Why didn't you just get your friend to rough him up for you?"

"I do not have the money to pay him."

She shook her head. "You have no idea who you are fooling around with when it comes to Aubrey. You shouldn't have snitched on him."

"He has not been back here. I feel better."

She rolled her eyes. "Of course he hasn't been back. Doesn't mean you're rid of him, though. That little call you made really pissed him off and he has friends too, Ceci. Friends who probably do things for free."

Cecilia swallowed, her gaze shifting to the floor. When she glanced back at Lorna, she shook her head. "You are the one in way over your head with him. Not me."

"Oh, you think?" She yanked a tiny magnetic disc from the machine, causing it to shut off instantly. She grabbed the bottled water in the cup holder and twisted off the cap. "Get out of my face, Cecilia."

She lifted the water to her lips and felt her hand trembling, hoped the other woman wouldn't notice. She *was* in over her head. Aubrey was going to kill Will McGomery over Sarah Chambers and she didn't know how to deal with that. She wasn't ready to call it quits on Will, was sure she could win him over to her side with just a little bit of luck and strategy.

She wasn't ready to come to terms with something else either. She was flat running out of ideas when it came to Slick Willie. She'd had enough of Aubrey, knew she should have never allowed herself to get involved him in the first place.

Now she just wanted out, but how? He wanted to see her

every night, was becoming increasingly possessive, increasingly unstable.

And then, of course, there was Maddie. She was going to be caught in the middle of all this. Nothing seemed to sink in with her when it came to Will, and though it made her exceedingly jealous, she didn't relish the thought of her own sister becoming a casualty of Aubrey's maniacal thinking.

She had to find a way to make her understand that the dog was nothing in comparison to what was coming. She had to make Maddie understand without Aubrey finding out.

It was not going to work, just coming out and telling her that he planned to kill McGomery and throw his body in the pond where they'd found Sarah. Maddie would do something stupid like go to the police. Then he would know, he'd know that his little Lorna Mae had betrayed him. And then he'd have Dwight Wray or one of his other flunkies kill her.

She tossed the towel at Cecilia Onate and stepped off the treadmill. "How much money we talking about, *Amiga*?"

****

Will was startled awake by an urgent voice, but it didn't belong to Madison.

*Sacrifice!*

Sarah Chambers shouted the word in his mind.

For a moment he lay there, unable to do anything but cling to the sensation of Madison spooned against his naked body. They had spent the entire evening in bed, finally succumbed to sleep, and now he was confused about what time it was.

His eyes adjusted to the shadows gradually, and he noticed the incandescent patterns playing over the room. Orange and red tinted phantoms flickering like transparent ribbons across the deep abyss of the ceiling and part way down the far wall.

It was as he tried to dismiss them as remnants of a dream that Sarah's voice came again, filling him with dread.

*Sacrifice.*

Suddenly terrified by the eerie light, knowing exactly what

was happening outside, he catapulted out of bed, jolting Madison out of her deep slumber. A coppery heat emanated from the room's one window and a trickle of acid fear entered his blood stream—adrenaline like an icy finger trailing along the inside of his veins.

He stepped in front of the window, gripped the casing on either side of it.

In the glow of his burning barn, he jerked on his overalls, only managing to hook one of the straps in his haste. Not taking the time to tie his boots, he bounded through the bathroom, and disappeared down the hallway. When he burst through the back door of the cabin, he was greeted by the sounds of his livestock being burned alive. He broke into a blind run.

He turned back only when the heat from the fire proved to be too much. Tears leapt into his eyes as he tripped across the yard toward the house, his lungs screamed for a respite from the seared air. He grappled for the door, his hands trembling as though he was inflicted by palsy.

Madison stood at the window in his bedroom. She wore his shirt and had her cell phone crammed to her ear.

"I called 911," she said breathlessly, glancing at him. She turned back to the window. "Yes, Daddy, his barn. Someone set his barn on fire."

Moving to the gun safe in the corner of the room, he had his 9millimeter within seconds.

"What are you going to do with that?" she asked, immediately disconnecting her call.

He didn't answer, could not put it in words. He left the house and she caught up with him in the yard.

This close to the fire, it was deafening, like the screaming turbines on a jet. She shouted and grabbed his arm, but before he could shrug her off, she seemed to hear it, the unmistakable sound of his animals being consumed by the fire—shrill cries that pierced the ears and the heart.

He knew she realized what the sounds were when he saw

the terror leap into her eyes. It mixed with the reflection of the flames, giving her the look of something primitive and wild.

She clapped her hands over her mouth.

"It's too late," he shouted. "I can't get to them."

She released his arm and fell back a step, shielded her face from the fluid-like waves of heat. He made it a couple more yards and had to stop due to the intensity of it.

He wanted to use the gun to put the animals out of their misery but it was impossible. He could get no closer, had no clear target. Whoever had done this—and he strongly suspected Madison's sister behind it—had secured the animals in the stable and made certain they could not escape. He directed the gun in that direction, squinting and forcing tears to slide down his cheeks.

He unloaded the weapon into the inferno of the barn, the report of it like firecrackers in the din of the hungry flames. Raw emotion ripped through his vocal cords, screams of outrage.

If Dwight Wray had known about this and not told him, he was basically screwed. Dwight had vowed his allegiance, and without his loyalty, Will had no hope. All his carefully laid plans would fall apart. He'd be back to ghostly whispers and dreams that he didn't even understand most of the time.

He staggered into the field away from the heat that singed his skin. Then, he felt himself go as limp as a damp flag. He owed Madison the truth about the past. If he were any kind of man at all, he would tell her. He would tell her the truth about what had happened to Sarah. But how?

*How?*

He loved her, didn't want to hurt her. He didn't want to lose her because he had to do what was right. For Sarah. For Molly. For Madison herself.

He sank down onto the ground, letting go of the gun and burying his face in his hands. After a moment, he detected her presence, shook his head back and forth without raising it.

"If you know what's best for you, you'll get as far away

from here as you can, Madison."

"And let whoever did this win?" She sank down, joining him on the dewy grass. "I don't hear the animals anymore. It's over." He couldn't believe she would be so stubborn in the face of such a truly malicious act. He ran the back of his hand across his eyes and said nothing.

"Do you think the firefighters will be able to navigate the road up here in their trucks?" she asked, and her voice was tremulous now.

He turned and looked at her, lifted a hand and pushed her hair behind her ear. A whistling sound within the flames engulfing the barn caught his attention, and he glanced away. With a resounding screech his barn folded, sending a spectacular eruption of sparks into the dark sky.

She leaned into him, shoving her face into the muscle of his arm. Then her head snapped up when a terrific explosion sent flames and sparks billowing up from the burning debris.

"The tractor was full of gas," he said.

She stared with glassy eyes as some of the sparks showered onto the roof of the cabin. As they dimmed into nothing over the ribbed steel, she shifted her focus onto him.

"Who is doing this to us?"

He gritted his teeth. "Do you not suspect your sister? Not even a little bit?"

Her face registered her shock. "I suspect Tritt Davidson, knowing what I know about him. Arson is like his signature."

"He was desperate back then," he said. "He needed to come up with a murderer before the investigation was taken from him and his son became a suspect. He would've done anything to make sure my cousin took the rap. Aubrey was trouble anyway, a problem that needed to be addressed, and framing him for the fire that destroyed my house was like putting money in the bank. He was going to put Aubrey away one way or another, and did, but he isn't grasping at straws now."

"Maybe he wants him back in prison because he knows he

is guilty of drowning Sarah, is willing to frame him yet again for arson to do it." Her voice dropped a notch. "Or maybe Aubrey did do this, and killed Clovis too. He made it clear to me that something bad was going to happen."

The sound of Marshy's truck distracted him, and his eyes cut across to the road dissecting the field. He took hold of the 9millimeter he'd dropped and hauled himself to his feet.

Without saying a word, he moved toward the house, leaving her sitting there in the tall, damp grass.

## CHAPTER TWENTY-EIGHT

When Will emerged from the cabin, Madison was in the backyard talking to Marshy, and she was immediately bothered by the fact he showed no interest in coming over.

He no longer had the gun he'd emptied into his barn. His hands shoved into the front pockets of his overalls, he watched the fire lap hungrily at the crumpled logs that had once comprised her great grandparents' cabin. She shifted her gaze and watched too, then glanced beyond the yard to the woods, uneasy at the thought that whoever had done this might be out there observing.

This part of the ridge had been cast in a weird light by the fire, the foliage of the nearby Poplars illuminated in shimmering pink, and the ground a burnished gold that seemed to glow through a haze of red. The place seemed cursed. Tangible vestiges of her heritage were going to be tarnished by these flames in her mind forever, some of them burned to nothing in reality.

"It was all I could do to convince your Mama to stay at the house," Marshy told her.

Her eyes honed in on his face. He was wearing a coat and already the shoulders of it were speckled with ash. She guessed that her hair was full of it.

"I told her you called for the fire department and she agreed that she should stay and make sure everyone found the way up here." His eyes moved over her carefully. "You want my coat? If you can believe it, they're calling for it to snow already. This'll feel good to you when this fire's doused."

She shook her head absently. Her attention had reverted back to Will and was locked on his stony expression.

"You ready to throw in the towel on this thing?" Marshy asked, jolting her. "I'd say it's way beyond time you came to your senses. This isn't a man you can have any kind of future with, Maddie, and you know that."

She looked at him, tears burning their way into her eyes. "You don't get it, do you, Dad? If I run away, the person who did this will win. I'm finished running away from things. I'm home and I'm staying." Her voice became a strained whisper. "No matter what."

His eyes were on the shirt she was wearing. "They've made it clear that you're the next target, and yet you refuse to listen to reason, are out in plain sight wearing his Goddamned clothes. They could be watching from the woods for all we know, and if they are, you think they're gonna be happy seeing you standing your ground like a stubborn fool brat?"

"What?" She shook her head in confusion. "What do you mean they've made it clear? They killed a mule, a horse, and a cow. How does that—?"

"You haven't seen your Jeep?"

She gaped at him, her heartbeat suddenly throbbing in her ears. "Oh God. What is it?"

A vehicle barreled across the field, the rumble of the engine drawing her attention. Marshy swiveled to look as well, then turned back to face her.

"The tires were slashed. All of them, and they spray-painted 'your next' in red across the driver's side. I spotted that first."

He took a step back, his eyes cutting to Will, who was still watching the barn. Shaking his head, he turned and started for the front of the cabin. "I beg you to think about this."

She watched the Explorer roll to an abrupt stop behind Marshy's truck, her fear like a feral cat slinking among her troubled thoughts. When Tritt Davidson slid out from behind the wheel of the SUV, she didn't know whether to feel relieved or more afraid.

She wished she could trust him, but knew she could not. Despite how desperate he may have felt at the time, the man had gone to inexcusable lengths to protect his son. He had taken everything away from Will McGomery, had sacrificed his reputation for that of Jacob Davidson.

A couple of marked Trailblazers from the sheriff's department pulled in behind the Explorer, and she heard something bigger motoring across the field. She wanted inexplicably to go to Will and put her arms around him.

Her cell began to ring and she glanced away from him to check the number, thankful the various sirens had been killed once the emergency vehicles had turned onto the road leading up the ridge. She pulled the Motorola from her pants and frowned at it.

On the display she saw a number and a name. The number meant nothing to her, but the letters spelled out '*McGomery, Will*'. She flipped open the phone and said hello, her eyes trained on the man who had become as important to her as air and water. He hadn't moved, still stood with his hands in his pockets and staring lost into what had been his barn.

She heard nothing. The phone was dead.

Marshy and Davidson were making their way over to Will. She snapped the cell closed, filing the incident away in her mind for later. She crossed over to the three men, studying Will's face. His angular features were a play of shadow and light, like the night at the fair when he'd been standing next to the sound stage. He awarded her a momentary look. She searched his eyes for any sign that he was reassured by her presence, but found nothing, just arctic waters in the depth of his gaze.

"It'll be a few hours before I can get the Fire Marshall up here," Davidson said. "After they put it out and rope off the area, I don't want any of you poking around in there."

The man had turned his attention to her, his eyes flashing the unmistakable and universal 'I told you so'. Then his gaze shifting back to Will, he sighed. "You have any idea why someone wanted to do this, William?"

A fire tanker, larger than anything Madison would have

guessed could make it up the ridge, lumbered across the side lawn. In the cacophony of noise that entailed as volunteer fire fighters swarmed it in preparation of hosing the fire, she barely caught Will's response.

And then she thought she'd misunderstood him.

"Did you just say what I thought you said?" Marshy asked, clearly of the same idea as she, his face crimson beneath his pink-tinted silver hair.

She shot Will a look and saw that a muscle in his temple had started to throb. His voice had the edge of sheet metal. "You heard me. I said get off my land. Madison may have wanted you up here, but I sure to hell don't."

"Wait a minute." Madison choked the words out, but then had a difficult time finding enough breath to say anything else. One hand pressed against her forehead, she divided a look between him and her father. "Would you both just calm down for a minute?"

"That's my daughter those words were intended for!" Marshy shouted, causing her to jump. "I won't stand for you allowing her to be next."

"What is he talking about?" Will's eyes cut back to hers, his dark brows bunched together in his confusion.

"Someone painted 'you're next' on the side of my Jeep," she explained.

"This is your fault," Marshy growled, planting a finger in the center of Will's chest.

Tritt Davidson put a hand in the space that separated them. With his other hand he gestured at Marshy. "You. Simmer down. This finger pointing don't help a thing." His head turned in Will's direction. "Both of you shut up."

Marshy started coughing fitfully, his eyes on Tritt. "I want you. To get the bastard who did this. Whoever. It is."

"You want him to find the one responsible? Then take him to your other daughter," Will said. "The one who's been stalking me for months."

Marshy's mouth opened to blast him, but Davidson shook his head in warning and stepped between them. Will spoke again, leaning around Davidson, but this time his voice was relatively calm.

"She's unstable and you know it, Owens. It's about time you faced the fact."

"It's that nut job cousin of yours who's doing this." he said, knocking Davidson out of his way with no more consideration of him than he might reserve for a mosquito. "Just because Lorna took it hard—you wanting nothing to do with her—doesn't mean she's capable of this."

He glanced at the fire, now being doused heavily with water. "She's not. She wouldn't have snuck up here in the dark and torched your barn or shot your dog in the head. She ain't got it in her, I'm telling you."

A couple of uniformed officers approached, flanking Davidson.

"You need some help, chief?" one of them asked.

"Everything's good," Tritt said, dividing a look between Will and Marshy. "Right boys?"

Will's steady gaze remained riveted on Marshy. "Who told you that the shot to my dog was in the head?"

Madison's stomach plummeted. She looked at her father and waited for him to answer. Everyone did.

"Madison did, of course." His eyes found hers and silently pleaded for her to collaborate this.

"You're just an old man that lies through his tobacco stained teeth," Will told him. "Lorna is the one who informed you and she knows because she paid someone to blow my dog's brains to smithereens."

"She's seeing your cousin," Marshy said, his mouth working as he searched for the words to make his point. "He told her. He did it and he bragged to her about it." His eyes cut to Davidson. "If you question her about it, I'm sure she will admit as much."

"Could you try any harder to defend her sorry ass?" Will retorted.

Their angry words were like daggers shooting back and forth, cutting Madison each time that they did. She broke away from the small crowd of men and fled to the quiet of the house.

She went to Will's bedroom and sat down on the side of the disheveled bed, covered her face with her hands. Her eyes and throat burned with the need to cry and she slumped over onto her side, felt something crunch beneath her weight. Sitting up, she grabbed up the photo of Sarah and Molly and stared stupidly at it in the weird glow of the fire.

Hand shaking, she reached over and switched on the lamp that sat on the nightstand, studied the youthful faces in the photo. The two women were locked in their eternal embrace. Molly with her dark, mysterious gaze and Sarah with her Robin's egg blue. Their smiles were flirtatious. Knowing.

What else could Sarah be trying to say to her except that Will was her murderer? Why would she haunt this place for any other reason?

She sat completely still and thought about it, then grabbed at the drawer in the nightstand, yanking it open. She dropped the photo inside it and moved her eyes to the window where she could still see flames dancing against a sea of black predawn.

It was a long time before she fell asleep, still hugging herself to chase away the chill.

## CHAPTER TWENTY-NINE

A ray of sunlight penetrated the thick canopy of dismal clouds and streaked through the grass, causing pinpoints of light to reflect from the frozen dewdrops and prick Madison's eyes. Somewhere a hawk cried out, a lonely sound that punctuated the desolate silence of the sky beyond the front porch of the cabin. She stepped over and leaned against a post, scanning the white gray above.

She saw only bleakness.

Will leaned against another post, further down, and stared blankly in the direction of his withered garden. She had discovered him here, hunkered in his coat, moments ago. Now, when she glanced at him, her attention was drawn instantly to the artwork defacing her vehicle.

"I'll check with my insurance as far as my Jeep goes," she said, looking away from the hideous sight of it. "What about your barn and everything else you lost in the fire?"

He didn't answer at first and when he did, his voice sounded parched and his words were not in regard to her question. "You've been in your room for hours. Did you get any sleep?"

She hesitated. "Yes. Finally."

"I'm sorry you had to hear that between your Pap and me," he said. "I know that it's why you came inside, and why you've been avoiding me."

She stepped back from the edge of the porch, shivered in her jacket. "I would probably suspect Lorna too if I were you. She's my sister though, and I can't see her doing these things."

"Well, someone sure to hell did them. After I took my shower, I took up residence in the living room with my Ruger. I don't feel like I can let my guard down as long as you are staying here."

His words ushered anger and pain. "So you would shoot my sister?"

"If she posed a threat to you," he said, his tone of voice suddenly volatile. "Whether you have the proof you need to believe it or not, she has given me reason to suspect she's untrustworthy."

Her voice unsteady, she took a step in his direction. "That stupid photo turned up again last night."

"Goddamn it," he muttered, licking his lips and turning his head away from her.

"That's not the answer I was hoping for," she said, hugging her body to ward off the cold morning.

He pushed off the post and headed toward the door. "Not now, Madison, I'm exhausted."

She watched him go inside. He left the door open, a good indication he expected her to follow suit.

The stubborn jerk. Why couldn't he just admit the truth? He knew something. She knew he did. That, or he was actually the one who had killed Sarah.

Feeling as if her unanswered questions were walls that were closing in on her, she came inside the cabin and found that he had already shut himself inside his bedroom. She milled about the kitchen, debating the wisdom of approaching him, and decided she wouldn't. They were both tired, with tempers too close to the surface.

She tried not to think of how good it had felt to be in his arms, lying next to him in his bed. Their intimacy, fragile as it had surely been, seemed damaged beyond repair by the events of the night before. It seemed that the deck had been stacked against them from the start.

Her eyes landed on his key ring hanging on the wall above the counter near the front door and she stopped pacing. She had noticed the keys before, but this morning they seemed to beckon to her. He had used one of them to unlock the door to his woodworking shop when he'd taken her out to see his new clocks.

She moved back into the living room and gently slipped them off the hook. She had nothing better to do and perhaps there would be something out there of interest, something that could help her understand Will.

It was a stretch, but she was strongly compelled by the idea and left the house quietly. She padded across the porch and headed over to the building, finding the correct key after several tries to the lock.

Once inside the chilled interior of the building, she spent long minutes just leaning against the door. She couldn't seem to get her heart to slow down. Her lungs burned in the cold air and her eyes smarted from unshed tears.

The small building was quiet, as quiet as a tomb, but she sensed Will's presence everywhere. She finally forced herself to move away from the door so that she could better examine this haven for his creativity.

For a long time, she didn't do anything other than look at his clocks. The wooden shells of at least fifty that resembled the one he'd given to her mother lined a long shelf. Another shelf housed the guts to them, boxes upon boxes of various parts and mechanisms, little gears with teeth and brass pendulums, less familiar, intricate gadgets.

She was impressed by how organized everything was, but hardly surprised. His cabin was small but immaculate. Will McGomery had been ensconced on this ridge for years now, and leading a tidy life. That was until she had come along.

Her eyes closed and she took a deep breath trying to stabilize her emotions. The aromatic smell of planed wood, Cedar predominantly, filled her head and left her feeling a little dizzy. She crouched, placing her forehead to her knees.

The imperative thing here was to pull her act together. Things could work out. Somehow they would have to.

Lorna had not done this to them. It wasn't possible. This had happened because of what Will knew, but wasn't saying about his past. How she knew this, she wasn't sure. She lifted her head, took another sustaining breath, and spotted a filing cabinet beneath a table filled with his smaller hand tools.

It was small, only a couple feet tall, most likely purchased from Wal-Mart or a store from a similar chain. She stared at it a long time before finally crawling on her hands and knees beneath the table. Unable to resist the allure of the concealed storage unit, she tried the top drawer and found it unlocked.

She opened it and pulled out a sheaf of papers—a bank statement—then slid them back into the stack of other documents. She moved on to the next and final drawer, saw more papers and what appeared to be a tape recorder.

The thing was an outdated model, perhaps five or six years old if she could go by the sheer size and design of it. Hand recorders, like cell phones, were getting ever smaller, sleeker, and thinner. This thing was a dinosaur, was made to use with full-sized cassettes. It felt wonderful in her hand though, like she was holding the proverbial pot of gold at the end of the rainbow.

*EVPs.*

If this thing held a tape, there would be EVPs on it. She was certain of it.

She examined the instrument and saw that a tape was, in fact, in place behind the clear plastic door. Her finger searched out the play button. Her heart began to pump wildly; she was on a runaway train headed for either a catastrophe of truth or simple disappointment.

The door to the building opened and she jumped, hitting her head on the table.

She closed her eyes for just a moment, then gripped the recorder like a lifeline. She scrambled out of the cramped space and stood, faced the man who had implied he was too exhausted to talk. Suspecting she appeared every bit as guilty as Judas had while sitting at a table with his fellow disciples and Christ, she tried to square her shoulders.

"You think you found something, do you?" Will's face

sported no expression, but his eyes were heated, reminding her of the blue in the flame of a blowtorch.

"I listened to it," she lied, the line of her jaw defiant.

He crossed over to her and took the recorder from her hand, smiling a brittle smile. "And?"

When she didn't say anything, he nodded. "That's what I thought."

She stared at him, tension building behind her eyes like steam. "You tell me this rubbish about EVPs and being haunted and expect me not to be curious?"

Her voice shaking like that of someone on the brink of hysteria, she plowed ahead. "You talk about Sarah's voice. Her ghost interrupts us when we make love. What am I supposed to think?"

She swiped at the tears that had found their way down her face in tiny rivers. "I want you to tell me why she's dogging you like this."

He paused in the act of removing the cassette from the recorder and gave her a look. "I wish I knew."

"You're lying to me. You do know."

He placed the recorder on the table next to a reciprocating saw and put the cassette in his coat pocket. He stared at her for so long, she was compelled to look away, but didn't dare.

She brought her arm up to dab at her moist nose with the sleeve of her jacket. "I put the photo in my room with the bookmarker. I'm going to piece this together somehow."

"Bookmarker?"

"Yes," she said, sighing. "A blue ribbon with scripture on it. *Surely goodness and mercy shall follow me all the days of my life.*"

"That was Molly's. I kept it in a Bible in the bookcase."

"Well then, maybe Molly haunts you too," she said caustically.

"I didn't kill Sarah, Madison. I didn't."

"And yet she haunts you, not her murderer." She lifted her

arms out from her sides and let them drop heavily, her laughter shrill and mocking. "Makes a lot of sense."

"Fucking fine. I killed her then. Will you shut up now?"

Feeling her face screw up and a sob rising in her throat, she looked at the floor. "I want to hear what you have on that tape."

"You're in no state of mind to listen to anything."

"Prove to me that Sarah talks to you. Let me hear what's on the tape or I'll leave…I'll never speak to you again."

He sighed. "It would be better if you did exactly that, Madison. For all involved. This is taking a toll on Marshy. I can see it in his face and in his eyes. Your being here is killing him. He's scared out of his mind for you, and though I'd give my life to protect you, I can't exactly say you're safe here with me, not after last night."

"Do you want me to go?" She raised her head and glared at him through her tears. "I'm not asking you if you think I *should* go. I'm asking if you *want* me to go."

His impatience with her was evident by the way his lips rolled inward. He turned, giving her his back, his breath coming out unevenly. Finally, he spoke into the tense space that her question had left.

"Yes. I want you to go."

Will thought Madison's expression was identical to one he'd seen recently on a flyer in his mail; that of a malnourished child in Indonesia—eyes huge and forlorn, lips poised in a half smile that only the curious and the afraid exhibit.

She had to know he was lying. Of course he didn't want her to go.

She must go.

Things were getting out of hand. Just like his dream had shown him, she would be trapped if she stayed.

As she moved passed him, he extended a hand and said her name softly, his tone apologetic. She flinched, hurried away.

Watching her leave the building, he wasn't surprised at all

when tears burned their way into his eyes.

# CHAPTER THIRTY

Madison drifted awake to darkness and the distant strains of a fiddle, and was instantly disgruntled over the fact she had fallen asleep. She was just as irritated with Will for not seeking her out after she had taken refuge in the guestroom.

She meandered out of the bedroom, watched him from the end of the hallway as he sat in the rocking chair in the living room and played his instrument. He looked ridiculous and rugged and so beautiful that it made her ache inside.

She immediately wanted to go to him.

"I recognize that song," she said, passing by the kitchen and entering the living room. "It's an old church hymn of which I can't, at this moment, remember the name."

He lowered the fiddle in increments until it rested on his lap. "Sorry if I disturbed you. I was trying to be quiet."

"It wasn't my intention to fall asleep anyway," she said. "And I definitely didn't intend to sleep this long. Did Davidson ever make it back with the Fire Marshall?"

He took the violin and bow over to the couch and put them in the case. "They came and so did your Pap. Again."

"Why am I not surprised he returned?" Resignation crept into her voice. "You're right. This is taking a toll on him, me being here."

"He told me that he wished he'd never sold me this place," he said quietly. "But then when he left, he offered to lend me the use of his tractor to remove what's left of my animals from the rubble."

Hope surged within her. "He did? That's a good sign. He's at least thinking about coming around."

He slid the fiddle case under the couch then turned to face her. "Let's just say your old man felt better after he landed me a solid punch in the gut. I think he even felt somewhat charitable after that."

"What?" Her eyes dropped to his abdomen.

He smiled a little. "I thought Davidson was going to deck him for it, but your Pap held up his hands and said, 'I'm entitled to that much, now let's get down to business finding who did this to him.'"

Unable to hide her amazement, she shook her head. "My father punched you. Incredible."

He shrugged. "I probably would have punched me too if I'd been in his shoes. Just so you know, Davidson's got some of his guys watching the place tonight. I guess he's feeling pretty charitable too these days, the wily fucker. I don't trust him as far as I could throw him."

"Are you okay, Will?"

His smile was sheepish. "Am now. Didn't feel too swell at the time though. I kind of sensed he was going to do something by the look in his eyes, thought he would aim for my jaw, but then he sacked me. I basically fell on him. It wasn't one of my more impressive moments, and I thought it was damn well over with for my spleen."

She crossed over to him, feeling herself go warm when she looked into his face. "You could've defended yourself, but you didn't. In spite of everything, you respect him."

"I do," he said. "He's your father and he loves you."

She bit into her lip. "What evil have I unleashed by coming up here?"

He extended a hand and caressed the apple of her cheek with the pad of his thumb. "We. What evil have we unleashed? We're in this together in case it's escaped you."

A tear spilled over the rim of her eye and he whisked it away.

"Madison, I'm sorry. I wish everything could be different. But for that to happen the past would have to be altered and that's impossible."

She searched his eyes, sniffed moistly. "Why does she do

it? Why?"

"You don't know what you're asking me."

"Yes, I think I'm very clear about what I'm asking you."

He rolled his head around his shoulders then slouched back into the couch. "I'm tired, Maddie."

"Your favorite excuse," she said. Placing her hand on his knee and applying light pressure, she implored him with her eyes. "You can tell me. You can tell me about Sarah, about the reason she haunts you, why someone doesn't think you deserve to have another shot at happiness."

"The past is a cross I have to carry," he said. "I don't expect anyone to help me bear it, least of all you. Especially not you."

At her look of frustration, he leaned forward and attempted to brush his lips across her cheek. She ducked her head and, for a moment, he remained close to her, rubbing his face against the sleeve of her shirt. She removed her hand from his knee, and he pulled back. She felt his gaze focused on her like a telescopic lens.

"I didn't expect Marshy to come around the way he did and I'm glad you didn't go." He touched her hair. "So glad."

She turned her head, met his eyes. He threaded his fingers through her hair. "Let's not ruin what time we have together with the past."

"I don't want to be in the dark, always wondering, Will."

"What if there is no light?" he asked quietly, causing her forearms to break out in gooseflesh.

His gaze was as steady as a blue laser, but cold, somehow detached. "What if in the end you find only darkness? Will you stay? Will you still let me touch you? I have little to offer you except what we share in bed…little that's good anyway."

He rose from the couch suddenly and went over to the logs stacked to the side of the stone fireplace. He added one to the fire he had built, then turned for the kitchen, pausing at the half wall to look back at her.

"I don't like the idea of you being in here without me after what happened last night. If you come with me to the bedroom, we don't have to have sex. Maybe you would like to read while I get some sleep?"

She leaned forward and wrapped her arms around her corduroy-clad knees. "Do you have a cell phone?"

His eyes went flat and then he rolled them toward the ceiling and laughed. "Have you seen one around here? Who the hell would I call?"

"Evidently me," she said. "Last night, before Davidson came over to talk to you outside, my phone rang and it was your name that popped up. No one was on the other end that I could tell. Like the photo and the bookmark, another piece to the puzzle?"

"I don't know what to say."

She smiled sadly. "I do. Goodnight, Will."

# CHAPTER THIRTY-ONE

Madison stood in a clearing, trees like looming witches behind her, a pond in front of her. Something was in the water. A fish on its side, swishing bugs from the surface.

No, it wasn't that.

It was a hand—bloodless, white fingers reaching blindly for the sky.

It had to be a dream. Had to be.

The dead woman rose from the water like a terrible mist and gasped for air. It was the bark of a raven—stark, harsh. Awful.

She couldn't look away from Sarah Chambers, couldn't look away from the wet hanks of blond hair covering the drowned woman's eyes. Lifting her blue-veined hands, she pushed the sodden hair back. Her eyes were dead, milked over like the eyes of the decomposing fish she had come upon while wading Clinch River with Lorna and Rachel as a girl.

She was sure that she was picking up something from this dream visage, this apparition. She heard it in her head, the buzz-tone of words, like a voice crackling over a faulty intercom.

*Sacrifice.*

What kind of sacrifice? Whose?

She wheeled around and slammed into something hard and yet pliant, a person.

Will.

She felt his shirt beneath her fingertips, saw the question burning in his eyes, eyes that were as purple as an Appalachian ridge set against a fading sun.

Why are you here?

This was the question his eyes asked, but she couldn't speak. She was terrified, galvanized by fear.

Wake up. She must wake up now.

*Wake. Up.*

Her eyes popped open and she drank in the absolute darkness of her surroundings, knowing where she was, but still feeling the chilled and damp air from the pond. This was black fear, cold fiberglass fear, and it penetrated her on a cellular level.

She shouldn't have been able to fall asleep. She'd slept all day.

The bed linens were twisted around her body and she felt trapped, as though caught in a tight, wet womb. She struggled out of the confines of her own sweat drenched sheets, breathing fast, her heart exploding in her chest. She clamored to the bathroom, making frantic sweeps at the wall until her hand made contact with the switch and the room was flooded with light.

Bracing herself against the sink, she murmured to herself, told herself she could talk her way out of any crazy dream. The trick was not allowing a cloud of panic to shroud her conscious mind.

Will McGomery was asleep in the next room. All she had to do to confirm this was go in there. She should go in there and set her mind at ease.

She splashed water on her face and it dripped from her chin into the basin of the sink. A violent shudder rolled through her. Her long t-shirt, soaked through with sweat, quivered over her skin. So cold. She was cold like Sarah must have been in that water.

Or maybe the fire had died down and the cabin had chilled. Either way, she was freezing. She was not okay. Something was wrong.

She stared at her reflection in the mirror of the medicine cabinet, exhaled slowly through chattering teeth, tried to rationalize the disturbing scenario that had assaulted her.

She had spent the evening reading the selections from Will's bookcase on Electronic Voice Phenomena. The last couple of days' upsetting turn of events and those damned books explained everything, and yet she couldn't shake the terror. He had been at the pond, had been startled to see her.

She felt like something was about to jump out at her, like something was...pending.

Her focus shifted from her reflection to the handle on the door of the medicine cabinet. She wanted to grasp it, didn't want to grasp it; was overcome with the dread she had experienced in the dream when she'd looked into Sarah Chambers' grotesque eyes.

Something was in the medicine cabinet.

Her hand lifted from the sink quickly, yanked open the door, and stifled a terrified scream. Behind McGomery's medication was the photo of Molly and Sarah, along with the blue ribbon bookmarker.

She sprung back from the sight of the objects, her eyes fixed over the glossy faces in the picture.

They seemed to be mocking her from the sunny scene in which they were frozen—fresh faces pressed cheek to cheek with twin smiles that teased. She inched along the wall until she felt the grainy wood of the door that led into Will's sleeping quarters. Her eyes never left the photo as she grappled for the doorknob.

She spilled out of the bathroom and into the next room, blinked into the shadows that shrouded an empty bed. She fell back a step, then moved quickly for the room's other door.

In the living room, she could see that the fire had not died down, was in fact lapping hungrily at a fresh log. He had been here, but wasn't now.

Panic, like a cold fist opening in her chest, caused her to glance around like someone in search of an escape route. Her eyes landed on the front door and she experienced a fleeting sense of relief. He had gone to get more wood. Yes, naturally. Certainly.

She glanced at the hearth. No. He had stacked plenty to the side of it.

"Will!" Her voice was a decibel below a scream and the sound terrified her. She knew she was on the brink of hysteria.

At the sound of the fire snapping over the grate, she swiveled her head, jumped backward when the burning log fell forward sending a shower of sparks up the flu. She lunged toward the front door, yanking it open, and skidded to a halt midway across the porch.

Will's building stood across from the house and a little to the right. Through the thin veil of snow that was falling, she saw light emanating from the couple of windows adorning the front of the building. It was like lifting her face to the sun. It filled her with painful relief.

She tripped down the steps and sprinted through the snow in her bare feet, scarcely aware of the biting cold. Taking hold of the knob on the door to the building, she twisted the icy dome of metal and burst into the warmth of the fire that was crackling in the Fisher stove.

A quick scan of the room brought her to Will McGomery. He was slumped against a leg of the table she had hit her head on just that morning, his legs straight out in front of him like he'd been propped there. The tape recorder was in his hand and he was gripping it so tightly in his fist that his knuckles had gone white.

His face was that of someone suffering from catatonia; his eyes glazed, mouth slightly gaping.

A seizure?

She rushed over and fell to her knees, grabbing hold of his shoulders and shaking him firmly. "Will!" *Please, oh God, please snap out of it.*

His lips moved, but barely. His eyes stared straight ahead, did not blink. She looked at the recorder in his fist; he clutched it like a lifeline, and yet he didn't seem to be there at all. He'd checked out.

She began to sob, tried to pry the recorder out of his fingers. His legs drew up and her head raised, her eyes stinging as they ravaged his face.

"Stop it," he said, his brows drawing down in his confusion. He pushed her away, causing her to fall backward. He blinked. Glancing down at his hand, he saw the recorder and looked at her fearfully, fumbled to switch it off.

"You were trying to catch something on tape and had a seizure, I think." She tugged her oversized tee over her bare thighs. "I just wanted to get that thing out of your hand before you broke it."

He began to tremble, his voice a thread of a whisper. "You were at the pond."

"Yes," she said breathlessly, her heart hammering. "She wanted me to be there. I think she tried to tell me something. When I looked into her eyes, I—"

"How could you have been there?" He leaned forward suddenly and clutched her arm in a fierce grip. Then, his face contorting, he hauled himself up and made a scramble for the door.

Barely making it beyond the threshold, he began retching into the scant layer of snow covering the grass. She heard the unmistakable sound and closed her eyes, wishing she could understand what was happening.

Suspicion ate at her. Sarah wanted closure, and he seemed to be the designated one to bring it, only she couldn't deal with that.

Tritt Davidson had told her about his alibi, but it wasn't airtight. At least, in her opinion it wasn't. Will might have been in West Virginia the week of Sarah's drowning, but couldn't he have made a discreet trip back, done something unthinkable, and returned?

She curled her fingers into fists, lowered her chin toward her chest. What if he hadn't been in West Virginia the whole time? What if Tritt had been so focused on Aubrey he'd overlooked the possibility that Will's family had covered for him, or at the very least, discounted the possibility of him being away during those critical hours surrounding the murder?

What was the truth and why the hell did Will McGomery want to catch Sarah on tape? The answers could be found as easily as pushing a button on his tape recorder.

She struggled up and glanced toward the door.

As fate would have it, he had taken the stupid thing with him.

# CHAPTER THIRTY-TWO

Will crouched in front of the stove. With quick motions so he wouldn't be burned, he used one hand to spin the dampers closed. Rising, he faced Madison.

"Let's go back to the house, your feet must be freezing."

She waited until they were in his living room and she had tucked herself into the corner of the couch before speaking again.

"I came looking for you after I was compelled to open your medicine cabinet in the bathroom and found the photo and the bookmarker."

He shook his head. "Where are they now?"

"I left them where they were, was still scared out of my mind over that dream."

His eyes remained locked over hers for a ponderous moment as he stood near the half wall, and then, recorder in hand, he left the room. When he returned a moment later, the recorder was no longer in his hand, but the photo of Molly and Sarah was, as well as the bookmarker. He crossed over to the fireplace and tossed them onto the half-burned log there, causing her to gasp softly.

"Do you think you should have done that?"

His expression was blank. "At this point, I don't really give a damn."

"Will," she said. "That dream terrified me."

"I can't control what you dream, but at least that photo of her and Molly won't turn up unexpectedly again."

She watched the flames lick at the paper, looked away when the faces of the two women began to melt and turn black.

"When I woke up in the hospital, I had no memory of the wreck that nearly killed me," he said, his eyes never straying from the fire. "I was told some kid ran a red light and plowed into the side of my truck. I found out later that it left him paralyzed from the waist down. Had he not been distracted and blown that traffic light, I'd have never started having the dreams and the seizures, would have never become this freak that I am. Isn't that selfish? The guy's still in a wheelchair, he will never walk again, and I can't work up the spit to say I feel sorry for him."

He took the poker from the stand sitting on the hearth and prodded at what was left of the bookmarker and the photo of his wife and her friend. The burnt pieces disintegrated and were lost in the glowing embers.

Ashes to ashes; dust to dust.

The thought chilled her.

He looked at her, a terrible sadness filling his eyes. "What exactly did you see in the dream?"

"I don't know," she said. "Sarah...and you. That awful black water."

"You don't remember what she said to you?" he asked.

She swallowed tightly. "No, something about sacrifice, I think. Why are you not willing to play that tape for me, or let me hear the EVPs you've recorded before? It scares the hell out of me, your refusal to let me in. It makes me feel like you have something terrible to hide."

"I was trying to catch Molly tonight," he said irritably. "I woke up, couldn't fall back asleep. It's a very personal thing, what I do with that recorder and I don't expect you to understand why I want to keep it private."

"In other words, you are not even close to getting over the loss of your wife." She rubbed her eyes and told herself to get a grip, not to lose it in front of him.

"I just want to hear her voice again," he said softly.

She jumped up from the couch, her fingers twisting the hem of her tee at her bare thighs. "Why were you at the pond in my dream if you're not Sarah's killer?"

"You don't suspect by now that she haunts me because I'm

a witness of sorts?"

She gaped at him. "You witnessed her death?"

"You think I did it," he said. "But I didn't. I see things in dreams, have every since I came out of the coma and started having seizures."

"You knew I was there. I wouldn't call that a dream. It was some kind of psychic connection. What the hell are you, Will?"

"You're not ready for the truth." He crossed over to the rocker, ran his fingers along the top if it and met her eyes again. "I'm sorry but I can't answer your question."

She blinked and then swiped at the tears as they rolled down her cheeks. "Then damn you, McGomery."

The guestroom had never seemed so far away, and when she finally reached it, she closed the door and shrank against it, terrified to know his truth.

More afraid not to know it.

****

The sun had not yet pierced the eastern horizon when Tritt Davidson pulled his Explorer into the hospital parking lot. Jacob was slotted for surgery in less than an hour, but had agreed to see him. The curious tone of his son's voice had been evident over the phone, but Tritt hadn't disclosed the reason he wanted to see him. He suspected his son had an idea anyway.

He found Jacob seated at his desk when he let himself into the spacious office. Jake turned his head away from the computer monitor, smiling uncertainly, and then swiveled around in the luxurious leather chair.

"Pop. Take a seat why don't you?"

He did immediately. He didn't think his knees were going to hold him up. His mind churned with disturbing thoughts, played over the decision to confront his son. Emily would hopefully never have to know about this conversation.

"Son, I'm not going to beat around the bush," he said in a voice that was shamefully unsteady. "I think you and I both have been doing that for way too long now."

Jacob's dark eyes dropped to his manicured hands, folded neatly over the ink blotter on his desk. His mahogany colored hair, just beginning to recede from his forehead, was run through with fine streaks of gold after a summer spent boating out on the lake. Tritt marveled at how beautiful and accomplished his son really was. He would never let anyone ruin his reputation.

"When you called the house so early, wanting to talk to me in private, you were using your drill sergeant voice," Jacob said. "It's the voice you use with people you perceive to be criminals." He frowned. "I figure after all these years, you've had enough of this walking on eggshells. Why now, though?"

Tritt looked at him in surprise. He hadn't expected Jake to be so forthright. He'd anticipated anything but candidness. He found he didn't know what to say in response to this, so he reverted to the original blueprint of their meeting.

"Jake, I'm gonna ask you a question and I want honesty. Nothing but. You're not young and reckless anymore, you—"

"You want to know if I pushed Sarah Chambers into old man McGomery's pond." Jacob ran a finger around the inside his crisply starched collar. Then flicking an imaginary speck off the white sleeve of his shirt, he smiled stiffly. "That's the question that's been eating at you?"

"I can see why you'd think that," Tritt said, swallowing hard. "Of course you would think that. You were fooling around with her, son. Several people told me they saw her with you out in town. Damn it, she was pregnant. We had big plans for you, your scholarship...medical school. I thought you didn't want to disappoint your mother and me. I thought that girl took you out there to tell you she was pregnant, got you in a panic and one thing led to another."

"I had no idea she was pregnant until you told me what the autopsy revealed," Jake said, his expression closed. He stared off into near space for a moment. "I appreciated the significance of her being pregnant and did exactly what you told me to do. I kept my mouth shut and my head down. I thought however, that maybe you believed me when I said I didn't kill her."

"You were my kid," Tritt qualified. "Whether I believed you or not, I had to protect you all the same. It didn't look good, that's for sure. I hate that I may have doubted you, but it wouldn't have mattered one way or the other. I still would've had to do the same things."

"Why now, Pop? Why are you coming to me now? Isn't all of this water under the bridge?"

"Not to Aubrey McGomery, it ain't. That asshole knows he took the rap for someone else and it's clear he thinks he knows who that someone else is, thanks to you. You went to visit him in prison shortly before he got out, must have thought if you gave him Chambers' killer, he'd leave you alone."

Massaging his left arm, he glared at his son. "Why didn't you tell me you knew the truth about what happened to that girl? That's the question I came here to ask, and don't even think of denying the truth. You know who killed that girl. You can hide it from me for a little while, but not forever."

Jacob Davidson stared speechlessly at him, then placed his head in his hands. "I was afraid someone would tell Aubrey about me and Sarah and he'd come after me. Back then, that was my fear, and when I went to see him in prison that was my fear. I needed assurance more than ever when I knew his sentence had almost been served. I had a family, a wife, and young son. You should be glad he brought this to your attention. He could have—"

"I'm furious that *you* didn't bring it to my attention, furious that I have to deal with all this again after so many years." Tritt rose from the chair. "You have no idea how much I don't want to deal with this. Do you realize your reputation is at stake, mine too, as well as my job? If I don't make sure all my ducks are in a row, this thing could explode in my face. He doesn't fool me one bit with his coming forward. He's going for blood. I have an informant that tells me so."

Jacob had lifted his head to stare at him but now lowered it back into his hands. "Better my reputation and your job than Aubrey McGomery hurting Gail or Ethan because I shagged his girlfriend."

"Did you not hear me? A lot is at stake here. All because you told that numbskull the truth you refused to tell me." Tritt moved for the door. "Aubrey never knew that I was the one who framed him for that house fire, but you did. You knew before I ever did it that I was going to and you never said a word to me about the truth, never tried to stop me."

"You wanted it to be him," Jacob said. "And you wouldn't have done anything differently if I had told you who really killed Sarah. You were too afraid of them doing a tell-all with that news reporter, and the world finding out about me being the possible Daddy of that baby. Face it, Pop. You couldn't stand the thought of me not being perfect. I always had to be spotless for you. I was the sheriff's son."

Tritt stood at the door, feeling betrayed as he looked at his son. Why couldn't Jacob appreciate how much he'd done for him? He was the sheriff's son. And he was being very ungrateful.

"If you'd told me the truth, Jake, I'd have taken care of the problem. We would never have had to worry about anyone finding out about that baby. Now I'm faced with having to take care of it anyway, and believe me, I intend to. Blood pressure, be damned."

Jacob shook his head back and forth. "Are you saying that putting the right person behind bars is not as important as making sure they don't talk about me? Let them talk! I had a summer fling with Sarah Chambers. Years ago. Big deal."

"What I'm saying is that no one, and I mean no one, makes a fool out of me." Tritt opened the door to the office, holding Jacob's gaze a moment longer before leaving. "Aubrey's already got his mind set on revenge. I'm going to leave it up to him to take care of the problem for me."

Rubbing his arm again, he added, "And then he's going to

be tried for murder and found guilty. Just as it should have been years ago."

# CHAPTER THIRTY-THREE

Will had immediately gone outside when he'd heard the low purr of her father's tractor coming across the field. They'd been outside for close to an hour now in the snow.

Madison stood at the guestroom window and watched in tearful silence as they worked to secure a rope around what was left of Cornflower's stiff and charred hindquarters.

Her father had already pulled Harlow and Dib across the field behind Will's house, carrying them beyond the old cemetery and over a slight rise, and left their remains to be picked at by the carrion eaters.

When he mounted the tractor yet again, she turned away from the window and went to the living room. She sat down in the rocking chair and listened to the fire popping in the fireplace, wondering if Will had gone back to picking through the ashes of the barn.

Why he bothered wasn't clear to her. It wasn't as if anyone would be able to find something that would lead to the perpetrator. Like the now-charred photo of Sarah and Molly, any evidence had been consumed by fire.

Feet pushing against the floor, she rocked herself back and forth in the rocker. Restless, she stood and moved back to guestroom to retrieve her phone.

She sat down on the edge of the bed and pulled up the call that had been made to her the night of the fire. Her eyes committed the number to memory even though she did not plan to erase it from the folder.

Dialing it, she held her breath. Four rings in her ear and then a recording told her that the cellular customer she was trying to reach was not available. Disconnecting, she dialed the number again and walked through the bathroom to Will's room, half-expecting to hear the muffled sound of a ring tone.

The house was silent. She disconnected before the automated voice kicked on again. She was in the laundry room, pulling clothes from the dryer when her phone made a beep, indicating she had a message waiting.

She pulled the cell from her pants pocket and hastily accessed her inbox.

*Closet floor.*

Her eyes stared stupidly at the text for a moment, and then she pulled up the number and name of the party who had sent it. She recognized the number immediately, and saw that the name below it read *'McGomery, Will'*.

Laundry abandoned, she raced back into Will's bedroom and flung open the closet door. Dropping to her hands and knees, she began inspecting the hardwood flooring, locating an irregularity in one of the boards.

It was loose. She used her fingernails to pry it up a quarter of an inch on one end and then with her other hand, she yanked it away. Will had cut through the particleboard that had been beneath the run of oak. A small hole was revealed to her, stuffed with pink insulation that looked like cotton candy.

She moved it to the side. Then, she reached into the black orifice, spreading her fingers wide and encountering icy cold concrete, along with several small objects.

Out came a cell phone and she looked at it in amazement. She reached back in and pulled out the recorder that Will had used the night before. Then she fumbled to replace the insulation and floorboard.

Her pulse was like a trapped moth beneath her skin. It fluttered wildly, in fragile anticipation of the unknown. She took everything to her bedroom and closed the door, immediately consulting the window.

Will was, as expected, combing through the blackened debris of the barn. She dumped everything but the recorder on the bed, and pushed the play button.

Nothing happened. She tinkered with the inexpensive piece

for a few seconds before deciding the problem was the batteries. She dropped it onto the quilt and picked up the cell phone, turning it on.

A message waited. She pulled up the inbox easily enough and accessed it, then read the text.

*I'll be there. Tonight. Seven sharp.*

She gasped when she saw the familiar cell phone number and name: *'Boardwine, Lorna'.*

Her sister had left the message only twenty minutes ago. She and Will were going to meet somewhere tonight?

Her mind reeling, hands trembling, she experimented with the phone until she was satisfied that Will had erased any and all other text messages he had received. She managed to pull up his contact list and frowned at the names—*Boardwine Lorna, Davidson Tritt, McGomery Dow*, and *Wray Douglas.*

Suddenly lightheaded, she lowered the phone and closed her eyes, took several deep breaths. When she felt up to it, she used his phone to text her sister. She punched out the words, *Where are you?* Then waited. She had a response within a minute.

*Why?*

Palms sweating, she responded. *I can meet you now. Name the place.*

She waited. Her heart pounded in such a way that she thought it was going explode inside her chest. Lorna's resulting message did not cause her fear to abate.

*You break it off with her yet?*

Will had told Lorna he was ending things with her? *Yes. I'm leaving now. Where?*

Lorna's text message came almost spontaneously.

*Not working today, but my car will be in the bank parking lot.*

Catapulting across the room, Madison snatched up her purse and came back to put the items on the bed inside it. She consulted her own phone, which was ringing, and saw Lorna's number, opting not to answer. This would be her sister checking to see if she'd been dumped and she didn't have the energy to be an actress with her.

Her brain working feverishly, she put on her jacket and went outside to face Will.

"I'm going to go visit my sister Rachel in Bristol," she announced, stepping gingerly around a chunk of burned wood and eyeing Will warily. "Think I could borrow your truck?"

He pivoted and looked at her, his eyes showing his surprise. "I'm going to Dow's this afternoon sometime."

*Liar.*

"Okay, so just tell Daddy I'm borrowing his. You can give him a ride home." She turned to leave, adrenaline pumping through her veins and making her feel wildly unpredictable.

"Madison." His voice was gruff. When she angled him a look, he frowned at her. "You okay?"

She nodded. "Just need to get out of here for a little while."

"Be careful," he said, and she hurried back toward the house, his words seeming somehow vulgar.

                              ****

Lorna spotted Marshy's truck as she wheeled her Volvo into the parking lot of New People's Bank, and Madison noted her sister's look of confused surprise. She waited for her to park and then got out of the truck and walked over.

"I've been trying to call you," Lorna said, her voice high and unnatural as Madison got inside her car. "What are you doing here?"

"You're not working today. I could ask you the same question."

Looking at her suspiciously, Lorna dropped her hand from the steering wheel. "It was you sending those messages, wasn't it?"

"I found his phone this morning," she said, her throat parched. "He had it stashed under the floor in his closet."

Lorna's mouth opened but, at first, no words came out. "I

told you you'd get hurt, Maddie."

"You are my sister," she said. "Tell me what in hell is going on with the two of you? Why does he want to meet with you tonight? What did his message to you say?"

Lorna looked almost pleased to be pressed for an answer. "He wants revenge. That's what he's all about, Mad. He said if I would come over to his side, help him bring Aubrey down, he would break things off with you for good. He wanted to meet with me so we could talk it over."

"Bring Aubrey down?" The words were like pieces of wood being forced up her throat. "Over the dog and the barn?"

"Duh, no. Over the drowning of Sarah Chambers."

"But you told me you thought Will himself was the one who drowned her." Her head hurt. She felt like pressing her fingertips into her eyes but instead stared unblinkingly at her sister.

Lorna shrugged. "I was just trying to scare you away from him. Will McGomery belongs with me, Little Sissa. Now that he's finally come to his senses and realizes you will never understand his need to set things right, we can make Aubrey pay for what he did all those years ago. Will lost everything because of Aubrey, and now Aubrey's going to get what he deserves. It's as simple as that and you are not going to stand in the way, understand?"

"Then why have you been playing around with Aubrey?"

"To make Will jealous and it worked. He can't stand the thought of me being with another man, especially the man who is wreaking havoc on his life once again."

Madison looked down, closed her eyes. "Oh, Lorna, what are you getting yourself—"

"It's true," Lorna interrupted. "You came along and turned Will's head. I can't deny that. I knew though. I knew that sooner or later he would see that you're just too much of a puritan to stand behind him. He's going to kill Aubrey and I'm going to watch him. And you are going to keep your mouth shut about what I've told you because you love me and you know what a monster his cousin really is. You know that he has to be stopped."

Astounded, Madison peered across the console at her sister. Just how delusional was Lorna? Did she really believe that being some kind of vigilante, or the girlfriend of a vigilante, was noble? Did Will really intend to meet with her? Was he willing to carry out his cousin's murder? Or did he have something else in mind, perhaps some plan to hurt Lorna because he believed she was the one harassing him?

Every fiber of her being denied the idea, yet the evidence did support it. Will had undeniably asked Lorna to meet him that night. He was up to something.

But what? Killing Aubrey? Why? Was it to silence the woman who haunted him? Or was he planning to rid himself of the problem that he perceived her sister to be?

"Don't do it. Don't meet him." She reached out and grasped Lorna's fingers. "I don't think you should trust what he's told you. Clearly I haven't been able to trust him. Think about it. Please."

Lorna smiled, her eyes sparkling like cheap rhinestones. "Maddie, get your junk and go back to Ohio. You don't have any dogs in this fight, honey."

Madison looked at her, revolted by her glibness. "*Primum Non Nocere*, Lorna."

"What the hell is that supposed to mean?" Lorna said, blinking.

"First do no harm," Madison replied. "If the two of you do this, then you are no longer my sister. We're strangers."

She opened the door and got out of the Volvo, thinking that Lorna did have a point. She really didn't have anything to do with the history between Will and his cousin.

Trouble was, she had never taken orders from Lorna and she wasn't going to start now.

## CHAPTER THIRTY-FOUR

Cecilia Onate took the bank envelope Lorna extended toward her.

"It's all there," Lorna said. "One thousand to your friend for the barn and the Jeep, and two hundred dollars for you."

Cecilia consulted the envelope, then removed the money and stuffed it into the front pocket of her jeans. She absently dropped the envelope onto the couch beside of her. "I will give it to him when I see him tomorrow."

Lorna nodded. It was incredible to think that her little lesbian *Amiga* had turned into such a Godsend. What had been intended to scare Maddie had in fact been the thing to turn Will around. He undoubtedly thought that Aubrey had been the one to do such awful things. He was determined to get him back, and having her on his side was one way of achieving that goal.

Everything was going to work out. Maddie would be too afraid to have anything to do with him now, and he would see that he'd been wasting time with the wrong sister. Lorna would move in with him and they would make Aubrey pay for hurting him. It didn't matter that Aubrey would pay for things that she herself had been responsible for. He was a sadist, and he deserved what was coming to him.

The cash advance on her Discover card would put her in a financial strain for a little while, but she had won. It was worth every penny.

She had *won*.

Cecilia looked at her contemplatively. "You know, *chica*, burning his animals was not something he liked doing. He said they were already in there. All he had to do was let them out, but you did not think that the barn was enough. You wanted them to die, did you not?"

"Your friend knew the deal. The animals were the reason I

paid a thousand bucks. It had to be drastic."

Cecilia smiled, her eyes looking beyond Lorna and befuddling her. Then she spoke and her words confused Lorna even more. "How did I look, *mi amor*?"

Lorna wheeled around and saw Aubrey propped against the doorway leading into the bedroom, a digital camera in one hand.

His eyes played over Cecilia, his smile quite affectionate. "Exotic as ever, honeybee." He crossed over to her and handed off the camera. "Get it onto the computer and make a DVD. If and when I need to, I'll give our noble, lard assed Sheriff Davidson a copy of it."

"*Sí*," she said, winking at Lorna. "With great pleasure."

Lorna's eyes played between the two of them, her thoughts spinning out of control. "What's going on?"

"Take a wild guess," he said, his voice flippant.

Her heart stopped. "You filmed me?"

"Of course I did, Blondie." He gestured behind him. "See that hole there in the wall. It's small, so you probably didn't. I drilled it this morning, and thanks to my little honeybee, I got everything right there on tape."

"Why?" It was all that would come out of her mouth.

He stepped up to her and trailed a lone finger down her cheek, his eyes moving from her to Cecilia. "Tell her, baby."

Cecilia giggled. "*Para divertirse solamente.*"

Lorna stared at her in horror. "What did she just—"

"Don't rightly know," he said, cutting her words off with his lips. Kissing her very softly, he then pulled back and gazed into her eyes. "What I do know is that you're not about to betray me. Not with that incriminating piece of evidence hanging over your head, you paying Ceci for those bad things you wanted done to Slick Willie."

"You're the friend? You did it and now you're framing me?"

"Very good. No one ever accused you of being a dumb blonde, just an overly trusting one." He smirked at her. "Did you really believe I was going to kill my own flesh and blood? Drown Willie in that pond?"

"Aubrey," she whispered. "Please. I—"

"I'd rather not hear your lies, Lorna Mae. I know the truth without you opening that deceitful little mouth of yours. You got the hots for Willie." He gripped her face and squeezed hard until her lips pouted toward him. "You think I don't know that? You've had the hots for him every since you found out he was camped out on your Daddy's mountain. You want to fix him, don't you, but there ain't no fixing in you, bitch. You're nothin' but a wrecking ball."

"I don't know what you're talking about," she said, barely coaxing the words from her unwilling vocal cords and through her protruding lips.

He slid his other hand down the front of her fitted blouse, cupped her pubis through her jeans. "Oh, I think you do. I really do."

Cecilia stepped close, leaned in and rubbed her lips back and forth across hers. "I betrayed you simply to amuse myself. That's what I said to you a second ago, *puta*."

Lorna couldn't think. Why were they doing this to her? And when had they hooked up behind her back?

Cecilia Onate was not who she had thought she was, clearly, but she had been honest about one thing.

Messing with Aubrey McGomery had been like dancing with the devil himself.

# CHAPTER THIRTY-FIVE

Will watched with steady blue eyes as Madison crossed over and sank down onto the couch, setting her purse down on the cushion beside her.

"You found everything I hid, took it with you," he said, moving over to the rocking chair and sitting down.

Madison sniffed, rubbed her nose. "I stopped and bought fresh batteries on my way back, listened to what you recorded, I presume in the building out there."

"In your opinion, what did the voice sound like it was saying?"

Her eyes filled with tears. "It sounded like, 'to the water'."

"Yeah, that's what I heard too." He leaned forward and placed his head in his hands. "All those stupid, damned questions I asked Molly and that's what I get. I get Sarah whispering about that stupid pond."

Her voice was a croak. "To the water? What does it mean?"

"Could be metaphorical," he said, lifting his head and looking at her through bleary eyes. "She may be referring to the truth when she says the water."

At her dubious look, his expression hardened. "You don't believe me? What, you don't think I've studied this stuff for years?"

"What is the truth? You know exactly who killed her, don't you?"

"Maybe I do, Maddie."

"Aubrey did it," she said. "And all this stuff he's doing is to keep you from talking. Scare tactics."

"Jesus," he whispered, his lips drawing down and baffling her.

"Where are all the other EVPs?" she asked. "The ones you've caught in the past? What did the voice whisper in them?"

"You don't want to know what Sarah said, baby. You really don't." His eyes were full of sudden, unmistakable tenderness for her, and it enraged her.

She lifted her hand and directed a finger at him. "Don't call me *baby*. You intend to meet with my sister tonight behind my back. You told her that if she would take your side and help you get revenge on your cousin, you would..."

The words would not come out. She stared at him, clamped her hands together over her mouth and waited—prayed—for the moment he would deny what Lorna had told her. When silence prevailed, she dropped her hands and burst into hysterical laughter. When it died, she was left with the tears.

"Tell me why you have Aubrey's number stored in your phone. And Lorna's. And the sheriff's. What kind of twisted game are you playing?"

"You went to see her," he said. "You went to see Lorna this morning."

"You better believe I did." She gripped the upholstered cushion on either side of her. "After reading her message to you, I sent her one back on your phone. I tricked her into meeting me."

His expression laced with anguish, he turned his head to the side. "Why do you have to insinuate yourself into everything? Jesus H. Christ, Maddie."

"Your dead girlfriend Sarah sent me a text message from your cell phone and told me to look in your closet. What the hell was I supposed to do? She's trying to tell me something that you don't have the guts to say!"

Her phone beeped and she instantly clamored to retrieve it from her pants. He was on top of her and wrenching it out of her hand before she could check her inbox.

She jumped up from the couch but he held it above her reach and when she finally slumped in front of him, her eyes full of her anger and defeat, he stepped back until there were several feet between them. He pulled up the message, stared intensely at it for several seconds, and then closed his eyes.

"What is it?" she cried. "For Christ sake, give me my phone."

Across the room, the stand, which held the broom, shovel and poker, once again toppled over. The loud clang caused her head to jerk around but then the erratic movement of the rocking chair snagged her attention and she stared at it in shock.

His own eyes widening at the sight of the chair's violent rocking, Will shook his head, raised his hands to his temples.

"Stop it!" he yelled, his voice a boom that instantly caused the chair to stop moving. His hand shaking so badly it appeared he was suffering from the early stages of hypothermia, he squeezed the bridge of his nose, said something beneath his breath.

He stood there like that a moment longer, then dropped his hand and approached her, handing her the phone. She snatched it from him and read the message that was still on the screen.

*Lorna. Lorna. Lorna.*

"I don't understand," she said, and then she did understand somehow. All substance seemed to leave her body and she collapsed onto the couch, the phone gripped tightly in her hand.

"That is what the voice caught on tape said," he told her, his voice unsteady. "When I first moved up here and strange things started happening—the dreams, Sarah's voice in my head—I started experimenting with the recorder. I asked Sarah all kinds of questions and finally I got the answer I was looking for. She said, Lorna. Lorna Owens."

He paused, his hands hanging limp at his sides. "I'm sure it wasn't just a coincidence that I couldn't get this place out of my mind after I saw it listed in the real estate section of the paper. Wasn't long after I moved up here that I realized exactly who Lorna Owens was and I've been working up to this day every since, biding my time, gathering more information from my dreams and seizures."

Taking a deep breath, he crouched in front of her. "While

you were asleep, I destroyed the tape that caught your sister's name—burned it—because I couldn't bear the thought of you finding it and hearing that awful monotone voice, being alone perhaps when you put it all together."

"No," she said and her voice was almost inaudible. She shrank away from him, pressed her back into the couch and stared through tears at the floor beyond him.

"Now you see why I didn't want to tell you the truth about the past?" he pressed. "I didn't want to hurt you."

She swallowed dryly. "No. A mistake, there's got to be some kind of a mistake. You're wrong."

"I wanted to believe that too, Madison, especially after meeting you and getting to know you. But there is no mistake and Sarah isn't going to stop until I bring her closure. She's been pushing even harder since you've been here. Surely you can agree with that."

Her eyes, bright and wild with fear, landed on his. "And closure means what? You trick my sister? You arrange to meet her so you can kill her? Is that what Sarah means by 'to the water'?"

"No," he said, placing his hands on her knees. "I told you. That is metaphorical. I'm meeting with your sister in an attempt to get her to admit the truth, to admit she was the one who pushed Sarah into that pond and watched her drown. When I leave here this evening, I'm going to meet with Tritt Davidson, who is going to fit me with a wire."

He sighed. "Davidson is a corrupt man, but he's agreed to reopen the case on the condition I vouch that Sarah's baby was mine and that Jacob's involvement with her wasn't until after she was already pregnant. I know all this is a shock, but Lorna's got to be held accountable for the things she's done…for Sarah's murder."

"Aubrey's in on it too," he continued. "Turns out he approached Davidson right after I did with suspicions about Lorna. Now we're working together as informants."

She blinked and tears burned two paths down her cheeks. "You've been working with Aubrey and Davidson behind my back this whole time?"

"I don't think Tritt really knew whether to believe my claim about Lorna until Aubrey told him to ask his son about her," he said. "I think he knew then that what Jacob's been hiding all these years isn't his guilt about killing Sarah, but his guilt over knowing who did kill her."

"Why?" she said, sobbing. "Why would she have done it? If anything, it was an accident. It must have been."

He simply looked at her, his eyes exuding sadness. "My seizures and dreams...the dead show me things, Madison. They show me places and events...people. Like the trap dream I had of you...it showed me this, showed me that you would be trapped in the middle of all this, would be badly hurt. I've seen Lorna. I've seen her—"

"Trap dream?" She blinked, placed her palm to her forehead and stared at him. "No. No. You saw something about Lorna and misconstrued it. You can't do this to my family. You can't just go on a hunch and crucify my parents. Lorna is a mother for Godsake. What do you think this will do to her already emotionally scarred children? No, you can't possibly believe this is—"

"I witnessed, in one of my episodes, your sister telling Jacob Davidson that she drowned Sarah. There was no mistake. She told him and I've been visited by his shame every since. I dream of him often, know that he is eaten up with guilt. Davidson said he was going to talk to him this morning and if Jacob concedes to what Aubrey said and what I've dreamed, he will agree to fit me with a wire. I'm waiting for his call."

He inched closer to her, gently pried the phone from her hand. She gripped his shoulders and released a tiny sob. "You will destroy my family, Will."

Suddenly, she jumped up from the couch and moved away from him. Glaring at him, she wiped at her eyes. "You could have told me up front what you were about. Then at least you could have spared me this awful regret. I will never forgive myself for opening up to you. Your betrayal is worse than Jim's."

"I didn't want to hurt you, Madison." He came to his feet. "I almost didn't go through with it, almost didn't send her those text messages because of you. Do you not think I would rather spare you this? I've tried so hard to spare you, but I can't. You see how determined Sarah is, and my seizures are getting worse. My only hope is to give her what she wants. And what she wants is for her death to be avenged."

"Well, you won't be avenging her tonight," she said. "Because I told Lorna you would not be coming, that I had sent the messages pretending to be you just to see how she would respond."

His jaw clenched, then he laughed quietly. "You have no idea what you're doing by trying to stop this. I told you the seizures are getting worse. You want me to die, or worse, lose what's left of my sanity? There is more to this than what you think. I have to go through with this or you may be hurt even worse than you already have been."

"I love my sister." She lifted her hands to her face, prayer fashion. "I want Sarah to be quiet. I…just want to silence her and forget the past, whatever happened."

She squeezed her eyes shut for a few seconds, then ventured a glance at him. "I didn't tell Lorna you wouldn't be meeting her. I tried—god knows I tried to convince her not to go."

"Your sister has to answer for what she did and I have to make sure that it is done the way it's supposed to be done."

She sucked in a breath. She wanted to hate Will for what he was saying. She wanted him to be a liar, but knew he wasn't. Lorna was a very sick woman. Had been for years.

*Oh, God.*

Will spoke, his voice breaking. "I believe that the only way

I can rectify what my wife did to herself is to make right the thing that was ultimately her undoing—Sarah's murder. Please, I'm begging you, Madison. Stay out of this. Let me do what has to be done. If not for me, then for Sarah, and for my wife whom Lorna helped to destroy."

She stood there a moment longer and then ran to the guestroom, shutting herself inside.

For the first time in her life, she truly felt without options.

And distinctly without hope.

# CHAPTER THIRTY-SIX

Dwight Wray stood at the window of Tritt's Ford Explorer and adjusted a John Deere cap over his freshly sheared head.

"You're absolutely sure?" Tritt asked, flexing his fingers over the steering wheel. He glanced beyond Dwight at the section of Clinch River visible from his vehicle, pleased he had chosen this remote gravel route in which to conduct their business.

"Absofuckinglutely," Dwight said, spitting onto the shoulder of the road.

Tritt mulled it over then leveled his eyes over Dwight's. "I have to say, I never really doubted it. Aubrey wanting to do things in a lawful manner never made sense."

"He told me that he burned McGomery's barn for you," Dwight said, scratching at his eyebrow. "He also said you bragged to him about killing that dog. What the hell is going on?"

"Well, despite what you've been telling me they plan to do, I have to assume you're wrong," Tritt said. "Even if they don't go through with their plan as Aubrey laid it out to you, I'll still have something to use against that psycho bitch. She's going down one way or another, and I can make the arson stick. The dog was just a message to scare her sister away, what little good that it did."

"You've got balls of steel taking such risks," Dwight said, laughing.

Tritt snorted with contempt. "My people believe I learned of the vandalism after it took place. They think Aubrey came to me with suspicions about her hitting a mutual friend up to do the barn and the Jeep. I'll be a hero when he provides me with this DVD he's got."

"And what if he tells Will McGomery that you had all that

done just so you could be a hero? I think you underestimate the fact they're blood."

"Nobody's going to believe a couple of fuck-ups like them. Besides, to tell on me is to tell on himself, and if what you say is true, Aubrey's got too much on his mind to fool with tattling on me anyway."

"You gonna let 'em go through with it?" Dwight glanced down the road one way and then the other. "You're gonna let everyone think you're putting a wire on McGomery to catch her in a confession when you know that he and Aubrey are scheming to kill her."

"She could have landed my son in prison for that girl's murder. No one would have been the wiser. As long as she's alive, she's a threat as far as I'm concerned."

He extended a beefy hand and offered Dwight an envelope. He arched his stone colored brows when the younger man reached for it. Pulling his hand back, he glared at Dwight. "I know everything, Douglas? You know you won't get the rest unless everything goes off as you say is planned." The dumb hillbilly needed to remember who was in charge. "If you don't get the rest of the money, you won't be able to feed that habit of yours for very long."

"I've been nothing but your whore since Aubrey got out of Wallens' Ridge," Dwight said. "You know that?"

"Boy, don't you be talking down to me," Tritt warned, feeling his face heating up. "I can always stop looking the other way when it comes to your lot. You want me to bust your kid brother, put an end to all that meth he's cranking out? You want to pull a good ten years, maybe more, in prison for dealing that shit? You better be on the up and up with me about things...about the things that are going down tonight."

For the first time since approaching Tritt's vehicle, Dwight's confidence seemed to falter. He leaned forward and put his palms together under his chin.

"I swear to you that what I've told you is the truth. She's

dead. They're going to take her to the water tonight, just like I told you, and drown her." He made a motion with his hand, like a bird flying. "Then they'll be heading straight to Mexico like bats out of Hell. That is, of course, unless you head them off. With me calling in an anonymous tip, I don't see how you won't be able to head them off. You get to be the big hero, just like you wanted."

Tritt offered the envelope again and this time allowed Dwight to take it. "You just make sure you call that tip in early enough. I'll need to get some people in place out there before the McGomerys show up."

Dwight smirked. "Got it, chief."

After Dwight had left, Tritt sat there, thinking about his plan and checking his rearview mirror for vehicles.

If Dwight didn't pull through for him, there wouldn't be a place by which the man would be able to escape his wrath. He would stop at nothing to make him pay. Informants of Wray's caliber were often exploited or sacrificed to some degree for the greater cause. It was a necessity in his world, and one he didn't lose any sleep over, but in this case, Dwight was being handed a sweet, sweet deal.

What Tritt would get in exchange was even sweeter. He would be rid of two very big thorns in his side. Lorna Owens was a diabolical fruit-loop. She had done him an enormous favor by eliminating the possibility of Sarah Chambers giving birth to what could have been dubbed his son's illegitimate bastard. But she could have cost Jacob everything, might have even been hoping that he would be charged with the Chambers murder.

She and Aubrey were definitely dangerous, ultimately a threat to anyone who stood in the way of what they wanted. Tonight, one would kill the other, and then he would put the one still standing away for a very, very long time.

Will McGomery was just an added bonus. People would talk for weeks about the recluse who'd finally joined ranks with his lunatic cousin, and drowned a woman at the infamous pond where Sarah Chambers had also died.

And the wily sheriff who'd brought the whole mess to light would come out smelling like a rose.

All was as it should be.

****

Madison's heart was like a heavy rock in her chest. She came out of the guest bedroom and made her way into the kitchen. There on the table, she spotted the tape recorder that had been in her purse.

"I took the liberty of retrieving my stuff from your pocket book," Will told her from the living room.

He had put the stand that had careened across the stone hearth back in order, and was now sitting in the rocking chair that had, for a short time, taken on a mind of its own. She slowly walked to the window next to the bookcase and stared out across the drab yard, now devoid of snow.

Earlier, when she had gone to meet Lorna, the temperature had risen to what she'd guessed was the low fifties, but Will had maintained the fire he had built in the fireplace that morning and she tried to draw warmth into her body from it.

"Madison, talk to me. Please."

She didn't turn to look at him, kept her eyes fixed on the dull-looking grass outside. "Why did she do it? I need to know why?"

His answer was prompt. "Her thinking hasn't been revealed to me, just her motive. She made a flippant remark to Jacob Davidson about being the one to put it to Sarah Chambers, and obviously, he never came forward about it."

"You're not hearing me, Will. I have to know." She pressed her knuckles to her lips, trying to stanch the tears that were always lurking just beneath the surface these days.

"Look how jealous and vindictive she's been in regard to me," he reminded. "I didn't even have intimate relations with her and she's become obsessive—psychotic, even. If she was in any kind of relationship with Jacob Davidson, and discovered that he was seeing Sarah on the side, it might have pushed her over the edge. She could have been following Sarah, stalking her, could have caught her out at the pond alone. The Chambers' land adjoined mine. She and Molly used to meet there all the time. It's reasonable to assume Sarah might have frequented the pond by herself."

"You don't even know if Lorna was behind what happened up here...the barn and the Jeep. Clovis."

"I talked to Dwight, who's been helping me from the inside on all this. He says he found out from Aubrey that the barn was Davidson's brainchild. He had someone that Lorna trusts—Aubrey's girlfriend Cecilia—suggest to her that you could be frightened away for a price and she jumped at the opportunity."

His voice gentle with compassion, he continued. "Aubrey, of course, was in on all of it; he pretended to be Cecilia's secret friend who would do things for money. He did what she wanted, right down to killing my livestock, and then he and Cecilia caught her on camera talking about what was done up here. They even recorded her giving Cecilia the money to give to the fictitious friend. This is how Tritt works. It's all so that in the end, he's made to look like the super lawman saving the day. Never mind that he constantly stacks the deck in his favor."

Now she turned and faced him. "This is making my head hurt. You and Aubrey are working together to bring my sister to justice, and yet he would betray you with Davidson, do malicious things to you just so Davidson can take the credit for catching Lorna in an act of duplicity? And what happens to this Cecilia character?"

"Dwight said that Davidson told Aubrey he'd let them both just disappear after I got a recorded confession from Lorna." He rubbed his jaw. "Aubrey and Davidson can't be trusted. You know that."

"You didn't tell Aubrey the truth about you and Sarah, did you? You let him think that you were just a philandering piece of shit."

"I told you," he said. "The truth won't matter to Aubrey. Bottom line is I crossed a boundary, screwed his girlfriend."

"You're too stubborn and too stupid to know what's best for you. You could have prevented Clovis and the rest of this mess if you'd just tried to evoke Aubrey's sympathy. He might have remained your ally instead of becoming Davidson's puppet."

"Are you kidding me?" He shot up from the rocking chair causing it to rock wildly, just as it had earlier when human force hadn't been a factor. His voice, suddenly tight with anger, chafed her already raw nerves.

"He would have seen it for what it was...betrayal. My brother doesn't care about the what-fors. He only cares about the what-happens. It's why when we started working together on this thing involving Lorna, I didn't tell him the part about Jacob being interested in Sarah. I told him that Sarah had confessed to Molly that she was crazy about Jacob, and that Lorna had noticed and gotten jealous. I thought if I told him the truth, he'd make that poor bastard's life miserable, but turns out Jacob told—"

"You said brother." The silence following her pronouncement was like the void in a deep cavern.

His phone began ringing. Clearly agitated, he fished it out of his pocket. His side of the conversation consisted of a handful of words: "Yeah. I'll be looking for him. You got it."

When he disconnected, his eyes met hers. "Davidson. He's sending Aubrey up here so that we can ride together in one vehicle."

"You said brother," she repeated stoically, and his shoulders slumped somewhat.

"He's my half-brother. It's obviously not something people know about."

"Why is it a secret?" she asked, knowing her expression conveyed her shock.

He shrugged. "Our mother was divorced from my pap

when she had relations with Dow. But she was still afraid of him, and when she discovered she was pregnant with Aubrey, she was sure that he would go nuts, with Dow being his brother and all. She moved away, and then somewhere along the line, she told Aubrey the truth and he came here to take up with Dow. For all intents and purposes, Aubrey was Dow's son from a previous marriage that no one around here knew about, but believe me, Pap at least suspected, because he lived to belittle and torture Aubrey."

She flinched when someone rapped on the door. She leaned close to the window and peered out, her heart skipping a beat when she saw Aubrey McGomery waiting on the porch.

"It's him...Aubrey," she said. "I don't see a vehicle though."

"He left his car at the Tignor place and walked up," he told her. "All prearranged. The last thing we need is for your Pap to see him."

Before she could give voice to the protest on her lips, he moved over to the door and opened it.

# CHAPTER THIRTY-SEVEN

"I've seen that truck somewhere." Aubrey said, looking over his shoulder at Marshy's pickup as he stepped inside the house.

Will closed the door and nodded in the direction of the bookcase. Madison folded her arms tightly across her chest and kept her eyes away from Aubrey's.

"Belongs to her Pap," Will said as he moved back to the rocking chair. After a heavy pause, he spoke again. "She knows we're working with Davidson to get evidence on her sister."

Aubrey stood there for a moment, and then slowly walked over to the couch, causing Madison to finally look at him. He sat down and raked her over with a suggestive look.

"What, no fancy schmancy duds today? I'm disappointed."

"Look at me," Will said, "not at her."

Aubrey complied, his expression conveying that he didn't want to. Madison stared at him, scarcely believing that his only reaction to her knowing about Lorna was to offer an insult.

"You trust this bitch?" Aubrey laughed. "Man, you got it bad, don't you?"

Will glared at him. "I trust her a helluva lot more than I trust you. She didn't burn my barn down."

He stared at Will for a long moment. "You can't prove that I got anywhere near your barn."

Will's fingers curled into fists over his lap. His eyes bored into Aubrey. "I thought we were going to work together to bring Sarah justice? Not stab each other in the back. I'm on your side. What more do you want?"

Aubrey eyes lit from within like Japanese lanterns. "What more do I want? Well, for starters, I want the future your old man took from me. While you were out sewing your wild oats with my girlfriend, I was living every single rotten day of my life knowing Sarah would never have any of *my* kids."

He leaned forward, bracing his elbows on his spread knees and popping his knuckles. "I want to go back and see you take the rap for that drowning instead of me, see you raked over the coals and—"

"Like I haven't suffered any?" Will interjected. "You're completely blind, or maybe just totally stupid."

"You didn't love her like I did," Aubrey said flatly. "You just used her, big brother. You knocked her up, and that psychopath bitch killed her because she got it in her head the whelp in Sarah's belly belonged to Jake Davidson."

Will's expression softened somewhat. "I had feelings for Sarah. I lost a close friend and I lost my wife…lost everything. After Davidson got finished with you and me, I didn't even have a house, or a picture of Molly. I didn't have a single thing of hers to hold on to. Face it, Aubrey, we both got the short end of the stick, pretty much our whole lives."

"Because we had a whore for a mother, and your Daddy liked to take it out on me that he'd been sharing his wife with his own brother?" Aubrey said, snorting. "No, I got the short end of the stick because you took the one thing that ever mattered to me and you shit all over it."

"You had Dow," Will said in a level voice, but in his eyes, Madison saw evidence of his anguish. He loved Aubrey.

"Dow was ten times the father my Pap ever was," he continued. "And I didn't take Sarah away from you. It wasn't like that."

Seeing that Aubrey was about to say something nasty, his lips pulling back into a sneer, Madison took a baby step out from the bookcase. "It really wasn't like that, Aubrey."

"Stay out of it, Madison," Will barked.

Aubrey divided a look between them, finally allowing his eyes to rest accusingly on her. "What, you think you're an expert when it comes to Slick Willie because you fuck him?"

Will's eyes cut back to him and Madison took advantage.

"I may not be an expert, but I know enough about him to know he doesn't deserve your scorn."

She braced for another outburst from Will and pressed her body back against the bookshelf when he jolted up from the rocking chair. He approached her, fists clenched, eyes popping.

"Would you mind staying the hell out of this?"

Her eyes sliced to Aubrey and she saw him lean back against the couch and cross his arms over his chest in apparent contemplation.

"Our little red-headed *Señora* has pinned her heart on you, Willie," he said, his bleached denim eyes narrowing over her.

For a second, Madison could see on Will's face, his resignation, then his expression hardened and he grabbed her shoulders and gave her a firm shake, enough to rattle her teeth.

"Why? Why did you have to come back to Virginia and get in the middle of all this?"

"You don't have to go through with this," she cried. "You will crush my family and break my heart."

He let go of her. Dazed, he took a step back, lowered his head. "You have to know by now how much I don't want to do this."

Aubrey leaned forward. "But he will do this and he'll make sure you don't talk about it either."

Will lunged for the other man, yanking him up off the couch by the front of his t-shirt. Pressing his face close to Aubrey's, his chest heaving, he spoke in a voice that chilled Madison.

"If you were not my brother, I would have killed you the day you hit her."

Paling, Aubrey darted his tongue out, licked his lips. "She would have been hurt less had my attempt to scare her off been successful. Now she's a threat to what we're doing."

"Tell her you're sorry," Will ground out, his lips almost touching Aubrey's. "Tell her you're sorry or I'm going to rip your throat out."

For several seconds it was a standoff, like animals vying for the dominant role—two lions, lean and rippling with intent. Aubrey, the devious of the two but perhaps not the bravest, grabbed the hands clutching his shirt and angled back.

"Fine man, whatever. Let me do it already."

Will released him, his body still straining with the effort to contain his outrage, and Madison felt her heart kick. Aubrey begrudgingly looked at her, smoothed his hands down over the screen-printed *Bass Pro Shop* logo on the front of his shirt.

"I'm sorry for smacking you, but you had no damn business getting yourself involved in—"

Will grabbed his ear and pulled on it viciously, causing Aubrey to cry out and double over.

"That isn't good enough," he said through clenched teeth. "Try again, asshole."

Gulping, Aubrey accommodated. "I apologize. I'm sorry I hurt... insulted you, Madison."

Will let go of his ear and shoved him away. Madison marveled over the sheer fact he had galvanized the younger man with something as simple as clutching his shirt and yanking his ear. The fact they were brothers was clear to her now, and it hurt her, made her realize that she and Lorna were not without their own impossible dynamics, and that so much could go wrong with people.

So much.

"Let's just do this," Aubrey said, worrying his ear between the pads of his grease-gray fingers. "Davidson called my cell and told me to get up. He wants us to come now. We bring her with us." His eyes cut to her and then back to Will. "Surely to Christ, you weren't thinking about leaving her here. She could blow this whole thing if she gets up with her sister."

She saw Will swallow. His eyes delved deep when he looked at her.

"I can't give you the benefit of the doubt," he said. "You'll have to give me your cell phone and stay with Davidson while

Aubrey and I do this."

Her throat constricted. Both of them were going to be involved? That could mean only one thing: Tritt had decided that a bully tactic was the best bet when it came to her sister.

Somehow she could make herself believe Will had the skill to finesse something out of Lorna, if there was in fact something to be finessed out of her, but the only thing fathomable when she added Aubrey to the equation was brute force. It was unbearable to think of Lorna being alone with the two men who sought to take her freedom away from her. No matter her sister's duplicity, it was because she was mentally unbalanced. She deserved better than to be cornered like some animal.

Didn't she?

"Leave us," Will said without even glancing at Aubrey. "Wait in the truck."

Aubrey hesitated, shook his head, and then headed for the door.

"Are you crazy?" she asked as soon as the door closed. "He's capable of anything and you let him go out there unsupervised?"

"He's had his little fun at my expense and won't do anything else to me. Now he's back on track, focused on this evening. I know him."

"Well, I don't trust him. And I have my doubts about Davidson and about everything that is supposed to happen this evening." She choked the words out, started to move toward the window but he grabbed her arm, pulled her toward him.

"Well, I think it's about time you started trusting me," he said, his voice suddenly gruff with emotion. "I'm trying to do what's right."

She blinked at him. A canyon yawned between them that would separate them forever. All because he was trying to do what was right. Once he went through with this scheme to vindicate Sarah Chambers, to liberate his wife from whatever spiritual purgatory he perceived her to be in, there would be no traversing this vast wasteland of injury and heartbreak.

At that particular moment, however, she could not coax herself to pull away from him, could tell he wanted to kiss her, and could tell that his heart was breaking.

"Please trust me." The words were whispered as he dragged his lips over hers.

Tears streamed down her face. Her words wet with them, she finally twisted her head away. "To do what? I don't want you to be the one to send my sister to prison. Not you."

"It has to be me," he said, his hands roving up and down her back, molding her to him. She buried her face in his shirt.

"Why does it have to be you? Let Davidson find someone else. Let Aubrey do it without you. He and Lorna are partners in crime anyway. Let him."

A long silence passed before he spoke raggedly near her ear. "He has plans to kill her, Madison. Davidson knows and is willing to stand aside and let it happen so that he won't have to deal with looking like an ass, one that let a murderer slip through his fingers years ago. I have to be involved. I'm the only one who may be able to save her life."

She pulled back and stared at him, filled with terror. "No."

"I've seen it in my dreams many times now and Dwight has confirmed it," he explained. "I know what my brother plans to do and so does Davidson. That's why I've had to make Aubrey think that I'm on board with him. I'm the only one who might be able to talk him out of killing her, and the only way I'll have an impact is if I can talk to him when he's in the act, and doesn't have time to doubt the things I tell him."

She pushed hard against his chest. "And if you can't? Then what? What happens to you? To Lorna?"

"We need to go now," he said, moving toward the door slowly.

She splayed her fingers over her face, sobbed. "What if you can't?"

He was at the door now. He looked back at her and she

thought that she could see a little bit of his soul in his eyes.
"I will."

## CHAPTER THIRTY-EIGHT

When Will passed through the door and left Tritt's office, Madison stared after him, wondering why he wouldn't look back.

Why couldn't he give her at least that? Was it because he knew that they had shared their last few moments together? He wanted to remember those moments instead of her fear and misgivings?

She pushed out of the chair where she had been slumped for what seemed an eternity, and shot out of the sheriff's office, feeling multiple sets of eyes sliding in her direction. Tritt's startled, "Hey!" reverberated in the background.

Aubrey was ahead of Will by a foot or two in the lobby and turned as he did. She never saw his expression though, only saw the light come on in Will's eyes. She stopped abruptly, hovered on some invisible precipice. Then, she took the dive.

Flinging her body, insubstantial as it felt, at the man who stood looking haphazard as ever, with his long, tousled hair and Red Pointer Overalls, she shook with terrible sobs.

"You better come back to me," she whispered, coming up on her toes and pushing her face into his hair near his ear.

He accepted her weight and held her close, bent his face into her neck. "I swear I will."

"I can't stand this, Will. I can't."

"You heard Davidson. No unnecessary force will be used." His voice was suddenly louder and she knew he was not really speaking to her at all, was role-playing. "We'll get what we can and it will be over with quick. Whether we get a confession or not, she'll be arrested for what was caught on that camera."

He buried his lips in her curls, took a breath and filled her ear with a whisper. "Be strong, Maddie. Trust me."

She sniffed wetly and pulled back from him, offered a brief

nod in response. Tritt's office seemed miles away and she knew she had made a spectacle of herself, but she tried to keep her shoulders squared as she walked the distance. An officer approached her with a cup of coffee and she accepted it gratefully. He didn't offer any verbal assurances and she was glad.

How many of them pitied her? How many surmised or had been told that she was a willing player in this awful plan to derail her sister? How many stupidly bought the song and dance that Davidson had put on about using an informant to catch Lorna with this Cecilia woman?

All of them, she suspected. Or maybe they were corrupt too.

What the hell was this going to do to her parents?

She was burning the last bridge when it came to them. Her divorce would be nothing at all in comparison to this. It had been a tiny stone in the road. The impenetrable Marshall Owens would not only consider this a complete and utter betrayal to their family; it was going to kill the man.

*Baa, baa black sheep.*

She would watch this bridge burn because she trusted Will McGomery, because somewhere deep inside she believed that Lorna was sick and dangerous, and that two of the very men who sought to bring her to justice also meant to kill her.

There was no point attempting to get another glimpse of Will. The hulking Davidson stood in his office doorway like a watchful and stern father. She looked at him instead.

She understood him despite the fact she knew they were as different as night and day.

He was not interested in bringing justice to Sarah Chambers. He was dead set on making sure that no one found out he had let a killer slip through his fingers.

It was about pride, saving face, and at the end of the day, looking like the hero.

And that scared her to death.

# CHAPTER THIRTY-NINE

It was something as simple as Tritt Davidson's brows drawing down that convinced Madison Aubrey's plans were now in motion.

"It's probably nothing, Will," he said into the phone that was crammed against his square head. "Let's give it—hey, don't even begin to tell me how to do my job. I can't have my people tailing this woman from daylight to dark when she's given us every reason to believe she intends to show up. We'll give it some time."

He was still for a moment, and then began rubbing his forehead in obvious irritation. "That numb nut cousin of yours better stay put if he wants this as badly as he says he does. Is he still across the street like we arranged? Good, you call him on that mobile right now and tell him he's not to get impatient and divert from our plan, then keep your ass off the line. She pulls in and sees you talking on a cell, she might suspect something's up."

He leaned forward and dropped the phone in its cradle, offering Madison a commiserating look. "She's late."

And he knew why.

Though her heart lurched in her chest at his actual words, Madison found it impossible to let her guard down, to let him see the anguish in her eyes. She kept her gaze leveled at the floor.

Tritt shifted in his swivel and the casters squeaked in protest. "You okay?"

"Would you be if you were me?" she said.

He reached for the pack of Tahoe's on the desk and her eyes caught the movement. Her lips pursing with an objection, she ultimately decided to say nothing as he proceeded to light up. It had been his third in twenty minutes and her lungs felt scorched, but if it kept him calm, then more power to him. She could barely cope in his presence as it was and she certainly didn't want to see him get agitated.

"You becoming involved with William McGomery was a big mistake," he said, shaking his head. "You just made what he has to do a hundred times more difficult."

She fidgeted with the scarred arms of her chair, the very chair she had sat in when the world hadn't been nearly as nightmarish, and recited what she had told Lorna, not bothering to say it in Latin. "First do no harm, sheriff. I have nothing to feel bad about because I didn't come into his life with intent to hurt him. I only wanted my land."

"There you have it," he said, blowing smoke toward the ceiling. "That little word...*want*. It gets people in trouble every time."

She glanced behind her at the open doorway, feeling claustrophobic.

Finally meeting his eyes, she made the decision to ask the question foremost on her mind. "Explain to me how it's supposed to go down. I know the general plan, but no one has told me the specifics. Will certainly hasn't offered to fill me in."

"You shouldn't concern yourself with the procedural part of this, sweetheart," he said. "What's the point?"

Her brow furrowed with her resentment. "The point is she's my sister."

"Precisely." He tapped off the small column of ash that had accumulated at the end of his cigarette into a cloudy glass tray on his desk. "She's your sister and William McGomery's the man you've pinned your tender little heart on. Complicated enough for you, I'd say."

"All the same, I'd like to know." She sat up in the chair, stabbed him with cold eyes. "Aubrey's your back up plan, isn't he? Have Will play on her fixation with him, attempt to finesse something out of her, and then Aubrey will make an appearance so they can bully her should the wooing fail. You're going to get something out of her no matter what."

He breathed in through his nose. "Then my boys will move in and take her off their hands. She will be brought in and you, my dear, can go home."

Asshole liar. He would let Aubrey kill her.

She got up from the chair and moved to the window, parted the blinds with fingers that were trembling. "And if they don't manage to get anything tonight? Any chance you'll let this go instead of reopening the Chambers' case?"

"I think you know as well as I do that your sister's got some serious issues. She's dangerous and I'm going to use whatever lawful means I can to get her out of the community." He cleared his throat. "There's a good chance she could benefit greatly from being incarcerated. A lot of—"

"Spare me," she said, clipping off his words and swiveling her head to look at him. "Nothing you say will make this any easier. You can't buffer the blow after it's already been delivered."

"You're right," he said, stretching back in the chair and taking another drag off his cigarette.

She turned back to the window and remained standing there for a long time with her back to the room. The minutes dragged on until it seemed like hours before the phone on his desk finally rang again. She turned, watched him snatch it up.

"Yeah, I know," he said after an interminable silence. "She probably ain't gonna show. Keep trying to get her on the phone and keep me posted. It's not like she's going to be too difficult to locate. I'll have a car go by the gym in Lebanon and another by her house."

A powerful undercurrent of foreboding tugged at her. Lorna was already dead. Will wouldn't get his chance to dissuade his brother. Aubrey and Davidson had taken no chances.

Lorna would die, if she wasn't dead already.

Tritt grunted and hung up. She moved to the corner of his

desk and folded her arms across her chest, her teeth chattering as an inexplicable chill swept through her body.

"Something's wrong," she choked. "When I spoke with her this morning, she was adamant about meeting up with Will. She seemed to be of the mind that they were going to pull a Bonnie and Clyde where Aubrey's concerned. She wouldn't just stand him up."

"There's no need to get in a panic," he said, texturing the deep timber of his voice with faux fatherly concern.

He started rambling off more stupid nonsense, but she didn't hear much of it. Her mind skirted his words, shot off down the dark corridors of endless, grim possibilities.

Lorna assaulted. Maybe strangled. Raped. Lorna being held under water and drowning like Sarah Chambers. What if Will had lied and he really was on board with Aubrey and Davidson? What if he had told her he wasn't because he hadn't wanted to see her horror and hatred? What if he was Davidson's willing ruse?

She wished Sarah would send another text message, but then the point would be moot. Will had taken her cell with him, had wanted to make sure she couldn't contact Lorna. If she could just think clearly, then maybe she could figure everything out; perhaps keep from going insane.

Where would they take Lorna?

Tritt was still talking, asking her something. She looked at him in confusion.

"What?"

"I said, do you think she could be at your parents' place or with some other family member?"

Ever the actor. "I have no idea."

He sighed. "Well, we might just have to reel your boyfriend back in so you can use your cell phone to check. With caller ID and all, I can't have your folks starting a ruckus over why you're using a phone from the sheriff's department."

*To the water.*

The thought popped into her mind unbidden.

Had the plan been to take Lorna to the pond? How ironic it would be. How perfect for seeking revenge.

Will had said 'to the water' was symbolic, but it was literal. Completely literal.

*To the water.*

She had to get out to that pond. Somehow she had to find a way. Her mind worked frantically and, at last, came up with a tentative plan.

# CHAPTER FORTY

"I'm going to be ill," Madison said, certain her appearance would support her claim. Her heart had kicked into overdrive. She was suddenly in a panic, her face filmed in a cold sweat from the boost of adrenaline to her system.

"You mean you're going to throw up?" Tritt came up out of his chair. "Now that you mention it, you do look a little peaked."

She moved toward the door. "I need to find the restroom."

He barked out directions and she hurried out of his office. She assumed he would be close behind, but blocked it from her mind. Approaching the ladies restroom near the end of the hallway, she pummeled the door and tripped into the quiet sanctum of the tiled room. At the end of the stalls was a miracle—a double-hung window with frosted glass.

No point thinking it over. She checked all the stalls by peeking beneath the doors, and seeing no occupants, walked into one of the cubicles, making enough commotion with the metal door that anyone in the hallway would be able to hear her.

She began coughing, to the best of her ability simulating the act of retching. So earnest in her endeavor to fool Tritt Davidson or anyone else he might have posted out there, she actually gagged herself unintentionally and thought, for a fleeting moment, she was going to make good on losing the contents of her stomach.

Flushing the toilet, she very quietly left the stall, exceedingly grateful that she was in her rubber soled Keds. She crossed to the window and slid the dual locks. She'd estimated the thing to be at least ten feet off the ground on the other side. When she raised the bottom sash and peered out, she was astonished to discover it was only about six.

Cars were moving down the street, a line of them just released from the traffic light, but the window was near the back of the building and it was near dusk. She thought that she stood a good chance of making it undetected.

If only the window would open a little further. Pushing it all the way up hadn't allowed quite enough space for her to fit through.

"You okay in there?" It was Tritt, the tone of his voice concerned or suspicious, she wasn't sure which.

"I'll be all right," she said. "Just give me a couple minutes."

It was unfathomable that the window, the very miracle she had been bestowed, was what also presented a dilemma. There was no possible way she could squeeze through the space provided by pushing open the bottom sash.

She began studying the structure of the window itself. Perhaps the sash could be removed. It made sense. Window sashes were broken all the time and surely people didn't have to replace the whole unit.

Her fingers slid over the top of the sash, encountered two hardly noticeable, plastic nodules that she knew would enable her to tilt the window to the inside of the building. She moved to the sink and turned the tap on full blast.

Praising the engineers who had developed a feature as wondrous as the tilting window sash, she approached the window again and slid in the plastic tabs. She pulled the sash toward her and in mere seconds, discovered that it could be removed by gently jimmying it back and forth in the track.

The window did not feature a screen, and after easing the sash to the floor and propping it against the wall, her hopes were vilified.

She could fit through the opening.

****

More than anything, Will wanted Aubrey to shut up.

Pulling the truck into the parking lot of the Sunoco at Rosedale, he knocked it into neutral and jammed the emergency brake.

"You're going to have to drive. I'm getting a migraine."

Aubrey scarcely missed a beat as he reached for the passenger door. "Hell, you probably just want to kick back and daydream about that piece of tail. You got too involved with that bitch and you know it."

Will exited the truck. "Just get us back to Lebanon so I can take her to her parents and we can get on with our plans."

"Our plans should have never gotten bungled up," Aubrey hurled over the hood of the old Ford. "You should have never taken up with her. What in fucking hell were you thinking?"

Will didn't have the energy to be irate. He was using what strength he did have to try to stave off what he knew was coming, had known was coming, for the better part of the last five minutes. He passed Aubrey at the front of his truck, reached out and touched the grill when he felt himself go, felt himself sink into the abyss of black beneath him that should have been the parking lot, but wasn't.

"You're pussy whipped, Willie," Aubrey said from a million miles away. "That's what you…

# CHAPTER FORTY-ONE

*The sun shining on the water makes it appear as a mirror reflecting heaven. He doesn't see the strings of algae or the dull brown murkiness that smells of cow urine and brine. He only notices occasional squiggles of black. These are ripples caused by a fickle breeze of stored memory and they are fading fast.*

*Maybe this isn't a dream. Maybe he's in heaven. Maybe he's dead.*

*Never has water been so saturated by light—pure, pristine light.*

*He turns and there she is, standing right in front of him on the water. Water is her only background, her only history. Her hair is a halo of white around her head, her small oval face made flawless, as precise as that of a Geisha's. She wears a pale blue dress, a dress a child wears, with black patent leather Mary Janes on her feet.*

*He feels a smile stretch his face. It's good to see her standing here. Good to see her whole and tranquil. Good to see her period. It's been years since Lorna pushed her in the water, stood over her like a small, dark ghoul from some morbid dreamscape constructed of splintered wood. It's good to see Sarah's face and not just her flailing arms and Lorna's blank stare.*

*She extends those slender arms out from her sides, closes her French blue eyes and exhales lightly.*

*His smile slips a notch because somehow, he knows that she is no more real, no more tangible than a dream. And he can't change what happened to her.*

*She slowly lowers her arms back to her sides, opens her eyes.* "Surely goodness and mercy shall follow me all the days of my life. Would you like to talk to the angel now?"

*A prickling sensation is in his chest, then something, like a caress, whispers along his spine. His voice is dry sounding, like rustling papers, like old parchment.*

"No, Sarah, I'm only here so that Molly's name can be put in the book with yours. How can I make this happen?"

"The angel bequeathed unto you the gift. You have not embraced this gift."

*He knows he is in a state of being that is between dead and alive, a psychic realm where water is a mirror and the dead breathe and speak. Here he sees the ones who have passed over, and yet he is as one of them.*

*Suddenly, he wants desperately to return to Madison Owens, whom he loves more than he ever thought possible. He's getting cold and a worm has begun to gnash microscopic teeth against his brain, creating a dull buzz of pain behind his eyes.*

*The black scribbles have returned. Everything goes dim, then black.*

*He hears another voice, an insistent whisper like the drone of an agitated insect. He recognizes the hoary sound of it—it is the whisper of Veronica Chambers.*

I want my name in that book, Sonny.

*The black curtain of his subconscious vision parts yet again and the pond, more like a small lake, stretches before him like a rose tinted mirage in the twilight. What is left of the sun has found its way through the bank of clouds, and creates a hidey-hole that is full of red, syrupy light.*

*He spots her on the shadowy dock, the dilapidated old boards still nailed together, years beyond the death of the old man who built the thing. She's at the end of it as though she's thinking of jumping in.*

*More a girl than woman, really, Sarah's blond hair catches the ornate pinks in the carnival midway hole in the sky and makes her head appear as though gilded by a little bit of heaven's light.*

*She turns and offers him more than just her lovely profile, offers him her face full on, and it radiates a smile that is more childish than it ever was while she was alive. A breeze stirs and lifts a wispy lock of pink white hair off her glowing cheek. Inside, he shudders with the purity of the moment.*

*A voice assaults him. It isn't Sarah's voice. This voice is loud, shoots through his eardrums and pierces the sleeping part of his brain.* "What the hell is wrong with you, Willie?"

*Sarah's happy expression collapses. Her mouth forms a perfect little inverted bow, like the pout on a doll's face. He is drawn back from the scene and he views the pond from a great distance. Sarah is but a tiny figure standing on the dock.*

*He wants to move toward her, see her plainly again. It seems to be of utmost importance to get back to the pond, back to her. Instead of willing himself to zoom back in with his third eye, though, he focuses on the sensation of being stared at from behind.*

*He knows before he turns that it is Molly who watches him.*

*When his eyes fall upon her, he sees that her face is bathed in the fading pink light of their final sunset together. How he knows this will be the last time he ever sees her, the last dream he ever has of her, he isn't sure. He just knows and it fills him with a great and consuming sadness.*

*She speaks his name, smiles and then calls him by the name she affectionately hung on him years ago. They had been on maybe their third date. She'd asked him what his middle name was and he had told her it was Joel. She laughingly called him Billy Joel then asked him if she'd always be a woman to him. He'd sung a line of the song to her and they'd laughed like kids and then made love in the tall summer grass behind his grandparents' barn.*

*A sound rips from his throat, a sob that has been years in the making.* "I'm sorry. Oh God, I'm so sorry. I shouldn't have left you alone that week. Please forgive me. Please forgive me, Molly."

*She places her finger over her lips. She says nothing, but he hears her thought and it is beautiful.*

*All is forgiven.*

*As though she is but a digital image, she jolts before him. Pixilated segments of her dance like fireflies with glowing pink tails. He tries to speak, to pull her back into clarity, but she explodes into a cloud of mist that blackens before his eyes like windblown soot.*

*Drawing breath into his lungs raggedly, he hears the intrusive voice again—concerned, somewhat frightened.* "Willie, come on, you stupid dumb shit, snap out of it.*"*

*The words meld together. Snapoutofit. Something about having to be with a pretty Señorita, a pretty little honeybee.*

*He doesn't want to listen to this nonsense. He wants to know how he can get Molly's name in that idiotic book, wants to know how to embrace this gift he has been given, but on and on, this voice is like loud applause in his head. Someone is clapping hands in front of his face. No, they are using their hands to slap his face.*

"Snap the hell out of it. The clock is ticking, man."

*He turns in his head and looks longingly at the pond. The pink reflection that sparked the spades of ripples in the water has faded. The sky has closed up and it is near to dark now.*

*Sarah isn't anywhere that he can see.*

*He has to leave, has to go with Aubrey to the pond. He knows it exists on another plane. Yes, he must indeed snap out of it.*

*He will give the dead what they want: absolution. He has already lost Madison. He senses it deeply, profoundly. He has nothing else to lose.*

*He closes his eyes, wills himself back into his conscious mind. Cannot.*

*A bleating sound has started up in the distance and he's afraid of what is behind it. It's a stark and hideous fear, and it has a coppery texture to it, like a penny in his mouth.*

*His hands are over his ears. He wills his legs to move, to take flight into the woods beyond, but he's immobile, seemingly paralyzed.*

*He knows it's behind him, hears the rustling, but hears Sarah's whisper as well.* "It is only the angel," *she says.*

*Instead of feeling the bite of his fear in his bones, he feels something else swelling in his subconscious mind like an enormous white bud on the brink of blossoming. Clarity. He sees Tritt Davidson clutching his chest and collapsing over his desk. He will be like Humpty Dumpty. All the king's horses and all the king's men will not be able to put him back together again.*

*It is a simple thing to turn and face the pond. Right before his eyes, a black mist is rapidly congealing into something that looks like a cross between an angel and a vampire. It has great raven black wings and they are still flapping, only the sound is the rustling not the thunderous claps from a moment ago.*

*The angel stands without garment, but with long platinum hair that cascades like a waterfall down its back. He sees that it is both male and female, with a phallus, but also breasts. Veins like intricate patterns of purple lace are visible beneath a sheathing of skin – skin that is translucent and white as a desert sky.*

*He waits for it to decide his fate, silently conveys what he wishes to happen. He wants this more than anything he's ever wanted—to return and have a normal life with Madison Owens.*

"You have embraced the gift of forgiveness," *the angel says to him,* "you have set them free."

*As foul smelling as a goat that has not been withered, the angel lifts a hand. It can only be described as the hand of a mighty seraph; it raises and one white fingertip is pressed into the center of his forehead.*

*All is eerily silent and then his mind fills with the sound of someone's voice, urgent, concerned.*

"You okay, buddy? You need us to call for help?"

Blinking up into a stranger's face, Will struggled to shake off the remnants of his seizure. A crowd of people hovered around him. The one closest to him, the one that has just asked him a question spoke again.

"Your friend just up and left you here, drove away. He said he didn't have time to fool with you."

Will's phone began to ring, and he fumbled to get his hands on it. Consulting the display window—blinking like mad to get his eyes to focus—he read the unfamiliar name and number, and decided to answer it anyway.

His heart banged against his ribs when he heard Madison's frantic voice.

# CHAPTER FORTY-TWO

"Where are you?" Acutely aware of the people still gathered around him, Will tried to steady his breathing, shook his head rapidly at the guy still waiting for him to answer his question. "No, I don't need an ambulance. I'm an epileptic, happens all the time. Just need a minute to get my wits about me."

Evidently Tritt's guys had not kept an eye on him and Aubrey after Tritt had told them to come back in. They would have no reason to. They didn't have a clue about what was going to happen later that night.

He heard Madison's excited voice in his ear. "I was able to sneak out of there. What's going on?"

"I had a seizure and Aubrey took off in my truck," he said, trying to wrap his mind around the fact that she had escaped the sheriff's office. "We were on our way back. I was going to take you to your parents and meet up with him later at the pond as planned. He's diverted from what we agreed on, he's panicked."

He gulped for air. "Tell me where you're at."

"I'm hitching a ride to my parents." Her breath was choppy, like she was scared out of her mind. "I'm telling Daddy what's going on. I can't do this by myself. I can't face this alone."

"How did you manage to get away from Davidson?" he said, feeling a wave of nausea roll over him. "Listen to me. Don't do anything stupid. Go to your parents if you must, but don't tell them anything. I may be awhile but I will come for you. Wait for me. Can you do that? Can you go to your parents and just wait for me? We'll tell them together, Madison."

Silence greeted him. She had lost signal or else hung up. He snapped the phone shut, too preoccupied with other things to deal with her and Marshy Owens. He couldn't call her back anyway. What could he say with all these people staring at him? I'm going to the pond to finish this thing once and for all?

*I love you, Maddie.*

He should call her back and tell her that, at least.

Glancing around, he saw that a few of his spectators had, in fact, moved away from the scene. He climbed to his feet unsteadily, looked at the three that remained, and cleared his throat.

"Anyone headed toward Big A Mountain? I need to get there fast."

****

Madison thanked the young woman profusely for the use of her cell phone and for the ride, and then got out of the Civic.

Just as he'd agreed to on the phone, Marshy had parked his Lincoln Town Car to the side of the Double Kwik Market at the mouth of New Garden. He leaned over and opened the door for her and she spilled into the passenger seat.

"I was on my way to meet you and I received a call on my cell," he said unceremoniously, his face pale beneath his silver hair. "It was made from McGomery's phone but it was a woman. All I could make out of what she was whispering was…"

His voice broke and she placed her hand on his arm, wanting to run from the car so she did not have hear whatever he was about to say.

She bit into her lower lip, sucked in air. "What did the woman say, Daddy?"

He shook his head, slow at first and then vigorously. "Tell me what's going on, Madison. You tell me right now. You call me from some stranger's phone, won't tell me anything, and then I get this other phone call from someone who shouldn't have any idea what my number is—McGomery doesn't even know this number unless you gave it to him. What is going on? Do you know where your sister is? We can't get hold of her."

"I think the plan wa—was to take her to the pond where

Sarah Chamber's drowned," she stammered, unable to give voice to all the horrible thoughts that filled her mind.

"Those bastards," he said between clenched teeth. His fingers squeezing over the steering wheel, he looked at her through tears. "I told her to leave them alone. And now here you're a part of it all. Right in the middle of it too."

"I never meant to be," she whispered, scarcely believing that she was, in fact, a part of it. "I only found out today that…"

She paused and looked at him, her chest aching. "I only found out today that Lorna drowned Sarah Chambers. Will told me. He said that he's been working with the sheriff to gather evidence against her, but then discovered that Tritt was actually aware of Aubrey's plan to kill her. Daddy, Tritt Davidson has no intention of stopping Aubrey. Will is going to try to stop him."

He rolled his lips inward, redirected his eyes to his lap. "You can't believe that. He's just told you that, but he's really a part of it."

"No," she said. "He does want Lorna to be held accountable for what she did to Sarah, but he believed that Tritt and Aubrey were on the same page as he was. He had a friend on the inside that told him what was really going on. This guy, this Dwight, told Will that Lorna paid someone to have all those things done…the barn, my Jeep, and Clovis. She's so messed up, Daddy. I think she's truly insane."

His fleshy cheeks trembled. "All my years of silence have done nothing to protect her." He placed his head to the steering wheel. "Maddie, I tried so hard to discourage you from seeing McGomery because of this Sarah Chambers mess. I was desperate, just wanted to scare you the hell away from there. The way he acted when Lorna developed that crush on him, I had a gut feeling that he knew about what she'd done. I was terrified that he had bought the land simply to get closer to her family, to her, and was eventually going to kill her."

She stared at him. "You've known all along that she killed Sarah Chambers."

He lifted his head and reached for the cell phone in the console. She grabbed it.

"We've got to call the state police, Maddie," he said, his expression conveying his shock. "You know we do."

She shoved the phone into her pants pocket and then drove her fingers into her hair, squeezed up fistfuls of it. "I can't take a chance of them showing up and thinking Will is involved. He told me to trust him. I think he can talk Aubrey out of it. I've seen them together. They're brothers, Daddy, not cousins, and Will can get through to him."

"What?" His eyes lit from within, incredulous.

She nodded fervently. "It's the truth. They have different fathers, but share a mother."

His face florid, Marshy started the car and entered the flow of traffic heading into Honaker. "I'm going to recover Lorna's body, that's what I'm doing. Whoever that woman he had calling me said as much. She said they were 'taking her to the water'. I'm telling you, McGomery is in on this, and I'm going to put a bullet in him as well as his brother. Screw the police."

She could not bring herself to tell him that it was a ghost that had called from Will's phone. Instead, she said the only thing she thought might break through his enraged thinking.

"He has given me his word. At least give him a chance to prove himself. Please, Daddy. I beg you."

He blinked several times before his expression softened. "I will give him one chance, Maddie. One. And if he blows it, then I'll kill him on the spot and gladly go to prison."

"How did you know she did it?" Her voice almost nonexistent, she leaned toward him. "Does Mama know?"

He shot her a look, wiped at his eyes with the back of one large hand. "Of course she doesn't know. Back when that Chambers girl drowned, I...I noticed something different about your sister. I can't explain it, but the change scared the hell out of me. I had this feeling that I couldn't shake, a feeling that she had had something to do with that girl's death. I kept her on such a long leash, and she could be so jealous and volatile at times. Your mother noticed the change in her as well after that drowning, noticed how she withdrew, and I assured her that I would talk to her and find out what was going on."

"And you did?" she asked, allowing her tears to slide down her face.

"I asked her why she was acting so strangely, holing up in her room instead of chasing after her friends as usual." He stared at the road ahead through tears that left his face shiny with moisture.

"She said, 'nothing Daddy. There ain't nothing going on'. I couldn't bear to know, couldn't bear to face it. I told her that I wasn't stupid, but if she would get her act together, marry and settle down, I'd never press the issue, that we'd make like I'd never asked her anything. She promised she would do whatever I wanted."

He gasped, his sob startling Madison. He shook his head back and forth and dragged a hand across his face again. "I couldn't tell your mother that she killed that girl. How? How could I have done that to her, told her that her baby was a cold blooded killer?"

"I know," she said, forcing the words out. "I wasn't able to speak of it either. I even tried to dissuade Will from going through with what he believed was the right thing because I couldn't bear the thought of what the truth would do to you and Mama. And then he told me the rest of it, how Aubrey planned to kill her, and I didn't know what to do."

He gestured at the glove compartment. "I don't want you coming down there with me. You stay in the car and wait for me or I let you out right now. I'll be damned if I lose two daughters in this."

She knew that to argue would serve to stress her father even more, and he already appeared dangerously close to a stroke. She would let him think that she was okay with staying in the car and when he was a few yards away, she would follow him.

She had to follow him.

"Daddy," she began, her voice crumbling like a sandcastle with the tide. "Maybe there's a chance we—you will be able to intervene. We have to hope—"

"We have to pray," he said, accelerating as soon as he crossed the railroad tracks that passed through the outskirts of town. Speeding up the first incline that would lead them into the series of easy curves that led into the foothills of Big A Mountain, he was silent for a moment.

When he spoke again, his words formed an anchor that pulled her heart down into the endless depths of despair.

"If my nightmares over the years prove right, I'll be too late."

# CHAPTER FORTY-THREE

"He said the pond is beyond the trees spanning the area behind where the house once stood," Madison told Marshy, her eyes adjusting to the darkness.

He had pulled the Lincoln off the road into the tall grass a good distance from the gated road that led to the pond. Now he clicked on the flashlight she'd handed him from the glove compartment and consulted the pistol she had also brought forth.

"I know, I used to frequent the pond as a boy," he said, snapping the cylinder on the gun closed. He motioned ahead of them.

"You can see the entrance to the road from here. If anyone comes out of there, you get down out of sight. I keep a small towel in the glove box. Hand it to me and I'll put it in the window to make it look like I was someone who broke down."

"What happens if you find her...?" She didn't think she could say the word *dead* so she didn't attempt it. "Should I call for the state police? We can't have that vulture Davidson circling."

He reached over—she knew possibly for the last time—and pulled her roughly against him. "If I make it back, we call the state boys and we take it as it comes, Maddie. I don't know how it will play out, but we'll do what we can to obtain justice in the days to come, even if I go to prison for murder. I intend to kill Aubrey McGomery, and the sheriff too if he makes an appearance tonight."

He pulled back and held her by the shoulders. "If I'm not back after thirty minutes, you call anyway and wait for them to arrive. I mean it. You don't come down there."

She nodded.

It was perhaps the biggest lie she never uttered.

****

The night was inky black without the moon's glow. A light breeze rustled through the trees that dotted the pastureland, stirring the leaves made crispy by the premature snow.

It wasn't balmy by any means, but it wasn't cold either.

Madison shivered anyway.

Marshy was somewhere ahead of her. She couldn't hear him, had given him a large lead, but she was acutely aware that he was heading into danger. Guilt was a factor, and she almost regretted calling him. But she had needed him to know the truth. She could not have gone through with this had she not let him know her part in all of it. She could not have risked her life, and also risked her parents thinking she had been conspiring against her sister.

She hadn't been, and now she was fighting to save Lorna's life. Will was fighting to save her as well, even though he must truly despise her. He had become her sister's only hope.

She moved down the dirt road, careful to stay in the tire ruts for the time being. The pungent smell of cow manure filled her nostrils, and she guessed that she had stepped in some of it. She was aware of everything, knew that she must keep her eyes peeled and her ears attuned to every sound, including her own.

She had to be a ghost.

The thought unnerved her. It was a ghost that had brought her here. Sarah Chambers. It was hardly an inconceivable notion at this point. The young woman's spirit had even reached out to her father.

*To the water.*

Now they were fulfilling a destiny. Sarah's. Their own.

Will had told her to stay at her parents' farmhouse. He had told her not to do something stupid.

Her actions weren't any more stupid than his.

So many times she had considered calling him again, but fear, like a razor sharp knife twisting through her thoughts, would not permit her too.

She could not call him, could not bear to hear something in

his voice that might make her aware that he had failed, could not bear the thought of him not answering her call at all. She would face this, head on. Pray she would find him whole, and Lorna.

Big Sissa Lorna.

It had been so long since she had prayed, but she was compelled to do so now.

Would God even listen to her? Could she even expect him to? She had turned her back on God about the same time she had started believing it was her fault that Jim had turned to another woman. She thought that God had turned his back on her as well.

*Please, if not for me, then for Mama and Daddy, for Lorna's children. Please don't let her be dead. Please. Please. Please.*

The breeze lifted a wisp of hair off her face. Perspiration, like a cold sheen of tangible fear, had gathered between her breasts, her thighs, soaked into her shirt and pants. Still, she moved down the road until she came to the area where she thought the old McGomery house had stood.

A barn, leaning precariously to the left, still remained. She slipped by it, the tall brittle Rye grass hissing with each cautious step. Her father had taken another route, for she was sure that she could not see a bend or a channel in this sea of gray. It occurred to her that she might get to the pond before him.

It didn't matter. She would hover at a distance until she saw him, until she saw something. She would act according to her instinct. She had the phone she had taken with her from the Lincoln. At any time she could call for the state police, hit Star 99.

Though her mind strongly doubted the idea, she told herself that Davidson could be brought down, exposed. Her knowledge of the semi-automatic handgun her father had taken with him was hardly a comfort. It was much easier to believe that Davidson would be the one making an arrest and that her father would be charged with multiple crimes.

How long had it even been since her father had fired a gun? She knew so little about him it seemed. Life had made them strangers and she was suddenly so ashamed that she had allowed it to happen. She had been so prideful and stupid with him. And he had done nothing but try to protect her from this.

He had known that she was in the midst of real danger, and she had snubbed her nose at him.

Tears filled her eyes and made the swaying grass around her seem like a churning sea of malcontent. She entered the cropping of Poplar trees, glad to be out of the whispering abyss where invisible hands snaked through the stalks and grasped at her ankles.

The maze of trees was more difficult to navigate than the grass, however, and several times she was forced to pick her way through Green briar that was both painful and tenacious. Her fingers bore the pricks, and beneath her clothing, her legs and torso obtained long, stinging scratches. She began to pray yet again, silent supplications emanating from her mind and leaving her vocal cords in the form of low whimpers that seemed to be not coming from her at all, but from the trees around her.

Be quiet. She had to be quiet, had to make the whispers stop. She reached the edge of the woods and saw the pond, an impressive bowl in the land that stretched far and ended at the edge of a forest that seemed to have no beginning or end.

She wrapped her arms around a tree, breathing like she had been chased by dogs. She pressed her cheek into the rough bark and stared at the black water. How far away was she from it? A hundred yards? She was a terrible judge of distance, something that hadn't improved with her elevating anxiety. She closed her eyes and tried to calm her senses.

Panic caused her eyelids to spring open wide. She must not squander even a moment. Lorna's life hung in the balance. So perhaps, did her father's, Will's, and her own. She scanned the perimeter of the pond. Saw nothing moving, heard only the slight rush of the leaves stirring in the poplars.

Close to her on the right, in the field leading up to the pond, she made out the shape of cattle, lying in the closely cropped grass. They were like white boulders, except she could suddenly hear them chewing cud, hear their heavy breaths riding on the night air.

Where was her father?

Where was anyone?

The gate she had crossed back on Route 80, the gate that blocked the road to the McGomery house ruins and the pond, had been padlocked. If Lorna had been brought here, then she had been brought by another route. Madison had no idea how many other gated roads there were leading to this property.

A standard issue cattle fence with a single strand of barbed wire skimming the top was within ten feet of her. She would have to cross it if she were to skirt the perimeter of the pond. Crossing it would put her at risk of being spotted. She stood there clinging to the tree, wishing the pressure of it against her breast would somehow suppress the erratic beat of her heart.

Then she heard it. Voices. The breeze had changed, wafting the sound toward her. It seemed from off the waters of the pond itself.

Men.

Her father? Aubrey? Will?

She scoured the bank of the pond, could just make out a fishing dock. How she had missed it, she didn't know. The night was so completely dense that, at times, it squeezed upon her eyes like pinching fingers.

She pushed away from the tree and moved up the fence line using the trees as cover. Then, she quite suddenly realized she had come into the presence of another entity, something that hovered in the darkness. Perhaps lying in wait. She came to a dead standstill, the hairs on her nape prickling in alarm.

They were behind her. She felt it with every fiber of her being, very slowly started to turn around. That was when a hand clamped over her mouth, and someone's lips pressed hotly against her ear, the words a mere whisper against her skin.

"Don't make a sound, Maddie."

## CHAPTER FORTY-FOUR

Madison wilted in her father's crushing embrace. After a moment, he released her, allowed her to turn around. Then he seized her shoulders and began to shake her.

"I told you to wait," he hissed.

She raised trembling hands and placed them over his. "I couldn't let you come alone, Daddy. I involved you in this. The least—"

"Hush, girl." He pulled her into a hug and pressed a kiss to the side of her head. "I've always been involved. From the moment I asked Lorna what was going on years ago and turned a blind eye, I've been involved."

His whisper was strained. "They're down there. I can make out four of them and I think one is your sister. I think they've bound her arms and legs. I'm going."

"Oh God, wait!" She clutched fistfuls of his shirt. "You can't go. Let's call—"

"Please, you have to stay calm," he whispered fiercely. He pulled back and swept her matted hair away from her forehead. "I'll be careful. They're not going to see me. I won't do anything unless they force me to. Call the state police and tell them you have information about a murder taking place out here and that the sheriff is involved."

He shook her again. "Okay, Maddie?"

Though his instructions had seemed outlandish, she nodded quickly and she fished the phone out of her pocket. After he had crossed the fence, and she let out the breath she had been holding, she crouched down and braced her quaking body against a sapling.

She made the call.

****

The sounds that Lorna Owens made behind the duct tape

slapped over her mouth were unnerving.

Will was glad he couldn't clearly see the horror and pleading in her eyes as she stood there on the dock that his grandfather had built, trembling in her restraints. He'd always known that his brother could be cruel, but somehow, he'd had it in his mind that Aubrey would be more humane when it came to taking the life of another human being, a woman no less.

What a fool he'd been about a lot of things, most especially about what he himself was doing at the moment. Aubrey was hesitating, giving thought to all that he had been saying to him, but he had underestimated the power that Cecilia Onate held over his brother.

He sensed Aubrey was anxious to take action, to do *something*. Panic had set in and Cecilia continued to exacerbate it. She had been spouting off in excited Spanish from the moment they had emerged from the woods, Lorna thrown over Aubrey's shoulder like something no more significant to him than a sack of potatoes.

Yes, it was very clear that Cecilia Onate was coming unglued and was making his younger brother incredibly nervous.

"*Empújela*," she said, nudging Lorna and causing a fresh torrent of whimpers to bubble up in the woman's slender throat. "Push her into the water."

Lorna almost fell against Aubrey, but managed to catch herself, weaving backward and forward in her tightened ropes to maintain her balance.

Cecilia grabbed hold of Aubrey's sleeve. By the tone of her voice, Will imagined that her dark eyes were as pleading as Lorna's. "*Por favor*. We must hurry, Aubrey. *Prisa*. Use the gun and be done with both of them."

Aubrey shrugged Cecilia off, and her voice erupted into sobs.

Will opened his mouth to speak again, but before he could, Cecilia shoved Lorna, causing the bound woman to pitch forward violently. Lorna fell into him and he lost his balance. They both tumbled into the water, she on top of him. It seemed like forever before he was able to surface with her.

He heard Cecilia first.

"*Prisa para arriba*, Aubrey! Hurry, shoot them, shoot them!"

Then came the unmistakable sound of a gun discharging. Lorna, close to his right ear, made a high-pitched sound as he struggled to tread the water while still supporting her weight.

"Be quiet," he growled, spitting water. "Or I'll let you drown, Lorna."

Her whimpers immediately tapered off. He hauled her toward the bank beneath the dock, relieved beyond measure that the tactic had worked and she was no longer making sounds that Aubrey could track.

He heard Cecilia sobbing, high frantic words he couldn't understand.

What the hell was happening up there? Had Aubrey shot her? Why was she carrying on like that?

Now struggling through the soft muck that made up the pond's sloping floor, he finally managed to wedge Lorna beneath the dock.

"Don't move or make a sound," he whispered harshly. "I don't know what's going on, but someone will be waiting for us to surface. I'd bet on it. You'll have a chance to make it through this alive if I leave you here."

She nodded her head up and down, her eyes wide with fear. He ducked down to leave, but turned back and leaned in close to her. His lips brushing her cheek, he whispered into the dank stench of mud and briny water.

"Just so we're clear, I'm not doing this for you. I'm doing this for Madison."

He sloshed his way up the bank, half expecting to be shot on the spot. When he came level with the field, the beam of a flashlight pelted him.

Cecilia still sobbed hysterically. "*Mi más querido*, Aubrey! No! Please no."

Aubrey was down, had to be, but who had shot him?

And who was it that had that same gun trained on him?


Madison stumbled into the clearing and ran headlong into the fracas, her breath leaving her lungs in a whoosh when her eyes honed in on what the flashlight in her father's hand revealed. Will, dripping wet and empty handed, squinted against the light. Her heart capsized and was flooded with liquid horror.

"Go back in and get her, Will!" Marshy screamed again. "I'll shoot you down like just like those two if you don't."

As Will stumbled back down the bank, she glanced to the dark figures on the ground a few feet away. The woman was crying piteously, murmuring in Spanish.

"*Mi amor, mi corazón. Te amo. No morir. Por favor...no morir*," she sobbed.

Madison swallowed tightly. She could see the woman hunched over what she suspected was the prone body of Aubrey McGomery.

"You can not die," she screamed, pounding her fists against him, the sound of it like a distant stampede to Madison's ears.

Was this the Cecilia she had heard about? Aubrey's girlfriend? And why had Will come out of the water without Lorna?

The beam of the flashlight shifted momentarily to the couple on the ground and she gasped. Aubrey was unquestionably dead, a round from Marshy's pistol having obliterated his larynx. A river of blood had flowed from the gaping hole, probably still seeping slowly into the ground. It covered the woman sprawled across his chest.

Aubrey's eyes were fixed, glazed over, his expression still twisted into a grimace of surprise and pain. The woman saw this and recoiled, trying to crawfish backward. Madison spotted the ugly bloom of blood on her jeans, just below the thigh. Marshy nudged her and she looked away from the disturbing scene.

"I got his gun," he said. "When he went down, he dropped it and I got it. Hold on to it."

She cringed, but took the weapon. The grip was warm. In a movie or a book, perhaps she would use it to make sure Aubrey's girlfriend, accomplice in murder, did not crawl away.

But in reality, she would not use the gun no matter what.

"Where the hell did he go?" Marshy asked no one in particular, and she knew he was referring to Will.

He waved the flashlight and a swath of light swept across the bank. The pond beyond was a black abyss, not glittering at all in the flashlight's weak beam. She heard something, wasn't sure what. It was like the soughing of the cattle she had heard while in the woods, a softly abrasive sound. Then whimpering. And grunting.

Marshy took several steps toward the bank and the gun quivered in his left hand, as did the flashlight in his right. She heard the sucking sound of Will's boots fighting the sticky muck along the bank.

The water had likely receded several feet down the bank that summer because it seemed to take him forever to make it to the top. When he did appear, he was holding her sister to his chest, severed ropes hanging from her wrists and ankles. Lorna was blinking furiously against the single glaring eye of the flashlight.

She had a sense of Marshy rushing forward, of herself sinking to the ground. Aubrey's heavy gun slipped from her fingers and she left it there on the ground beside of her. A sound bubbled up and out of her throat, like the strangled cry of a bird, and she forced herself up, hurried toward the three of them. Will eased Lorna's feet to the ground and brought a hand up to rip off the tape covering her mouth.

Lorna gasped at the night air, the sound of it automatically reminding Madison of the sounds Sarah Chambers had made in her nightmare. Clutching Lorna to her and feeling Marshy embrace them both, she sobbed, wept for Sarah and for her sister, whose lives were both over in one way or another. Lorna's own voice was a hoarse sound near her ear, hardly audible. "Aubrey and Cecilia...they were going to drown me, Maddie. Will hid me under the dock."

"It's okay," she croaked, squeezing her eyes closed. "Everything is going to be all right. We'll get you help. You'll see. We will get—"

"Madison," Will said huskily from behind Lorna. His face was cast in deep shadow and she realized that her father had dropped the flashlight, realized also that her father had sunk down onto the ground.

She instantly dropped to her knees. "Daddy? Are you okay?"

"I will be. You and McGomery make sure Aubrey's woman stays put."

She picked up the flashlight and moved toward Cecilia, ascertained that she was still on the ground. The woman squinted at the light and continued to sob, more quietly than before. She swung the light toward Will and Lorna then and her heart stopped at the sight of them.

Will was using his pocketknife to cut the ropes the rest of the way off of her and Lorna's eyes were on his face, radiating her love for him. When he was finished, she flung them weakly around his neck, and reflexively his arms came around her, causing Madison to take a step back.

"I love you, Will," Lorna cried. "You saved my life. You saved me."

Madison lowered the flashlight, her mind churning at her sister's words. She heard the Hispanic woman's hiccups and aimed the light back at her.

Cecilia was now lying flat on her back, her chest rising and falling with irregular breaths. Perhaps she was dying. The idea of comforting the woman was repulsive; yet a part of her needed to, needed to make her human, make her a person instead of this thing that had wanted to kill her sister.

Her heart. Her love. That was what she had called Aubrey. She had loved him, enough to stand by him while he committed murder. This Cecilia had been no less heartless than her lover, and yet was likely just another victim in this whole mess her sister had started many years ago.

"Stop it, Lorna. You sicken me." It was Will, and she turned at his mumbled words, knew then just how much he detested the woman clinging to him. Knew also just what kind of risk he had taken to save Lorna's life.

He was a man riddled with guilt, haunted by his past and by the girl that had been his one downfall in life.

She would never love any man as much.

## CHAPTER FORTY-FIVE

Will took the flashlight from Madison and she watched him move over to where Aubrey lay motionless in the grass.

"Goddamn it," he said, his voice a slither of rancorous anger. "He was listening to me, he was listening to reason."

He sliced the light to Cecilia, still whimpering a short distance away. Going over to her, he knelt and surveyed her wound.

"Here," he said extending Madison the light. "Hold this."

She came over immediately and held it for him as he removed his shirt. "You're going to make a tourniquet?"

"Yes," he said. "Hold the light on her."

While he did just that, she watched in a sort of trance, watched as the muscles in his damp arms worked beneath the skin. The woman watched as well. Several times her eyes clashed with Will's and once, in virulent Spanish, she asked him if he was proud that he'd killed his own flesh and blood for Madison's sake.

He chose not to answer.

Marshy began to weep, rough sounds that were like sandpaper to Madison's heart. He didn't understand Spanish, as far as she knew, but the woman's tone must have conveyed her despairing rage.

"I had to do it," he said, casting Cecilia's dim form an anguished look. "You should count your blessings you're still breathing."

Again, she turned her attention to Will, watched him tie a second strip of his ripped shirt around the woman's leg. Perplexed that he might hate her father for defending Lorna, she spoke into the unpredictable silence.

"Will, do you really think you were making any headway with Aubrey? I think he was going to kill Lorna no matter what."

He stood and faced her. "He was listening to everything I said. I think if gunslinger there hadn't panicked and started shooting, Aubrey would have allowed me to turn your sister over to the authorities. He and Cecilia could have left, gone on to Mexico to live with her family as they'd planned all along."

Marshy approached and his voice trembled when he spoke. "What was I supposed to think? That woman was hollering things I couldn't understand and then I heard the splash. Wasn't any of you going to stand in my way of saving my daughter. I can tell you that right now."

Cecilia laughed behind Will. "Serves you right, Tonto. Now you will rot in prison for killing my Aubrey."

Madison heard sirens. She felt suddenly off kilter like she had been on an amusement park ride. She was going to be sick. Or maybe pass out.

God, had Aubrey really been reconsidering?

Will's eyes narrowed against the light she held unsteadily over him, "It doesn't matter now. The three of us will say that Aubrey was shot only because Marshy thought both his life and Lorna's was at risk, as well as mine. He only acted as a last resort."

Cecilia started cursing in Spanish and Marshy spoke over top of her. "It's the truth! I had no choice but to try to protect my own."

The sirens were getting louder. Will looked beseechingly into the glare. He swallowed, his Adam's apple bobbing and his blue eyes sparkling with tears. "Maddie, I'm sorry I yelled at you just now. I know that your Pap was against a rock and a hard place. I just hate that Aubrey is...I...loved him."

She opened her mouth to tell him that she was sorry too, so very sorry that his brother was gone, but a deafening blast caused her to drop the flashlight and fall to the ground, hands over her head. She heard a heavy thud like a bag of cement mix being dropped from a few feet above the ground.

She knew instinctively it was Will.

She grappled for the flashlight and screamed when she saw him crumpled on his side, blood seeping rapidly into the denim bib over his chest.

The sirens were so close now, and something else was encroaching upon the scene as well. A helicopter. Its powerful searchlight dissected the field beyond the pond.

Reflexively, she arched the light around until it landed on Lorna, who was still holding Aubrey's gun, the gun Madison hadn't wanted to touch. The gun that she had left on the ground.

Her voice competing with the percussive *whoop-whoop* of the helicopter, Lorna smiled vacantly. "I was crazy about Jacob and that stupid bitch Sarah ruined my chances with him. He didn't want me, but I wasn't about to let him embarrass me with that little twit. She was so stupid. She thought I had trespassed to go swimming, when really, I followed her that day. She thought we could be friends, started telling me her problems and told me that she didn't know whose baby she carried, Jake's or Will McGomery's."

Madison scrambled over to Will, keeping the light trained on Lorna, but seeking out his hand with her fingers. His grasp was weak, his breath shallow gasps. Cecilia rambled in Spanish. It suddenly sounded as foreign to her as Mandarin Chinese.

"I won't go to prison," Lorna said, causing Madison's heart to jolt with terror. Her sister placed the barrel of Aubrey's gun beneath her chin, pointing it upward toward the roof of her mouth. Her smile faded from her lips until her face was a blank mask under the white glare of the flashlight.

No sound would come out of Madison's vocal cords, but she heard their father speaking. He spoke in a voice she had never heard before, that of a frightened little boy.

"Please don't do it. Please, baby."

"Sorry, Daddy." Lorna blinked, her finger tightening over the trigger. Her voice and her eyes were empty, as devoid of life as a Martian landscape. Then her gaze locked with Madison's.

"Looks like we both lose, Little Sissa."

Madison's scream reverberated through her mind in an endless echo as Lorna closed her eyes, and pulled the trigger.

## CHAPTER FORTY-SIX

He had said to trust him.

Madison ceased the motion of Will's rocking chair—a chair she knew he had made with his own hands—and stared at the bookcase full of books on the paranormal. She hadn't been able to tell him she was sorry that fateful night, sorry about Aubrey, sorry for not trusting him.

Her throat constricted. The simple act of swallowing was incredibly painful, like she had rust in her throat. Why hadn't she trusted him? He had known what he was doing. He had said that Aubrey was listening to him. Now it was too late for pathetic words of apology.

She had been the cause of so much heartbreak and loss.

Within days, she had assumed the role of recluse on the ridge, had become the outcast with the ugly and painful history. Her sister was dead because she had, in blind relief and joy, left Aubrey's gun lying on the ground. Lorna had been able to put a bullet in Will's chest because of those same damnable emotions.

Her sister had been a psychopath, had murdered Sarah Chambers, but been found worth sparing in Will McGomery's eyes. And she, so stupid, so untrusting, had left him wide open to Lorna's insane plotting.

Her hands folding over her heart, she began to cry. Cried as she had every evening since her sister had taken him down.

Since her life had been forever altered.

****

Amid the balmy night air, water and sky competed to provide the most spectacular canvas for the evening, but actually, they only managed to compliment one another. Like lovers that only truly blossomed in the presence of the other.

A woman walked gingerly along the long fishing dock, like she did most evenings, and he knew that before it was all over, he would be with her.

She had the same lost quality about her that he felt in himself. They were loners, each a recluse from the troubled world they had abandoned. He gazed wistfully at her red-blond hair, made into a flaming torch by the setting sun and wondered if like him, she came out to the water every night because it called to her with its surf, with its million voices.

Had she been reborn like him? Was she searching for a new identity in this place with the bitchin' sunsets and tequila-vibrant waters?

Under what circumstances had she wound up here in this empty paradise with a Jack-of-all-trades scoundrel like him?

She looked innocent, approachable, and he realized he really had nothing to hide from her at all.

He was a clean slate. He'd wager that she was too.

Dwight Wray stood and brushed the Cancun sand off his Bermuda shorts. He'd never made that phone call for Tritt, that anonymous tip that the sheriff had been counting on so much. Instead he'd boarded the flight that had ultimately landed him here. He was ever grateful for the money Will McGomery had given him to be his informant. That was for damn sure.

McGomery's savings had given him this life of the brilliant sunsets, had given him freedom from his bondage.

He wouldn't have to worry with being Tritt Davidson's puppy on a string ever again.

He started walking toward the dock, a greeting on his lips, and a future on his horizon.

# CHAPTER FORTY-SEVEN

Marshy's truck slowly backed around to leave. Will raised his hand in a wave, and winced at the familiar pinch in his chest. It would be awhile yet before his body let him do anything without registering a complaint.

He opened the front door of the cabin and stood in the threshold, looking inside at the woman sitting in his rocking chair. The table lamp was the only source of light in the room, and she looked warm and soft, like pure heaven sitting in golden, forty-watt sunshine.

"Your Pap said you sat with me every evening for days until you learned I had regained consciousness."

She blinked. Just once and then looked down from his eyes. "When Dow came up here and told me you'd regained consciousness, I was...so glad."

"That's it?" he said, smiling a smile she didn't glance up to see. "You were glad, Owens?"

Her face twisted into a grimace and he instantly regretted his attempt at a joke. She had lost her sister. He had failed her and he thought to make light of her?

*Jesus Christ.*

He had come out of the fog this time without a lick of common sense apparently.

He was nervous. No, he was scared to death. She hadn't been back to see him since he'd awakened and that could mean only one thing. She was damaged, had been broken into pieces. He should have believed it. Marshy had tried to tell him and his dreams in the past about the trap had forewarned of it.

As fate would have it, Sarah's prophetic words had proven to be true. Madison was the sacrifice.

"I'm sorry," he said, stepping through the door and closing it softly.

The room was chilled. He moved to the hearth and examined the stack of kindling on the grate. There wasn't much. He would have to go outside and get more if he wanted to maintain a decent fire. He crouched and began laying on the few pieces anyway. Her voice came to him, clipped.

"It's not cold in here."

He finished and moved to the door. "Guess I chill easily these days. I'm going to get some more kindling."

She shot up from the rocker. "You can't do that in your condition. Sit down. I'll get the kindling."

As she moved passed him, he reached for her. She flinched away from his touch. He tried to hide the pain this caused him, rubbed his jaw with one hand.

"I know. I need to shave. Give me ten minutes and I'll be as good as new."

Her eyes promptly filled with tears. She shook her head. "Stop it, Will. Please just stop it."

"Stop trying to talk to you?" He scratched his ear, dropped his hand from his face and sighed deeply. "I think the only reason I pulled through this was because I wanted so much to talk to you again and now you want to deny me that."

Her eyes popped open wide and her cheeks brightened, giving him hope that the Madison he had once known still existed somewhere beneath the grief and injury.

"Deny you that? I begged you to wake up and speak to me!" Her voice shattered and the pieces tinkled around them in the form of sobs. "Every night I sat in that hospital chair next to your bed and I begged you to open your eyes, to hear me and respond."

He stared at her, felt his heart pounding in his chest with love for her.

"I thought I was going to lose my mind, watching you lay there in that damned bed," she said. She took a few steps back from him until her spine was almost touching the bookcase. "No one could say why you wouldn't gain consciousness. Your vitals were good. Your body began to heal." She wiped savagely at her tears, now coursing down her cheeks. "I prayed for you to hear me."

He took one step toward her and she bumped into the bookcase. He held up his hands. "Fine. I won't touch you, but I want you to look at me. You're looking everywhere but into my eyes. I'm alive and I want you to damn well act like it."

Her eyes slid up to his and he searched them imploringly. She shook terrible, like a tiny house on an active fault line. He took a breath and it hitched in his throat.

"I did hear you. All those times at the hospital, I heard you, Maddie. Why do you think I'm standing here right now?"

"You almost died because of me," she said. "I dropped that gun. I was stupid."

"And I thought I could actually head-shrink my brother out of avenging Sarah's murder." He shrugged and winced at the pain it caused him. "I was the fool, but a fool that survived nonetheless, and I want to be here with you, want to make things right."

He tried to keep his voice level. "I made a pact with a ghost and I wasn't promised anything. In fact, I was shown that you would be the one hurt and you were. I want a chance, just one chance. I'll make it up to you."

"Me?" She pressed her fingers into her eyes and made a sound that was painful to hear. "I wasn't the one who almost bled out on the ground because you left a gun within my psychotic sister's reach!"

He said nothing, could think of nothing to say. Her defenses were firmly in place, and he feared that no words of his would ever be able to break down this wall she had constructed between them.

It was so unfair as to be cruel, this fate that he was left with. In his quest to silence Sarah, and give his precious but tormented Molly closure, he had set off a chain of events that had caused pain and devastation to the one woman he was sure he had been sent back to watch over and love. If Lorna had been destined to die anyway, then why not by the hands of his malice-filled brother?

His intervention had pushed Lorna to kill herself, and her ultimate act of selfishness was to be the deathblow to her sister. Madison was not okay.

They were not okay.

None of them would ever be the same, not Marshy, and not Marshy's wife, who Will heard was being treated by a psychiatrist and kept under sedation. And Madison would bear the worst of it because she blamed herself for it all. His little trooper with the wild auburn hair looked at him with mortally wounded eyes, eyes that were as haunted as he'd ever been.

"I wanted to bring silence to my dreams, to my life," he said, "and what I did was fulfill the prophecy of that damned dream I had of you. Now I have to turn away? Watch you bleed in this trap I custom made for you? I don't know how to do that. I think it will have to be you to walk away."

She nodded, then wiping her face again, she sniffed. "Davidson died of a massive heart attack that night. Did Daddy tell you?"

"I was informed." He frowned, crossed over to the rocking chair and sat down.

She hugged herself tightly, he figured either to hold herself together or to keep him out. Or both. Her voice was delicate and tattered like lace curtains that had endured too many seasons in the sun.

"You've lost so much weight, Will. Your cheeks are sallow."

He smiled gently at her. "I look like a bum."

Instead of smiling back and easing the heavy weight in his chest, she scowled at him. "Dwight Wray left a text message on your phone a few days ago. It was a line from a Jimmy Buffet song. I take it he's on some kind of vacation."

"You could say that."

He shifted in the chair, exhausted from the simple ride home. "Dwight was essential to me, kept me informed. I just wish he hadn't underestimated Cecilia Onate. I wasn't expecting her to be with Aubrey at the pond, and to be so determined to get rid of me and Lorna."

Madison shuddered, chafed her arms at the memory of the woman who had been Aubrey's accomplice. The woman's fate was up in the air, but certainly did not look favorable.

She dropped her arms. "I'll go for the kindling now."

"Madison," he said, his voice as soft as a down pillow. "Sarah's gone. When I embraced my gift, an angel came to me and I was healed of this infliction I've had, the seizures, the dreams. Molly's name…it's been written into the book and her spirit is freed. It's over."

She looked at him with fear shining in her eyes. "If you won't allow me to fix you a fire, then I will go." She pulled her upper lip through her teeth as though she was precariously close to tears again. "I don't know about angels, Will. Or God."

"Hey," he said, drawing her eyes back to his when they strayed. "There is no black and white in any of this. Your sister was not evil to the core and Sarah's quest for closure wasn't simply about me making right a wrong for her. I'm convinced that we are dealing with more here, destinies beyond theirs alone. I don't know how else to explain it."

She laughed and it broke his heart to hear it, for it was not Madison at all that he heard, but someone utterly broken, perhaps beyond repair.

Like Molly when she'd been alive.

"My sister was rotten through and through," she said. "Stop treating me like I'm an imbecile." She moved quickly for the door.

His voice tore from his throat like a ragged hangnail, hurting him. "Wait."

She turned and looked at him, her hand on the doorknob, her fingers already twisting it. He smiled and knew it was the sorriest smile he'd ever tried to pass off as genuine.

"Give me a few weeks to get my feet back under me and I'll get a lawyer." He forced himself to stop gripping the arms of the rocking chair, placed his hands on his thighs. "This place was destined to be yours. I want to deed it to you."

## CHAPTER FORTY-EIGHT

Madison tripped down the steps and across the dark yard into her Jeep.

Just the sight of it made her want to cry and since she was already falling apart, she lay her head on the steering wheel and let herself completely unravel. Despite unbearable grief and worry and stress, her father had taken the vehicle and fixed it, tires as well as the paint, and now Will McGomery was giving her his land.

She didn't want them to try to fix what couldn't be mended. She didn't want the land. She didn't want Marshy Owens to pity her because she had to witness her genetically and fatally flawed sister blow the top of her head off.

Pity did not change the fact he had turned away from what Lorna had done to Sarah Chambers, did not change the fact she carried in her womb Will's baby—a child she would most likely miscarry after several weeks because she couldn't seem to take care of herself as she should.

So Sarah was gone, silenced, but in her own head, the inner voice of fear and shame refused to be quiet. It wouldn't stop, hounded her constantly.

She was afraid of the panic attacks that polluted her days and nights. She was afraid of the post-traumatic stress she knew was affecting every aspect of her life at the moment—that would maybe affect her life forever. She was afraid of losing her mind and having Will McGomery witness it. Failing him, failing their unborn child.

Failing.

She had to leave, get out of there before she jumped out of the Jeep and ran to him anyway. Before she fell at his feet and offered up to him all her bloodied hopes and dreams, dashed to hell and doomed, stained and reeking with the decay of her guilt.

Her fingers fumbled with the key in the ignition and the engine came to life. Tires crunched over gravel and she heard the voice in her head, pleading with her.

*Don't go. Goddamn it, don't go!*

Her foot jammed down hard on the brake. She lurched forward, swiveled her head to the left.

He was coming across the yard. He was the voice—Will McGomery, her peculiar, fiddle-playing psychic was telling her not to go.

She didn't reach for the door. She couldn't. Suddenly, her fingers were useless digits of flesh and bone in her lap.

He ripped the door open and pulled her out, like a man who had never had a bullet tear through him within an inch of his heart. His arms were tight, yet impossibly gentle as he rocked her against him.

She felt small, but not lost in this cradle of protective male strength. She felt found.

"Oh, God, don't you know how much I love you?" he breathed against her neck, filling her hair with a magical warmth, a warmth that seeped into her very thoughts, that calmed that wild hiss of fear in the synapses of her brain.

He set her down, cupped her head in his palms and began raining kisses upon her face and then her mouth. Kissed her deeply. Wetly. Madly and noisily.

"I love you, Madison. I've been in love with you, I think, from the moment I laid eyes on you." It was murmured against her teeth and her tongue. "I can't live without you, not a day, not an hour, not even a minute. Don't go. Please. Don't go."

Her spirit was a flower opening to the hot sun. She kissed him back, clutched fistfuls of his soft and worn button-down shirt. It was a beautiful shirt beneath beautiful denim overalls.

"I'm afraid," she said, but then maybe it was only in her mind that she said the words because her lips and tongue were otherwise engaged.

He groaned against the moist and swollen words not yet

spoken between them. Dipping his head and burying his face in her hair again, his whole body shook.

And she held on to him.

"It's gonna be all right," he said, breathing deeply of her neck.

Suddenly, she knew.

Knew.

She realized that what they needed, all they had ever needed was each other. And with that dawning upon her fully, she slid her fingers into his hair and anchored herself to him, found his ear and spoke to him in a whisper that sounded to her both brave and timid.

"I can't live without you either. I've tried and I can't."

"You don't have to," he said, his voice hushed, tremulous. "You don't, Maddie."

After a heartbeat, she found her voice. "I'm pregnant, Will."

His hands moved down to the small of her back, pressing her closer to him. His chest rumbled with a sob. "My God. That day in the shower. I can't believe it."

Arms coming around his neck, she wept softly. "You're happy then?"

"Happy?" He searched out her lips and kissed them tenderly. "I want to marry you, Madison Owens, give you tons of babies and happiness, and my loyalty and my heart. I've waited a lifetime for this, for a second chance, and now I'm going to grab it and never let it go."

Pulling back she looked deep into the blue gray shadows of his eyes. "This gift...what is the gift that you embraced? I have to know."

"Forgiveness," he said, swallowing. "Molly's forgiveness. And my own."

She continued to stare at him. Then she lifted on her toes and kissed him on the forehead in the area that she knew was referred to as the third eye.

They were awakening to a future that was uncertain, but that she was certain would not be devoid of love. It was a future that began to unfurl with her next words.

"Take me inside, Will."

THE END

# NOTE TO READERS

*Silencing Sarah is the culmination of a two-year journey.*

*It began as just another episode of writing in June of 2005 but quickly manifested into something – an obsession if you will – that I could not set aside. Perhaps it was because the idea for the book, like a delicate purple butterfly, emerged from the cocoon of my subconscious in the form of a dream that refused to fly away.*

*That summer, I missed the rustic sound of the Cicadas that surely filled the balmy night air. I didn't witness many of the breathtaking sunsets bleeding across the skies over Big A Mountain. For eight weeks I simply recorded what played through my conscious mind like a movie and when the last page was written, I couldn't rest easy, say I'm done, and move on. I spent the next several months looking for that special place by which I could place my fledgling purple butterfly.*

*I knew from the very beginning that this book was intended for someone and it is my belief that it has finally reached that individual. Through the support of many and the faith of a few, I have finally awakened to the reality of Silencing Sarah. And it is you.*

*I thank you deeply for being a part of my readership.*

Love,
Marla Cordle

1211482

Made in the USA